I DREW MY ELF SWORD, DRAGON'S DEATH. . . .

"Trolls," my captive elf said in a loud stage whisper. "All around, moving in like soldiers. And something else, some*one* else."

"One of your kin?" I asked.

"I think not." He was silent for a moment. "They are close."

My danger sense started screaming as the first wave of trolls came toward us in a solid line. Numbers? It's hard to count in the middle of a fight, even if you've got light, which we didn't. I started to think that an estimate of one hundred couldn't be far wrong. In any case, there were too many trolls, even for a Hero, his elf sword, and his three valiant companions. We could slow them down, make their victory expensive, but there didn't seem to be any way to actually beat them.

Then my danger sense hit me with an extra twist. . . .

THE HERO OF VARAY

RICK SHELLEY

A ROC BOOK

ROC
Published by the Penguin Group
Penguin Books USA Inc., 375 Hudson Street,
New York, New York 10014, U.S.A.
Penguin Books Ltd, 27 Wrights Lane,
London W8 5TZ, England
Penguin Books Australia Ltd, Ringwood,
Victoria, Australia
Penguin Books Canada Ltd, 2801 John Street,
Markham, Ontario, Canada L3R 1B4
Penguin Books (N.Z.) Ltd, 182-190 Wairau Road,
Auckland 10, New Zealand

Penguin Books Ltd, Registered Offices:
Harmondsworth, Middlesex, England

First published by Roc, an imprint of New American Library,
a division of Penguin Books USA Inc.

First Printing, July, 1991
10 9 8 7 6 5 4 3 2 1

Printed in the United States of America

1

Hangover

Parthet, Lesh, and I walked down to the town of Basil after supper in the castle. *Down.* The main gate of the castle is nearly a hundred feet above the town's streets. Castle Basil sits on a big hunk of naked rock, and the road curves back and forth down the southern face of Basil Rock through five hairpin switchbacks. That road—eight feet wide on the straightaway, twelve on the turns—was hand-hewn, carved out of the rock without the benefit of any explosives or power tools like jackhammers. A lot of that stone was hoisted to the top and used in the construction of the castle. Most of the rest, according to Parthet, became part of various fireplaces and chimneys in and around town.

Parthet groused about walking, but my uncle the wizard would have complained just as much about riding. "We could have taken the doorway down," he said when we were just a single turn below the castle gate.

"It's a beautiful summer evening," I replied, gesturing expansively, "and we can all use the exercise." After being cramped up on a boat for three weeks, returning from a goodwill tour of the kingdoms west of Varay in the buffer zone, I wanted to get out where I could do more than pace back and forth a dozen yards at a time.

"At my age, cranking my eyes open in the morning is exercise enough," Parthet said.

"How many centuries have you been sliding by on that excuse?" I asked.

"Trade secret. Speaking of secrets, you pick up any on your travels?"

"One dandy rumor is all. In Telemon they're saying that the blind wizard of the late Etevar of Dorthin is the bastard son of the Elfking and Xayber's wife . . . or maybe it's the other way around. I heard both versions."

The man the Dorthinis had simply called "The Wizard" was still roaming around Fairy or the buffer zone—somewhere. Blind, he was no threat to anyone, so I had seen no reason to punish him any further when we captured him after the Battle of Thyme. Sure, he had made it possible for the Etevar's soldiers to kill my father, and he had done his best to give me the same treatment, but my first few weeks as Hero had made me . . . well, if not more tolerant, certainly less eager for "a life for a life" revenge, and after three years I had seen no reason to regret my clemency.

Parthet snorted. "Where'd they pick up *that* kind of trash?"

"Seems they do a little trading across the Mist now and then," I said. "The story apparently came from the sailors. They did know about the Battle of Thyme and the fall of the Etevar."

"Not from *their* sailors," Lesh said. "*They* won't sail out of sight of land for fear that they won't be able to find their way back. But the Elflord of Something-or-other sends a trading ship across the Sea of Fairy every year or so, so they say."

"The voice of doubt?" Parthet asked in a laughing voice.

"When did Fairy folk ever take to being merchants?" Lesh asked. He was a veteran soldier, and his view of Varay's habitual foes was rather narrow.

"Whenever it suited their purpose," Parthet said with a chuckle. "It isn't always war over in Fairy. Those folks have to eat just like us, and slaves can't grow it all. And anyway, traders can be spies at the same time."

"Even the Vikings back in my world turned to honest trading when that looked more profitable than raiding," I said. I had mentioned Vikings to Lesh during our "cruise." The trading ship we sailed on had a vague resemblance to a Viking dragon ship.

The pub we were aiming for was the Bald Rock, the larger of the two inns in town, the one with the best beer (by almost unanimous agreement among everyone but the proprietor of the other inn, the Castrated Dragon, and his regulars). Still, the differences weren't great, and I tried to divide my patronage as equally as I could.

We were given the big table in the front corner as usual,

and the landlord's lads brought out the best mugs in the house, then plopped a ten-gallon keg in the center of the table and tapped it so we could serve ourselves and not have to waste a second waiting for refills. Bowls of nuts and pretzels were set up for us also, so we would have something to nosh on and so the salt would keep us thirsty and drinking—as if we were likely to need help. At least Old Baldy didn't salt his beer. It was a nice, homey arrangement.

The lighting was a dirty yellow glow that came from a series of oil lamps set high enough to keep them out of the way of the occasional brawl. The room was always a little smoky. By the end of a long evening's debauch, a person's eyes could be stinging madly and watering continuously.

Make no mistake. The three of us set out to get blind, stinking drunk that night. Lesh and I were unwinding from our long travels—the goodwill tour had gone on for a total of three months altogether—and Parthet doesn't need an excuse to match anyone in the kingdom drink for drink. But it isn't all that easy to get blind, stinking drunk in Varay. The same force that causes everyone to eat so much also hurries up the conversion of alcohol to sugar and burns those calories as fast as all the rest to fuel the basic magic of the land. There was never any real doubt that we would empty the first keg of beer. Quite likely, we would make a good start on a second. And before you strain something trying to figure it out, let me save you the math. A ten-gallon keg split three ways works out to about thirty-six twelve-ounce bottles or cans apiece . . . or about fourteen trips to the latrine, out back. To be honest, though, it was never just the three of us who emptied a keg. Every time the landlord came over to see how we were doing, we would invite him to share a mug with us. And other people would stop by our table now and then to pay their respects, say hello, or whatever, and they always got the same hospitality. When we drank down in town, it was almost drinks on the crown for everyone. But I wasn't causing a scandal by showing the "common" touch. That is, I wasn't doing anything unheard-of. Parthet was willing to drink with anyone to anything, and he had often said that my father was the same way. That's how we sometimes got deep into the second keg in an evening's drinking.

People *liked* to see us come into the pub.

"Dieth having any special trouble in Dorthin?" I asked Parthet after we were settled at our table and into our first round.

"About like always," Parthet said through a foam mustache. He shrugged. "Some of the warlords are still unhappy about the situation. There's a half-dozen of them thought they should have stepped into the Etevar's shoes, and they still won't acknowledge Dieth or you. They cause trouble for Dieth. They cause trouble for Mauroc." Mauroc-by-the-Sea, east of Dorthin, was the seventh of the seven kingdoms.

"Anything serious?" I asked. There was really nothing new in what Parthet had to say. Dorthin had been plagued by occasional fighting, mostly raids among neighbors, since the death of the Etevar. On two different occasions I had been forced to travel to Dorthin to help Duke Dieth put down bloody feuds and hold the kingdom for me. I still hadn't found a way to dump Dorthin permanently on Dieth or anybody else, and I really didn't have the motivation to spend the time it would take to fully "pacify" the country. I didn't care to go looking for unnecessary trouble.

"He hasn't asked for help," Parthet said. "He knows how you feel about Dorthin." I just grunted and took another drink.

"At least we don't have to worry about the Elflord of Xayber yet," Parthet said an hour or so later, returning to the thread of threats as if there hadn't been sixty minutes of irrelevant conversation in between. "Far as we can tell, the civil war in Fairy is still raging." He laughed loud enough to draw stares and ignored them. "Xayber has had his hands full since we sent your message to the Elfking three years back."

"And if Xayber finally wins up there, he's going to be at our throats in a hurry," I reminded Parthet. I hadn't forgotten Xayber's vow of vengeance against me for a minute, and I didn't care to do any intermediate gloating over the elflord's problems.

"You connected with your young lady since you got back?" Parthet asked near the bottom of the first keg.

I growled. I knew damn well that he was using *connected* as a euphemism for *screwed* . . . which is the euphemism I normally use for . . . well, you get the idea. Some nights, Parthet would carry on at length about his thousand-plus years of *connections.* "Just because a wizard can't sire children doesn't mean that he can't play the game," he liked to say. It was the only time he was likely to refer to the sterility that his vocation caused.

"Joy's in St. Louis, at her folks'," I said. "I talked to her on the telephone this afternoon. She's flying back to Chicago tomorrow."

Parthet nodded. "Oh, by the way, Annick made a visit to Arrowroot a few weeks back." There was no *by the way* about it. Parthet had led up to that bit of news intentionally. I had never told Parthet—or anyone else—that Annick and I had made love that night while we were waiting to bring the army through to Thyme from Arrowroot and Coriander, but he always seemed to know. And every time a new sighting or rumor about Annick came to his ears, he made sure to tell me about it.

"Oh? What's she been up to?" I asked, casually enough to disappoint my uncle. Annick. I was no closer to understanding her than I had been three years before when she made it clear that she wasn't going to stop hunting for her elf-warrior father . . . so she could kill him.

"No idea," Parthet said. "There are the usual stories that she's been off on another foray in Xayber, killing any Fairy folk she could get to." Parthet shrugged. "Unless she starts the tales herself, it would be hard to put much faith in them."

"I wouldn't find it hard," I said. I had seen her in action up on the isthmus. "But what about this visit?"

"She visited her mother, then disappeared again."

"Probably off in Fairy slitting sleeping throats again," I said.

"Hear, hear," Lesh said, one of his few contributions to the table talk that night. He prefers to concentrate on the beer. That night, he was doing a wonderful job. Every few minutes his head started to sag toward the table, but he always got a mug in place before he could pass out.

"By the way," I said, throwing the phrase back at Uncle Parthet, "isn't it about time for you to start training an apprentice? You're not getting any younger, you know. That's what you keep telling everyone, anyway.''

Parthet's instant pique was almost strong enough to sober him up.

''Don't start *that* again,'' he said, slamming his mug down on the table. ''Believe me, I'll *know* when it's time to train an apprentice.''

I like an occasional night out like that, but not too often—because I always suffer from hangovers of truly heroic proportions. I need time between binges to forget how bad the hangovers are. A good drunk can put me out of action for half the following day, and out of sorts even longer. But while the glow is warming me, it's great. I don't even get upset when the talk turns to Annick . . . as long as it doesn't turn before I've got at least two sheets to the wind.

People came and went from the Bald Rock. As the evening got later, it was more people going and fewer coming in. Most of Old Baldy's customers had to get up early to work the next day—farmers, shopkeepers, craftsmen. By most folks' standards, Varay isn't very civilized. Life is still dominated by nature, by the sun and the seasons. No electricity. Parthet, Lesh, and I were the only ones down from the castle. Most of the people who live and work up on the rock also do most of their eating and drinking up there, because it doesn't cost them anything. Trips down to the town's public houses are for special occasions. Of course, most of the beer consumed in the castle is purchased from Basil's two publican/brewers.

We were well into our second keg of the evening when trouble walked in, though my danger sense didn't warn me as quickly as it might have. It wasn't just that I was drunk, though that contributed to it. The stranger was disguised by a powerful magic. I glanced at the man when he came through the door and didn't get any kind of warning at all. He stood just inside the door for a moment and looked around. There were only a couple of people left in the Bald Rock besides Parthet, Lesh, me, and the innkeeper and his lads. The stranger looked rather fuzzy. I was willing to lay that entirely on the beer. I squinted to get a better look, but the stranger didn't come into focus.

"Ever see him before?" I asked my companions. I think I was speaking softly, but I can't be sure. Lesh and Parthet both shook their heads. They had turned to look at the stranger too, though it had been quite an effort for Lesh. He had been going at the beer as if Prohibition were going to take effect in the morning.

The innkeeper came out from behind his bar to greet the stranger, who just waved him off. Old Baldy shrugged and went back to his place.

The stranger looked my way and started toward our table, moving very casually—at first. But then things happened very quickly.

I sobered up instantly. That was the work of my danger sense, once the danger got so close that my peril was immediate.

The fuzziness around the stranger disappeared, leaving him strongly defined in the dirty yellow light of the Bald Rock. He was an elf warrior, as tall and fair as all of them are, and his sword was making a blurred arc as he drew it from a shoulder rig—a rig just like mine. He couldn't pull it straight over his head because of the low ceiling. The motion was more like a baseball pitcher with a three-quarter delivery. It was still a quick draw.

I leaped to my feet and over to my left, away from the table, and pulled my own sword on the move. The elf's first blow bit into one of the beams in the wall. By the time he got it free, I was ready to meet him.

Fighting with six-foot swords under the eight-foot ceiling of the Bald Rock called for a particular concentration. Some techniques are worse than useless without full swinging room. But perhaps I had done more practicing at that sort of fighting than the elf had. It was a slight advantage, perhaps the only one I had. The elf was bigger than me, stronger, and likely a lot older and more experienced, though he didn't look especially old. Elves don't particularly show their age. The fact that he was an elf warrior meant that the intrinsic danger sense and the other magics of the Hero of Varay were matched or exceeded going in.

We were both humming sword chants. That was still an involuntary reflex on my part. Whenever I used the elf sword I had won on that beach in Xayber, the melody came out of my throat. The tune wasn't always exactly the same. When I was just practicing, it sounded quite different from when I was fighting for real, and the dragon-fighting version was distinct from this one. But they were all variations on a common theme.

I was also vaguely aware of Parthet going into a magic chant. He was drunker than I had been, and I wasn't sure that his conjuring would have any effect on an elf warrior in any case. It couldn't hurt, though. And Lesh was too far gone to be any help. I hoped he was too drunk to *try* to get involved. He certainly couldn't defend himself in his condition.

The elf warrior fought with the fierce abandon of someone who was absolutely convinced of his own immortality and invincibility. I had no such assurance. Heroes of Varay died regularly. I had come close enough myself in the Battle of Thyme, and before that, when I faced the Elflord of Xayber in a long-distance duel. Even after three years, I spent a lot of time in the burial crypt below Castle Basil meditating along the line of dead kings and Heroes. Even Vara, founder of the kingdom, had died. His bones were there in the crypt with all of the others. At least there was a niche with his name on the capstone.

But I had also seen one "immortal" elf warrior die, so I knew that the immortality this elf warrior seemed to rely on so heavily wasn't absolute. That's how I got my elf sword. Maybe I was no dragon, but knowing that my opponent wasn't as immortal as he thought he was gave me another very slight advantage. Maybe.

Time means very little in an engagement like that. Neither of us was likely to tire soon enough to make a difference. The endurance of elf warriors goes even beyond legend, but the magic of the Hero of Varay is more than sleight of hand as well. And I had a lot of available calories to burn. Sure, sobering up quickly had included breaking out in about three gallons of sweat, but my body had converted all that alcohol to sugar, so I was on a sugar high, with more energy than sense.

The end came quickly. The elf's sword bit into our keg, and while he was freeing his sword and wiping beer from his eyes, I swung Dragon's Death in a flat arc that took his head completely off his shoulders. But while I was doing that, his sword came free and the tip ripped into my abdomen.

I felt a tugging, and then a fire, I spun away and through a complete circle, but it was too late to avoid damage. The elf's head bounced off the splintered keg and came to rest on our table, right side up, eyes open and facing me, a fierce scowl frozen to the face. I lowered my blade and leaned on the hilt like a crutch, fighting against the waves of pain that were flowing up from my gut.

The elf's eyes were moving, looking around. The mouth opened.

"Before you die, I give you the greetings of my father, the Elflord of Xayber," the elf warrior said. Then his jaw dropped, his eyes closed, and he died.

I pressed my hand against the tear in my gut, futilely trying to hold in my blood. It wasn't the sort of homecoming I had planned at all. . . .

I had returned from my goodwill tour of the buffer zone that afternoon. I had learned something new about myself. My stock of goodwill wasn't enough to hold me through a three-month goodwill tour. A long diplomatic gig wasn't the kind of job that would normally be given to a Hero, but I was also heir apparent to King Pregel, so I was stuck with the job. I did my best to weasel out of it, but when Pregel insisted, there wasn't much I could do but smile and accept the inevitable. My great-grandfather might be 128 years old and in questionable health, but he was still in charge, and when he said go, I went. He told me that the tour would be part of my continuing education about life in the seven kingdoms.

He was right, though perhaps not entirely in the way he meant it. I learned that nobody in the seven kingdoms had running water, decent plumbing, or a common magic to fend off lice, bedbugs, and assorted other pests. The buffer zone has a lot of little creepers never seen back in the real world, and the bites or stings of a few of them can produce downright peculiar effects. The only other thing I learned was that appetites and meal sizes seemed to decrease in proportion to the distance from Fairy. I wasn't sure what the hell that meant, and my survey was hardly scientific, but it was obvious. At Basil and in the northern border fortresses of Varay, people pigged out as often as they could and nobody got fat. In my tour through the four kingdoms west of Varay—Belorz, Caderack, Montray, and Telemon, in that order—I found that the farther west and south I went, the less food people had to eat in order to get by. And in the far southwest (the Titan Mountains took a big bend to the south, so much of Montray and Telemon was farther south than anywhere in Varay), obesity was an occasional problem.

During the last two months of my tour, I had plenty of time to consider that phenomenon. After all, the actual diplomatic nonsense rarely took more than a few hours every now and then, since we were on the road most of the time, and I couldn't spend *every* waking moment swearing that I would never let myself be suckered into such an extended stay in the buffer zone again. I was too far from the magic doors to zip back to my own world for an occasional shower and the other amenities. The primitive life is a great place to visit . . . as long as you can get back to civilization now and then.

When I got back from my tour, I had been the official Hero of Varay for three years and a couple of months. On the whole, they had been peaceful years, and I had managed to divide my time between the buffer zone and my own world, with the emphasis on the latter. After facing the Etevar of Dorthin, we had quite a stock of fresh sea-silver left, so I put it to good use, setting up quite a few new magic doorways to let me gad about a little more freely. Now I had an apartment, a condo overlooking Lake Michigan, in Chicago; a small castle in southern Varay, a simple tower with no bailey or curtain wall or anything, like the castle in that movie *The War Lord;* and magic doorways connected all of my places to Basil and to my mother's house in Louisville. Yes, she still lived there, most of the time. Twenty-odd years of electricity and modern plumbing had spoiled her for the full-time primitive splendor of Varay too.

Heading west on my tour, I had been on horseback. Lesh, Harkane, and Timon had accompanied me. Letters had been sent ahead months in advance, setting up what arrangements could be made in the seven kingdoms. There is virtually no postal service in the buffer zone, particularly not between kingdoms. The occasional wandering merchant or minstrel would be hired to take letters along and find a way to direct them closer to their goal. Sometimes a letter might pass through five or six different messengers before it reached its destination. Remarkably, none of the letters setting up my tour got misplaced. The tour took us to each of the capitals and some of the other major towns and castles in the kingdoms west of Varay. In between stops, we often spent several nights in a row camped out or bedded down in village inns that were infested with a variety of unpleasant bugs and rodents.

At least getting back to Varay once we reached the far west was faster than the trip out. We hired the largest coastal trading ship available and sailed the Mist home. We started out on the west coast of Telemon, sailed north around a peninsula shaped something like Iberia, then east, all of the way to Arrowroot. The sailors of the buffer zone were cautious men, though. They sailed by day and tied up on shore every night, afraid of being blown too far out into the waters of Fairy. Even though I was in a hurry to get home by then, I kept my impatience at bay. I wasn't entirely comfortable about the voyage. Other than a couple of short day cruises, I had never been on a boat before. At least we didn't run into any storms or rough seas. The Hero of Varay did not disgrace himself by getting seasick.

We docked at Arrowroot after twenty-three days at sea, got our horses and luggage unloaded, made arrangements to pay the ship's master the remainder of his fee, and went to the castle to transfer back to Basil. I grabbed a flagon of beer as we passed through the great hall, something to drink on my way up to King Pregel's private quarters. As usual, Baron Kardeen was aware that I had returned almost before I was. He always seemed to know just who was in the castle and where. The chamberlain met me before I got to my great-grandfather's rooms.

"How is he?" I asked, a normal question.

"Not bad, considering," Kardeen said. *Considering*—Pregel was 128 or thereabouts, so the standards for "not bad" weren't extremely high. The king's health fluctuated quite dramatically at times. He could go from chest-thumping health to critical condition and back again almost overnight.

Kardeen and I went in together. Pregel was sitting up in bed reading—a book, not a scroll. Mother had been bringing him large-print books for years, something to keep him occupied. Occasionally, I brought him a few books I thought he might enjoy, things Mother would probably never think to get for him.

"Ah, you're back," he said when he saw me. He marked his place carefully with a Garfield bookmark and set the book aside. "Is it just three months?"

"I wouldn't say 'just,' " I said. "The way I itch and all, it feels more like a couple of years."

Pregel chuckled. "Any difficulties along the way?" Even though he was in bed in the middle of the day, Pregel seemed to be at the top of one of his health swings.

"Nothing special, I guess. Nobody tried to tar and feather me or anything like that." I gave him the stack of letters that the various kings and lords of our western neighbors had sent for him. Pregel tossed them aside without a glance.

"That's good. It's been far too long since we've done a tour of our western neighbors. I haven't felt up to that kind of trip for years."

"I can see why. Is it okay if we hold off on the full report for a day or two?" I asked. "I'd like to spend some time soaking in a hot tub and start feeling human again."

"Yes, I imagine you would." Pregel chuckled again. "What was her name again?"

"Joy." I shook my head to keep from grinning. Pregel might be old, but he wasn't completely out of touch.

"Ah, yes, a wonderful name for a young lady. Yes, we can wait a few days before we ask all the questions. That will give me time to read all these letters. As long as there's nothing urgent."

"There isn't. Nobody's declaring war or anything."

"Must have been dull for you. You'll have to bring your young lady by to say hello one of these days."

I just nodded. That was easier than admitting that I hadn't told Joy word one about the buffer zone or my job. I wasn't sure about telling her yet. It isn't that I wasn't sure of Joy, I just hadn't come up with a way to tell her about Varay without either convincing her that I was crazy or scaring her out of her gourd. Joy was special enough that I didn't want to take any stupid chance of spoiling our relationship.

Most times, I enjoyed sitting around and chatting with Pregel. His mind was clear, his sense of humor surprising. But that afternoon, I was itching so badly that I couldn't wait to get home and soak myself until I looked like a prune, maybe baste myself liberally with baby oil or whatever it was going to take to get rid of my itching and discomfort. While I was soaking, I would call Joy and set up something for the next day. It wasn't just that I wanted to let the anticipation build, I had a prior commitment for my first night back.

I got out of the king's room as quickly as I could and went around to see if Parthet had popped in while Kardeen and I were with the king. The chamberlain had told me that Parthet hadn't been at Basil since breakfast, which was quite in keeping with the wizard's habits. He rarely took all three meals in the castle. At lunchtime he could more often be found in one of the various pubs that met his approval. He had used some of that excess seasilver too.

"He knows you're due, so he'll be along early for dinner," Kardeen said as we headed toward his office. "He's been looking for you for the last week or more."

"I should be back by supper," I said. I was developing a feel for time in the buffer zone, even without a watch. "Maybe I won't be here at the start of the meal, but I'll be along in time to eat." I had a solid two hours, closer to three, before supper would begin in the great hall, and it wasn't as if I would lose time in transit. Kardeen and I nodded each other off, then I headed for my bedroom in Castle Basil to go home. I left Lesh at Basil to get an early start on the evening's drinking, dropped Timon off at my Castle Cayenne in the southernmost part of Varay, then popped through to my Michigan Avenue condo in Chicago.

My place in Chicago is thirty-eight stories up, on the east side of the building, looking right out over Lake Michigan—a classy home in a classy neighborhood. I took frequent guilt trips over it, but the Hero of Varay has more money than he can possibly spend sanely, and gold from the buffer zone spends very well in the "real" world. So much for turning away the Elflord of Xayber, so much for defeating the Etevar of Dorthin, plus never-before-claimed bounties for killing two dragons, and a monthly salary to boot. Baron Kardeen's chancery clerk kept very strict accounts even if the entries would send a CPA into fibrillation. I didn't even have to draw on my status as heir for money. On top of everything else, I also drew a small income from Dorthin. Duke Dieth did his best there, but not all of the feudal lords of Dorthin had accepted the new hierarchy yet.

The master bath in my apartment is appropriately decadent for such an upscale Gold Coast address. The tub will do everything but scratch your back, and it comes close to doing that with directed jets of water circulating just the way you want it. I showered, rinsed the tub out, then filled it for that long soak. While the water was running, I phoned Joy.

Joy Bennett and I had been going together for a year before my goodwill tour. Being away from her for those three months was the main reason why my goodwill ran out before the tour did. Joy had been near the end of her last semester for a B.S. in computer science when I left on my tour—about the same point in her studies that I had been at when I stumbled into my new job and kissed college goodbye. Joy told me that she was going to be exceptionally busy for the last few weeks of school, so she didn't object too strenuously when I told her I was going to be gone for ages on a mysterious mission that I couldn't tell her about. She joked about it now and then during the ten days between the time I told her that I was going and the time I left, but I'm pretty certain that she halfway thought that I was working for the CIA, just the way I used to think that my father was a spy because of his periodic disappearances.

I had offered Joy the use of my condo while I was gone, but the dorm at school was more convenient through the end of the semester, and she decided that she would rather use the time after the end of school to go home for a visit with her parents. I promised to call her as soon as I got home, and she promised to get on a plane to come back to Chicago the next morning. We were in that deep about each other. Marriage hadn't *quite* been discussed, but we had talked around the fringes of the subject now and then, and it seemed to be a likely prospect . . . if I managed to get the subject of Varay across without scaring her off, at least. I knew I couldn't put that conversation off much longer.

The phone in St. Louis rang four times, then a fifth. I had a sinking feeling that no one was home, but then Joy answered. After a round of long-distance greetings that I wouldn't dare confide to paper, I said, "I'm home."

"It's about time."

"Way past time," I told her. "I've missed you so much."

"Not even a postcard in three months."

"I wasn't anywhere I could count on mail service," I said.

"Oh? I didn't see you on campus." A private joke.

"Still coming back to see me?" I asked.

"I'll be at O'Hare fifteen minutes after noon tomorrow."

"You have the schedule handy?"

"Don't need it. I memorized it weeks ago."

"Twelve-fifteen. I'll be there. I love you, Joy."

"After three months, you're going to have to prove that all over again, you know."

"Ummm. I can hardly wait."

No, the bathtub wasn't overflowing when I got back to the bathroom. It *can't* overflow. It says so right on the guarantee. An electronic eye shuts the water off when it gets to the fill level. Other sensors adjust the hot and cold water to whatever temperature I set the thermostat for. And there is a panel just out of reach of the faucets that gives me a telephone, intercom to the front door, five-inch television, and speakers to bring the comfort of my stereo into the comfort of my tub.

I listened to the elevator music of WLAK while I soaked—relaxing music to help me unwind. It put me to sleep, as usual. But I didn't doze for long. My danger sense won't let me be when I fall asleep in the tub. The instant I start to slide down a little, it wakes me with an annoying little jerk. And then my stomach started growling, so I knew it was time to head for supper.

My entryway to Castle Basil is in the hall closet of the

apartment in Chicago. Leaving my bedroom there takes me to my bedroom on the fifth floor of Castle Cayenne. Going from dining room to kitchen takes me to my mother's home in Louisville. And the kitchen–dining room direction takes me to a small office I keep on West Washington in Chicago's Loop. I only keep the office as a place for the doorway, a shortcut to get downtown. We had a *lot* of sea-silver left after my foray into Xayber, and the stuff is useless if it isn't used within three months after it's harvested, so we used it.

I went through Cayenne on my way to Basil to pick up Timon again. The Hero of Varay must be properly accompanied. Timon was still my page. And I had to appear fully armed as always. Most times I didn't worry about wearing both of my swords. The elf blade, Dragon's Death, had stood me in good stead when I needed it, and during the intervening years I had practiced extensively with the claymore until it was almost second nature for me to use it. Besides that, it was a much more impressive weapon. A big part of the secret to avoiding trouble is making people think that you can return more than they can serve up.

There were already people eating when I reached the great hall of Basil. I took my customary seat at the head table, and Timon started dishing up the food for me. I didn't accept that kind of service in my own castle, but in "public" I had to put up with it. Varay can be very tradition-bound about some things.

Naturally, Uncle Parthet was one of the people who had started eating as soon as the first platters and pitchers were hauled in. He waved a spoon my way when he saw me coming in, but our dinner talk was severely limited. Our mouths were always full. Someday, I'd like to do a real study of just how much food people eat in Basil. As the roughest estimate, I'd say that people eat their weight every two to three weeks—and that might be overly conservative.

Weight Watchers would find no business in Varay, though. I asked Uncle Parthet about all of the eating once, back while I was recovering from my injuries after the battle around Castle Thyme. "It's all the magic, lad," he told me. "The energy has to come from somewhere, and mostly it comes directly from the people who live here."

At just about any dinner at Castle Basil, you'll find beef and pork roasts; ham; sausage; chicken and/or turkey and/or duck and/or goose; potatoes fixed three or four different ways; a selection of vegetables, salad items, and fruits—fresh in season, canned, dried, or otherwise preserved the rest of the year; bread, rolls, and desserts—usually fried or baked desserts, as fattening as possible; beer, wine, and coffee; and on and on, including "side dishes" of stew and soup. The buffer zone is a glutton's paradise. Just sampling everything at a meal puts your calorie count well into four digits, and nobody "just" samples it all. It's like having Thanksgiving dinner three times a day, *every* day, and the cooks of Varay have never heard of things like low-fat, cholesterol-free, salt-free, "light" foods, sugar substitutes, margarine, and the like.

People don't drop dead young from heart attacks or strokes either. Go figure.

Dinner takes time when it's that full of treats. Ninety minutes, even two hours, isn't rare for a meal in Basil. It was dusk before Parthet, Lesh, and I broke away from supper and headed for the main gate. The "welcome home" bash was on me.

And then that damn elf warrior walked in and spoiled the party.

2

Joy

I don't *think* that I lost consciousness for even a second, but I didn't take an active part in any of the immediate proceedings. I looked down, saw the blood on my shirt and blue jeans, reached down, and felt the wound. The cut started about three inches to the right of my navel and quit about three inches short of including a vasectomy. I didn't even feel any real pain at first. The shock of being wounded numbed me, if only for a moment. I stared at the wound like a fool, touched it, managed to feel a certain amazement at it all. My assailant seemed pretty confident that I was going to die from it. Or maybe it was just a rehearsed speech, something he was supposed to say when it was my head lying on the table. I certainly *hoped* that it was nothing more than that.

The Elflord of Xayber had not forgotten me—not that I had expected him to. He had sent his son to do me in.

I stood there wondering what to do next, and I didn't have a clue. I saw the elf's head on the table, his body on the floor and across a stool, and I *think* I actually took time to think about falling down myself. I was slow in realizing that Parthet and Lesh were talking about me, that Lesh was at my side now, holding me up—and seemingly having trouble holding himself up. We were weaving back and forth, and I didn't remember wavering that way just a moment before. That was when the pain finally got to me and I came close to passing out. I sagged, but Lesh was there and somehow managed to keep us both on our feet.

"We've got to get him through to a hospital," Parthet said. "That wound looks too dangerous for home remedies, even mine."

"Hospital?" Lesh asked. The word had trouble getting out past all of the alcohol.

"We'll take him through to his mother's house. She can get him to help. Hang on just a second. I've got to stop the bleeding first."

Parthet went into one of his mumbo-jumbo chants. I was still staring at my wound, not up to speaking . . . or even to falling down yet. The circle of blood quit growing, and I got numb again, this time just from the waist to my knees—an anesthetic numbness, not shock numbness. When the feeling went out of me, I started to fall again, but Lesh still managed to keep me from hitting the floor.

Parthet finished his conjuring, then got on the other side of me from Lesh. As small as he was, Parthet wasn't completely helpless. Parthet also carried along the head of the dead elf.

"Get some lads to carry the body up to the castle, tonight," Parthet told Old Baldy. "The king will want to see him without any bits and pieces hacked off for souvenirs or charms. If *anything's* missing, be it so little as a fingernail, your beer will taste like vinegar for a year." Sometime later, I heard Parthet mumble, "Old Baldy would sell him off by the ounce and retire if he could. Where would I go for beer then?"

I didn't notice at the time that Parthet had also fetched along the elf's sword.

There was a magic passage from the back room of the Bald Rock up to the castle, a passageway put in by Parthet and my father a couple of decades back. That was the route Parthet had wanted us to take when we started out after supper. We did use it going back. Parthet opened the way and Lesh hauled me through into the castle and started shouting for help.

I didn't pay much attention to the step-by-step drag or my reception in the castle. Things got kind of dreamy for me, but I'm sure that I was still at least partly conscious. Even at the time, I wasn't worried about dying. I didn't have an instant's doubt about my eventual recovery—once I managed to forget the elf's message. After all, I didn't die on the spot, and the elf did. I had been through worse. I had certainly *felt* worse. I didn't see Vara or any of the other members of the congregation of Heroes that had haunted me before and during the Battle of Thyme. Parthet had said that it was all nonsense, but I still couldn't write off my experiences to imagination.

I recall seeing Baron Kardeen looking anxiously at me, and I felt surprise that we were already back at the castle. I thought to smile, to reassure the chamberlain, but I don't know if the thought reached my face.

There was some kind of delay then. We didn't pop straight through to Louisville. Lesh got me stretched out on a bench and sat by my head, holding on to make sure I didn't roll off. Parthet and Kardeen conferred for a moment, off to the side, out of earshot for me in the shape I was in. Parthet examined the dead elf's sword closely and then shook his head. He picked the elf's head up and shook it. He set the head on a small table, facing him, and touched his rings to the elf's temples.

There was some chanting.

"Talk to me, you bastard," Parthet said.

"I can't," the head replied—quite clearly.

"If you don't, we'll bury you in chicken shit."

I guess that was some sort of ultimate threat to make to a dead elf warrior. His eyes opened wide and his face grew a look of supreme terror.

"You wouldn't!"

"In a second, with the greatest glee," Parthet assured him. "Tell me, was your blade poisoned?"

"I am the son of Xayber! I have no need of poisons."

Parthet spit in his eye. "You ain't the hot shit you thought you were, or you'd still have a body beneath your wagging chin."

"Enough," Baron Kardeen said softly. I was thinking the same thing, but my mouth was still on strike. I had never seen Uncle Parthet behave so crudely.

"For now," Parthet said, sighing. "But fill a crock with the strongest whiskey you can locate and put this head in it. We may need to talk to him again later. It depends on how Gil fares in the hospital. If there was more than steel to his blade, we may have to question him again."

"We'll keep him available," Kardeen said. His voice sounded oddly strained, *taut*.

Maybe I was the only one shocked by the head of a dead man, or dead elf, talking. He had no lungs to push air through a larynx. In fact, I doubted very much that he had a larynx left. Dragon's Death had caught him extremely high in the throat. I had a lot of questions that I wanted to ask, but I couldn't ask them. I had all the parts the elf was missing, but he could talk and I couldn't. What's fair about that?

But then they started moving me again. I could no more move on my own than that elf could. We went through a doorway to Louisville and woke Mother. She got her chance to fuss over me, but she didn't take long at it. She knew enough about medicine to know that my wound was out of her league. She got clothes on and led the way to the garage. They stretched me out in the back of her Dodge van. We all went to the hospital. Mother didn't bother calling an ambulance. I doubt that she even considered it. She preferred to do the driving—like a maniac, but Mother always drives that way. I was too numb to cringe, but I was still conscious enough to worry about her driving.

My first hours in the hospital are a blank. After an initial examination, x-rays, and other tests, they decided that I had to have immediate surgery, and for that, they turned out my lights. I have a feeling that they were surprised by how difficult it was to put me under, and at the time, I thought that my danger sense was fighting them with every bit of magic it had. But we were in Louisville, not in the buffer zone, and the magic lost.

When I came to, I was in a private room with two IV bags dripping clear fluid into my left arm. I woke quickly, without any drowsy, dreamy period. *Snap.* It wasn't until I started to reach for the elf sword that wasn't over my shoulder that I noticed the tubes to my arm. Memory flooded in to fill the gaps. I looked around. I was alone, but not for long. Mother and Parthet must have just stepped out for a drink of water or something. They came back in.

"How are you feeling?" Mother asked.

I was still taking stock. "Not bad, considering," I said after a moment, and then I realized that I had echoed Kardeen's assessment of Pregel's condition. I shook my head, but didn't bother to explain the gesture to Mother and Parthet. I still felt some pain, but less than just after the fight—and it could not *begin* to compare to the pain I felt after the dragon fell on me outside Castle Thyme.

The needles in my arms were more annoying than the pain from where the sword had slashed me. I mentioned that.

"The surgeon said that you were extremely lucky. All she had to do was sew up everything that was cut."

"How long have I been out?"

"Less than four hours altogether. The doctor said that you wouldn't be waking up for another hour or more and that you would probably be groggy all day." Mother shrugged. "I didn't take that too seriously. I saw your father wounded too many times."

"How long am I going to be cooped up here?"

"A few days. The doctor wasn't too specific. She said it depended on how you respond to the surgery, and whether there's any drainage infection."

I turned my head toward Uncle Parthet. Even with the wound and surgery, my mind was working a lot better than it normally does the morning after a good drunk. "Joy is going to be at O'Hare Airport in Chicago, just a few minutes after noon. She expects me to pick her up."

"You can't . . ." Mother started before she realized that I wasn't talking about going to meet her myself.

"I think there's probably time to catch her at her parents' house," I said. "It doesn't take very long to fly from St. Louis to Chicago."

"It's not six o'clock yet," Mother said. "She's probably not out of bed."

"I don't see a telephone in here," I said, looking around again.

"This is just the recovery ward," Mother told me. "You won't be moved to a regular room until later this morning."

"How much later?"

"I don't know. I'll have to check." I stared at her without speaking and she said that she would check on it right away and left.

"Where's Lesh?" I asked Parthet.

"Out with the automobile. I just went down there a bit ago to tell him that you're okay. He didn't want to come up, dressed for Varay. He's probably in more pain than you seem to be. I don't have any of the fixings for my hangover cure along."

"And I suppose your head's throbbing too."

"Not so bad, lad, not so bad. Now, what did you want to tell me that you chased your mother out for?"

"I'm going to need you to pick up Joy at the airport. I imagine she'll want to come here. If I can reach her at home, she can fly here instead of to Chicago. If not . . ."

"You want me to pick her up in Chicago and fetch her here."

"She doesn't know anything about Varay yet, Uncle," I said. "Not one word."

Parthet was quick on the uptake. "You mean I can't bring her down by doorway from your apartment."

"That's exactly what I mean."

"You want me to get on an *airplane* and bring her? I've never been on an airplane."

"You don't know what you're missing."

"And happy at that." He hesitated, but then he nodded. "I do hope you can get her on the telephone in time, though," he said.

"If they're not going to move me to a regular room in time for me to make the call, you could do it, but don't scare her to death. Tell her I'm okay before you tell her I'm in the hospital."

My surgeon came in then and bustled Parthet out of the room so she could examine me. She identified herself as Dr. Barlow as if "Doctor" were her first name and said that I shouldn't be awake yet. That came out almost like an accusation. She wanted to know how I felt, and how I happened to get stabbed so badly. Among other things.

I didn't answer any of the questions right away. She hardly gave me a chance to talk. But the delay was useful. It gave me time to try to remember if anything had been said about an "official" story. An urban hospital in the "real" world meant bureaucracy, a police report at the very least, maybe even a cop in to ask questions and be generally nosy. And I couldn't remember that we had agreed on any kind of lie to tell.

"I was out last night and got jumped," I said when I couldn't avoid the question any longer. "It was dark and I didn't see much." Keep it short. Keep it simple. We could do any necessary embellishing later.

Dr. Barlow nodded absently while she investigated the sutures she had stitched in my hide and the drain tube hanging out. "You were lucky," she said when she finished. She went to the sink at the side of the room and scrubbed her hands. "When I saw the wound, I expected to find more internal trauma than there was. The wound was deep but clean. It could almost have been made with a large scalpel. There were no severed sections of intestine, no damage to other internal organs. I stitched up the cut skin and muscles, the abdominal wall. Not much more complicated than a hernia operation, as it turned out."

"No permanent damage of *any* kind?" I asked.

She didn't look at me directly. "The reproductive system was not involved."

Well, I guess that was what I was referring to. I wasn't used to women doctors, even older, dumpy ones like Barlow.

"How long until I get out of the hospital?"

"Figure four or five days, if there are no complications."

"Can I get rid of these tubes? They're driving me crazy."

"Not yet. How about pain?"

"Not enough to distract me from these damn needles."

I guess I was too lucid or something. Dr. Barlow did all of the easily recognizable medical things on me without calling in a nurse to help. She checked my respiration and pulse, blood pressure, adjusted the drip on the IVs, and made a long entry in the metal-jacketed chart.

"I must be a better surgeon than I thought," she mumbled.

"Why do you say that?"

"No pain, too much energy. You shouldn't even be awake yet, and if you were awake, you should be groggy, hurting, and looking for a shot to put you back out."

"Just a waste of time," I said. "How soon can I get to a regular room? I've got an important phone call to make."

She stopped fiddling with the chart then and stared at me. "Do you *ever* feel pain?" she asked. The question startled me, but she wasn't being sarcastic. She was serious.

"Oh, yes, I feel pain," I told her. There were flashbacks to the Isthmus of Xayber and to the field next to Castle Thyme when I hurt so bad that death would have been welcome. "I've felt much worse pain than this."

I got to a room in plenty of time to make the call to Joy myself.

"Don't tell me you've decided that you don't want me to come back," she said as soon as she got on the line.

"I won't," I said. "It's just that I'm not going to be able to meet you at the airport. I had a little accident last night. I'm in the hospital, in Louisville. I'm okay, but it's going to be a few days before they let me out."

There was a silence that seemed to go on for quite a while before Joy said, "You sure it's not a nut house?"

"I'm sure."

"How badly are you hurt?"

"They had to operate on me during the night. Nothing major."

After another long silence, Joy said, "So, tell me just exactly where you are. I'll change my ticket and meet you there."

I told her. "My Uncle Parker will meet you at the airport," I said. "He's short, a little stooped, wears huge glasses about three inches thick, and he's something over twelve hundred years old." That was my latest estimate. Joy giggled, obviously assuming that I was making a joke. "He looks harmless, but don't let that fool you."

Joy called back twenty minutes later with her new schedule. It would take her until late afternoon to get to Louisville. I assured her that Uncle Parker would meet her and bring her straight to the hospital, and that she could stay with my mother until I got out of the hospital. I didn't clear that with Mother first, but there was no problem.

"Joy's all right," Mother said when I told her afterward. "She's not like that other creature." She tried never to refer to Annick by name. She hadn't liked Annick from their first meeting, before Annick and I had our one-night fling. At the time, I was surprised that Mother could even think that I would be attracted to anyone who got her jollies cutting the throats of sleeping men.

"What's involved in making a new set of rings?" I

asked. Mother didn't pick up on the hint there right away. The family rings operate the magic doorways. The passages are a *family* magic, but you don't have to be born to it. After all, Dad wasn't born to it, and he could use the doorways. The family magic came from Mother's family. She made it possible for Dad to use it . . . and I had already made it possible for Joy. In bed.

Mother shook her head. "That's Parthet's domain. You'd have to ask him."

Parthet had gone back downstairs, to keep Lesh company, I think. Lesh had made several previous trips to our world with me, a couple of them rather extended. The translation magic in the buffer zone makes language instruction impossible there, so we had to come out of the buffer zone before I could start teaching him English. And I wanted to learn the language of the buffer zone, which turned out to sound a lot like Old English or some early, mixed version of German and English. Lesh might not be the best teacher around, but having him to practice with helped, and I also had Mother and Parthet to draw on. That meant that I could pick up more vocabulary than you find in an army barracks. One of the flaws I had noticed in the translation magic during my first excursion as Hero of Varay was that it lumped together a lot of only vaguely similar creatures as *trolls*. Back in my world, without the magic to confuse things, Lesh had fourteen different terms for varieties of the creatures, and Parthet added a half-dozen more.

A moment passed before Mother said, "The rings. This girl from St. Louis?"

"Maybe." I shrugged. "I guess I won't know for sure until I see how she reacts to learning about Varay."

"A word of advice?" Mother waited, and I didn't object. "Be *very* certain of her before you try to explain."

I smiled. "I sort of figured that out, Mother. The fact is, I'm scared to tell her. I keep telling myself that she'll think I'm crazy if I just tell her about it, and if I just take her through one of the doorways without any warning or explanation, it'll scare her away, or make her think that *she's* flipped out."

"I called Dr. McCreary last night." There was a *long* silence before Mother said that.

"No need to phony up a death certificate for me yet,"

I said quietly. Hank McCreary was a Varayan expatriate living in Denver. After Dad's death in Varay, McCreary signed a certificate saying that Dad died on a mountain-climbing expedition, an accidental death, body recovered, examined, and cremated.

"No, but he's also had experience treating Varayan medical problems. I didn't know yet just how serious your injuries were, just that they were beyond my limits." Mother was something of a doctor herself, up to a point. Doc McCreary had done most of her training. In a place like Varay, it doesn't take much to be leagues above everyone else in medicine.

"So, what, have you got him flying up here?"

Mother shook her head. "I called him back after your doctor finished with you."

It wasn't quite the reunion I had been looking forward to for the past three months. The location of my wound would have made that temporarily impossible even though I wasn't in any great amount of pain. Parthet brought Joy in and then he left with Mother.

Joy was all shook up, and I could see that she had been crying. She was still sniffling when she came into the room.

"I'm okay, Joy, really," I told her.

She came over to the edge of the bed, but she seemed to be afraid to even touch me. I reached for her hand, and her instinct seemed to be to jerk away. And when we did hold hands, she didn't want to put any pressure on me.

"I'm not going to break into small pieces or start screaming in pain," I said, patiently, not sarcastically—not with Joy.

"He said you've got a big, long cut in your stomach."

"All sewed up, as secure as the seams of your jeans."

Joy didn't know whether to laugh or sob. The sound that came out had a little of each in it.

"Come a little closer," I told her. She did and I finally pulled her down for a good kiss. There was nothing wrong with my mouth.

Joy Bennett, the joy of my life. She went crazy whenever I made that kind of pun. After a year together, I couldn't find many new variations. Joy was twenty-one, slender, five-three, and light enough that she never even got on a bathroom scale. Her waist was *almost* small enough for me to get my hands all the way around it and made the other measurements look more exaggerated than they were. Her hair was in that vague borderline range between dark blond and light brown. Her eyes were a bluish gray, the kind of eyes that thriller writers like to call "steely-cold killer's eyes," but there was nothing steely or cold about Joy's eyes. Like me, Joy was something of a computer whiz, bending a natural talent to the rigors of formal training in college. At odd moments, I wondered if she would be able to step away from it cold turkey the way I did. The answer to that might be important.

The strength of my kiss finally convinced her that I didn't need to have FRAGILE stamped all over me. She relaxed and even managed to return the kiss with adequate warmth.

"So what happened?" she asked after we finished a fitting welcome-back-after-three-lonely-months kiss. "And how come you were in Louisville getting in trouble when you were supposed to be in Chicago getting all hot and bothered while you waited to pick me up?"

"I ran into a guy with a six-foot sword," I said. She started laughing, but I pulled the sheet aside and showed her the length of the cut. Her face when pale when she saw the bandage and the drain hanging out and all, but after a moment some color came back to her cheeks and she moved the sheet to look down a little farther.

"Just making sure," she said. I stopped her when she reached down to touch me a few inches below the bandage. I didn't want to press my luck yet. If I got an erection, it might lead to pain I didn't need, and if I didn't get one, I'd worry about it. Some complications are better avoided.

"How long are you going to be in here?" Joy asked, transferring her busy hands to my chest and arms. I adjusted the bed to sit me up and she hopped up next to me—but carefully—when I patted the sheet. We got our arms around each other and kissed again.

"A few more days, according to the doctor," I said. "I don't know how much longer we'll have to wait for anything else. Not too much, I think."

"Are you sure?"

"I'm sure," I told her, but I was mentally knocking on wood. "I'm a resilient kind of guy, and I've been waiting three months to get home to you."

"This kind of thing happen to you often?" she asked. Joy had seen the scar on my back, where the spear got me while I was on the "rampage" in Fairy, and she had seen the spot where the compound fracture of the left leg I got when the dragon fell on me outside Castle Thyme had popped through the skin, and the various other scars I had picked up during those weeks. A Hero of Varay might heal quickly, but the healing didn't do away with scars.

"Not too often," I said, pulling her close for another kiss. That seemed to be the best way to change the subject. I had told her that the scar on my back came from getting poked by a sharp stick—technically true, if evasive—and merely wrote the leg scar off as coming from a broken bone, without ever saying how I broke it.

Mother and Parthet gave us a good long time alone together, and Mother knocked and waited before she came back into the room. Everything was decorous by then. Even if I had felt up to anything, I wouldn't have tried it when I knew that Mother was in the hallway just outside the door.

Joy spent every minute she could in the hospital with me. She snuck in before visiting hours started at noon and didn't leave until the nurses chased her out after they ended—*long* after they ended. Mother and Parthet kept coming around. Lesh visited for a few minutes a couple of times, after he had what he considered a more suitable wardrobe, but everyone pretty much gave Joy and me all the time together we wanted.

By the third morning after the operation, Dr. Barlow was talking to herself almost constantly—at least when she came in to check on my condition. I wasn't just making a timely recovery, I was healing impossibly fast. The word "impossible" was finding its way into the doctor's conversation about every other sentence. I declined her request to stick around long enough for her to run a few extra tests on me and I told her that I wouldn't at all be happy to be part of a paper in the medical journal of her choice. Actually, I was somewhat more pointed about that, maybe a touch on the rude side. She didn't come by to say so long when she signed my release that afternoon.

Mother assumed, without asking, that I would want or need to stick around Louisville for a few extra days just to be sure that there weren't any complications. Dr. Barlow wanted to see me in five days to check on her artwork, and so forth. But since I was doing fine at that point, I didn't expect any later complications, and I didn't plan to spend even one more night in Louisville. Joy and I had things to do back in Chicago—or just about anywhere but in my mother's home.

That gave me another slight problem, getting back to Chicago with Joy. The problem? My danger sense goes completely berserk if I even get *near* an airplane, any airplane. You can't reason with magic. My danger sense didn't give a damn about all of those statistics that claim that air travel is the safest kind. And Joy didn't know about the magic passageways, so we couldn't very well just pop through to my apartment that way, not without spoiling the mood, no matter how well Joy took the experience. And I couldn't put Joy on an airplane and then pop through the doorway myself and beat her to Chicago.

There was only one real solution to the dilemma. No matter how much it disrupted my danger sense, we both had to take the airplane. Before we left for the airport, Uncle Parthet got me away from Joy long enough to tell me that he would make sure that my hardware got home safely. It wasn't until then that I remembered that he had brought my elf sword through with us the night I was hurt. I couldn't very well cart that along on the airplane.

Joy and I took a late-afternoon flight. It's only a short hop by air from Louisville to Chicago. We spent a lot more time on the ground than we did in the air, waiting for clearance to take off from Louisville, then getting from the runway to the terminal at O'Hare. The flight isn't even long enough for a meal (for small blessings . . .) and just long enough for a single drink (that the doctor had said I shouldn't try for at least two weeks).

As I expected, my danger sense raised hell from the time I first *saw* our aircraft, and it kicked up such an extra fuss near the end of the flight that I was almost convinced that we were going to crash. The seat-belt sign had already gone on for the landing, but I put my arm around Joy and held her as tightly as I could under the circumstances.

"What's the matter?" she asked.

"I hate airplanes," I whispered through clenched teeth. I hoped that there was nothing more to it than that.

"You're scared of flying?"

"Just the takeoffs and landings."

There was none of the usual friendly chatter from the pilot during the last part of the flight, which added to my apprehension, but neither was there any kind of dire warning. Our approach felt a little too steep, a little too fast, but then, my danger sense didn't like anything at all about the flight.

Once we were on the ground, I knew that there *had* been *something* wrong, somewhere along the way. I could hear it in the pilot's terse "Thank you for flying with us" speech and in the drawn faces of the stewardesses at the door as we left the plane and took the walk through the umbilical to the concourse. Once we were in the airport, the feeling of danger got as strong as it was that day when I opened the passage from Coriander to Arrowroot and felt the waves of danger flooding over me.

"Something's wrong," I told Joy as I hurried her along the concourse to the main part of the terminal and the baggage-claim area. "Something is terribly wrong. I can feel it."

"What?" Joy asked, a little out of breath. She was having trouble keeping up with me, and I finally had to either slow down or pull her off her feet. Her "Gil, what's the matter?" had an uneasy edge to it.

"I don't know yet," I told her, "but it has to be something really big."

I didn't give her time to question how I could "know" something like that, but it didn't take us long to find out what it was. Airports try to shield passengers from unsettling news, but this was just too big. I heard talk, and pretty soon I heard official talk. People were clustered around several of those coin-operated televisions that they have in the waiting areas.

The cruise ship *Coral Lady* had just been nuked by terrorists in Tampa Bay. A lot of people were dead. And panic was spreading faster than the mushroom cloud.

3

Red Pepper

Despite my involvement with Varay, I like to think that basically I'm a rational, intelligent human being. Consequently, the eruption of one hostile nuclear device conjured up nightmarish fears of a mushroom salad being tossed all around the globe. It was as if Gorbachev and his reforms had never existed, as if the reforms in Eastern Europe had never begun. All of the years of scare tactics that went before remained too strong, too close to the surface of my memory. I was terrified, and so was everyone around me. Many of the people in the airport seemed to be literally scared stiff, too petrified to even move. When my danger sense gave me an extra nudge, I figured that it was a just a reaction to the fear all around Joy and me. A crowd of people in a panic is a mob, a dangerous place to be.

For a few minutes, Joy and I stood and listened to the television reports along with a crowd of other rational, intelligent, *terrified* people. Hard facts were still scant. A "small" nuclear device had definitely vaporized the cruise ship *Coral Lady,* which may have been carrying as many as two thousand people, passengers and crew. The explosion had taken place, approximately, as the ship passed under the Sunshine Skyway Bridge, entering Tampa Bay. The extent of damages and casualties on shore wasn't even being estimated yet. The TV news people were having trouble doing their work. Phrases like "This is just terrible" and "I can't believe it" were getting in the way of reporting. The news people were as frightened as anyone else, and it was impossible to get reports from anywhere close to the center of the disaster. In the first spasm of official reaction, the military restricted all air space within a hundred miles of the site of the explosion, so reporters couldn't even move in with helicopters to get tape of the disaster scene.

After I collected the basic news—what little there was—I started to notice something even more frightening. Some people, on the television and in the crowd watching, refused to believe that the blast could have been an isolated act of terrorism committed by a small band of fanatics without some kind of governmental sanction and support. Calls for retaliation—against one group or nation or another—were already sounding. Different people had different ideas about who "must" have been responsible. The Soviets, Iranians, and PLO all had their accusers. There were a few instant arguments, one of which led quickly to a fistfight.

Chicago didn't feel like a very safe place to be just then. I started pulling Joy along again, away from the televisions . . . and away from the fight. No, I had no intention of getting involved or trying to stop it. I was "out of my jurisdiction," as the saying goes.

"What do we do?" Joy asked. She had to shout so I could hear her over the din in the terminal.

"The first thing to do is get to my place. The biggest problem right now will probably be panic." At least I hoped that there would be nothing worse than panic to cope with right away. That could be bad enough.

"What if there are more explosions?" Joy asked.

"One step at a time," I said.

We managed to snag Joy's two suitcases from the baggage carousel, which was a major surprise in itself. Even without a major catastrophe in the news, recovering luggage right away is never certain. But there wasn't a taxi or limo to be had outside the terminal. There were crowds of people waiting to mob any cab that did dare to drive up. The traffic cops and airport security couldn't hope to handle that kind of action. There were no CTA buses in sight either.

Joy and I went back inside and headed for the car-rental booths, but they were all swamped. We couldn't get within ten yards of a counter. It was pointless to wait. There wouldn't be a car left by the time we could get halfway through the lines.

"How are we going to get out of here?" Joy asked. She was starting to sound a little panicky herself.

I shook my head, but I was already pulling her along again. There was only one possibility left that I could think of, the El. If we could get aboard a train into the city, we could ride to within a mile of my condo, close enough to walk the rest of the way if we had to.

The elevated was apparently the last route anyone thought of. Possibly a lot of out-of-towners didn't know that there was a line running from the airport to the Loop, or they just weren't geared to thinking of that kind of transportation. There was still a crowd waiting, but not as large as the crowds trying to rent cars or flag down taxis that weren't there. Joy and I were able to move far enough through this crowd to squeeze aboard the first train.

Squeeze. There was scarcely room for everyone to inhale at the same time. Not even a world-class pickpocket could have operated in that car. Our ride into the city was long, uncomfortable, and more than a little terrifying. Each stop brought the risk of a riot as some people inside tried to get out and more people outside tried to cram in. The stops weren't long enough for passengers to get off if they weren't already near a door, and no one could move toward the doors until some of the passengers in front of them got off.

By the time we got near the Loop, Joy and I were able to get out. We just took the first opportunity that came up, even though we were still quite a distance from my place. We had to walk for a few blocks then, but conditions weren't nearly as chaotic in the city as they were out at the airport. In fact, things may have been calmer in the streets than usual. There were people out on the sidewalk talking to neighbors and strangers, everyone wondering what was going on, but more people must have been inside, glued to their televisions and radios. Eventually, we were able to flag down a cabbie who was still working, though he had a boom box on the front seat next to him and it was blasting out the news. When we pulled up at the entrance to the apartment building, I gave the cabbie a fifty and told him to keep the change. He almost smiled.

There was no security guard on duty in the lobby, but I wasn't about to call the building manager to complain about the lapse. Joy and I went right on through and had an elevator to ourselves. Still, the elevator seemed to move as slowly as if it had to stop at every floor between the lobby and thirty-eight.

Once we were in my apartment with the door locked behind us, I started to relax, just a little. In the apartment, no matter what happened, we were only a few steps away from safety. I dropped Joy's suitcases in the foyer and we stood there, just clinging to each other at first.

"I'm scared," Joy said, her voice muffled because she was talking half into my shirt.

"Me too, a little," I conceded, "but we'll be safe now." I still needed a couple of minutes to calm down to only halfway panicked myself. Scared? You bet. Hero or not, I was damn scared. With any luck at all, my danger sense would give us enough time to escape through one of my magic doorways even if an H-bomb was about to go off overhead. The danger sense worked just as well in the real world as it did in the buffer zone. But the fear was still there.

"I'll turn on the TV so we can find out what's going on," I said after I got myself more or less under control. "You see if you can get through to your parents on the telephone." I figured that the phone lines would all be jammed, but if Joy didn't try, she might be sorry later. I was starting to think properly again, and that relaxed me a little more.

"If you do get through, tell them that you're safe and that I'll make damn sure you stay safe." I didn't turn loose of Joy right away, though. "You might suggest that they put together whatever food and survival gear they can pack into their car and get ready to head out into the country if things get any worse." If war did come, running to the country might not help, but it had to offer more hope than sitting around in a major metropolitan area waiting to be vaporized.

Despite *glasnost* and *perestroika* and the disintegration of Communism in Eastern Europe, there was still a chance for all hell to break loose. The remaining hardliners might seize the opportunity to try to reestablish themselves. I couldn't forget how the optimism of that May in Beijing had turned to horror in Tiananmen

Square, the bloodshed that Romania had gone through, or the continuing difficulties within the Soviet republics.

"Is that what we're going to do?" Joy asked.

"Something like that." I didn't even smile. I was too tense for that. "We've got a safe bolt hole we can get to in a hurry." How long the buffer zone would remain safe if our world fell into a stupid general war I couldn't guess . . . but I didn't expect to see mushroom clouds over Varay.

Joy went to the telephone while I turned on the televisions in the living room and master bedroom. There didn't seem to be anything new on about the *Coral Lady* at the moment. In the bedroom, I spotted two six-foot swords lying on the bed. *Two* of them. I had forgotten the second sword, the one that Xayber's son had used on me, and it had been a long time since I had heard the line that an abandoned elf sword would return to kill whoever abandoned it. That was why I started carrying the first one, Dragon's Death. Now, it seemed, I had a second to worry about.

There was a sheet of Uncle Parthet's three-by-five spiral notebook paper with the swords, but all it said was: "See you at Basil."

Louisville! I hoped that everyone there had hopped back to Varay at the first word of trouble.

"I can't get through on the telephone," Joy said when I rejoined her in the living room. "I can't even get long distance. All I get is a busy signal when I dial the one."

"Did you try the operator?"

"All lines are busy, please try again later."

"Then we'll just have to keep trying," I said, giving her a quick kiss.

Joy nodded, too vaguely, then excused herself. As soon as I heard the bathroom door close, I hurried through the dining room and hit the silver tracing on the door to the kitchen and stepped through to Mother's house. I started shouting and running through the place, but there was no one there. When I spotted both cars in the garage, I figured that they had all scrammed back to Varay. I hoped so. I even got home to Chicago before Joy came out of the bathroom.

She went right to the telephone again and had no luck. She hung up and tried again. And again.

"Give it a few minutes," I suggested. I went to her and led her back to the sofa. "It can't help to keep dialing over and over. That may be what's keeping the lines tied up, everybody trying over and over like that."

She nodded. We sat on the sofa and watched the news on the television for a time. I held Joy close to me, but she hardly seemed aware of me. I could understand that. She was scared, really *scared,* for maybe the first time in her life. I was scared too, but fear was no stranger to me.

The TV networks were all staying exclusively with coverage of the terrorist attack and the reactions to it around the world—obviously. They didn't have a lot of information from anywhere near the scene yet: some tape taken from helicopters before the Air Force chased them away, a long way from the scene of the explosion, and the first radio reports from on the ground in west Florida—not very close to the scene either. Mostly, the networks were reduced to covering press conferences and briefings in Washington and Tallahassee. No one held out even the slightest hope for any of the people who had been on the *Coral Lady,* but the lists of passengers and crew weren't being made public until an effort could be made to contact all of the families. A large section of the Sunshine Skyway Bridge crossing Tampa Bay had disappeared, and the remaining sections were just so much twisted wreckage. No one had any idea how many people and vehicles might have been lost on the bridge. Afternoon traffic had been heavy, according to one traffic helicopter that managed to escape the blast and land safely after the explosion. The blast had sent the waters of Tampa Bay crashing up on shore, then sucked the water level down as water streamed in to fill the hole left in the sea by the nuclear explosion. A second tidal wave flowed ashore then, swamping boats and low-lying coastal areas, causing more as-yet-unknown casualties and damage.

At least the early diplomatic news was less terrifying. No one seemed ready to start throwing missiles around. Everyone was talking—saying "Not me" and generally condemning terrorism in general and the attack on the *Coral Lady* in particular. It wasn't just the "man on the street" who was frightened by the possibilities. This time it was more than politics that got the various heads of state in front of the cameras and microphones.

The networks had to fill most of their time covering the reactions of people like the ones Joy and I had seen at the airport and on the elevated coming in from O'Hare. The same kind of crowd scenes had been played out in most of the major cities of the United States to one degree or another, and there were some reports of panic overseas as well. People had been hurt, trampled. At least three had been killed in separate incidents. The initial panic was slow in passing, but conditions were already improving—according to one network anchorman who was just beginning to get his own emotions under control.

Nearly a half hour passed before Joy decided to try calling her parents again. The network had gone to a rehash of Three Mile Island and Chernobyl and the problems following those. They even started talking about Hiroshima and Nagasaki, the only cities to suffer nuclear explosions previously. Joy only had to try twice to get through to St. Louis this time.

I busied myself checking to see if there was anything I wanted to take along to Varay. Sure, the immediate danger seemed less than it had just an hour before, but I wasn't ready to accept even the remaining risk. I was going to get Joy somewhere safe. That still presented its own problems, but I couldn't slough them off any longer.

The telephone conversation sounded like a disaster of its own. Joy was talking and sobbing at the same time. I don't know if her parents could understand a word she was saying. I couldn't understand some of them. But she did calm down a little before she finished. Her parents had to know that she was safe, and she knew that they were safe. Since there were still no dangerous alarms of additional explosions coming over the television, that had to be enough for the moment.

I handed Joy a box of tissues when she got off the telephone and she went through about half the box. Then she hugged me and put her head against my shoulder and I just held her until she was ready to talk.

"They're okay," she said.

I smiled. "Yeah, I could tell. You feeling better?"

She nodded. "We're still not having much of a reunion, are we?"

"It'll get better." I took her back to the sofa and we sat down again. I wasn't sure yet how to break the news about Varay to her, but I didn't want to put it off any longer. I guess I hemmed and hawed around the fringes for several minutes before I really took the plunge.

"You remember that I said that I have a safe place for us to go?" I started. Joy nodded.

"I've been trying to find a way to tell you about this place since we started getting serious about each other."

She got a mildly puzzled look on her face but didn't say anything.

"I love you," I said. There was a long silence between us then. Joy's puzzled look got deeper. I started feeling frustrated. I wasn't getting anywhere.

"I love you too," Joy finally said, but she sounded hesitant, worried about where I was heading with the talk, I guess.

"The problem is, if I just tell you about this place you'll think I'm crazy. And if I take you there without telling you a little about it first, you'll think *you're* crazy. Or maybe you'll just get scared."

"I've been scared since we heard about that bomb going off," she said.

Good point. Let's try again, I told myself.

"You know the story of *Alice in Wonderland?* She falls down a rabbit hole, then goes through a door into a crazy, magical world?"

"I saw it on TV last year. What in the world are you getting at?"

But I was running out of words. "I think it's time to show you," I said, getting up from the sofa. "Just remember *Alice in Wonderland.*"

"Where are we going?"

"We're going someplace safe. And we start in the bedroom." I had hold of her hand and half-pulled her up from the sofa. Joy started giggling. I guess she was ready to write off all the strange talk as the start of a new sex game. That would do for the moment.

"You had me worried," she said.

We detoured to pick up her bags. I carried them into the master bedroom and left them right by the door.

"Should I unpack anything first?" Joy asked.

"Not yet." I pulled her to me and kissed her with all the fervor and passion I could muster, then broke the clinch.

"Just a second. I've got to get something before we go."

Specifically, I had to get the two elf swords. I slipped the straps for the shoulder rigs in place and the blades clattered together. Joy's eyes expanded.

"I told you that I ran into a guy with a six-foot sword," I said, trying to make it sound light, like a joke. "The one with the ebony handle was his."

"And the other one?" She wanted it spelled out.

"That's mine." I kept my eyes on Joy. Her smile had already evaporated. Now, fear started to crawl across her face again. It was time to hurry.

"You'd better carry one of your bags. That will make this a little faster."

She nodded automatically and picked up the smaller suitcase, still looking at the hilts of the swords sticking up behind my shoulder. I used my rings to open the doorway into Castle Cayenne, then held it open with just my left hand. I used the right hand to urge Joy through the door. Her eyes went blank as soon as I opened the passage, but she didn't resist. Then I pushed her other suitcase through with my foot and stepped through behind it.

Joy turned to stare at me, and past me, again. When I took my left hand from the silver tracing and my Chicago bedroom disappeared, she screamed.

She screamed.

In the movies, the hero slaps the heroine's face when she screams hysterically. She stops and after a dramatic pause for a close-up, she says, "Thanks, I needed that," or something equally trite. Maybe real life was even like that once upon a time, but women's lib and the modern horror of even minor violence on a personal scale have killed that kind of reaction. People get more upset if a man slaps a woman he knows than they do if he murders twenty or thirty strangers. In any case, I don't think I could ever bring myself to hit Joy, certainly not for screaming in reasonable terror.

I shouted her name, then took her in my arms and held her tight—with almost crushing force. The scream stopped, but the blank look of horror remained. I shook her, very gently, just enough to get her attention.

"Joy, you're safe here." I spoke rather loudly to make sure that I was getting through. "I love you. I love you." I didn't know what else to say. I had never had to deal with hysterics before.

I started to get scared again myself. I had worried about Joy's reaction to Varay from the beginning, but I had never dreamed that her reaction might be this extreme, that she would go hysterical or catatonic on me. I held on to her until her shaking slowed down, then led her to the bed, and we sat on the edge of it. Joy moved as if she were in a trance. I continued to hold her tight.

"This is Castle Cayenne, my home in the kingdom of Varay. That's in a buffer zone between our world and Fairy," I said, speaking slowly. All I could think to do was to tell her as much of the story as I could, in simple terms, and hope that some of it would penetrate the shock and start her back to an even keel. I thought that she would be able to cope very well, once she got used to the idea, if we could just get past this initial fright.

"*Alice in Wonderland. The Wizard of Oz.* The idea shouldn't be all that impossible to accept," I said.

"We're not in Kansas anymore, Toto," Joy misquoted dully. At least she was talking again.

There was a sudden pounding at the door, and Joy jumped just as Lesh swung the door open and charged in with his sword in his hand. He saw me, us, and stopped. He started backing toward the door at once.

"Sorry, lord," he said, sheathing his blade. "We heard a scream. I didn't know you were back."

"It's okay, Lesh. We just got here," I said. I looked from him to Joy, then back. "You might fetch a bottle of the Bushmills, some water, and a couple of glasses."

"Aye, lord." Lesh backed the rest of the way to the door, half-bowing several times. "Are you feeling well now, lord?" he asked.

"Well enough," I said, nodding. Lesh closed the door as he left. Joy stared at the door, then turned her head to look at me.

"Lesh?" she said.

"You've met him before," I reminded her. "A couple of times. He was at the hospital, and before that, in Chicago, during Mardi Gras."

"Am I going crazy or is this all a dream like *The Wizard of Oz?*"

"Neither. You're not going crazy and this isn't a dream. This is all for real."

Joy shuddered, then put her head on my shoulder for a moment. She was still trembling, but not as wildly as before.

"He kept calling you 'lord,' " she said after a moment, and her voice was beginning to sound a little more normal as well.

I took a deep breath. "He calls me that because he knows it doesn't bother me as much as being called 'Your Highness.' "

"Gil, what's going on?" Plaintive, still frightened, but not in the same way as before.

"The 'lord' is because I'm the Hero of Varay. Capital H. It's a formal title. But my great-grandfather is the king, and I'm also his heir."

She didn't respond to that.

"I didn't learn about any of this until my twenty-first birthday," I said. I started to tell her about that, but I didn't get very far before Lesh knocked at the door and brought in a tray with a bottle of Bushmills Irish whiskey, a pitcher of water, and two small crystal glasses filled with ice cubes. Lesh and Parthet must have brought a load of ice through from Louisville.

Lesh set the tray on the nightstand and left without speaking. I poured whiskey for both Joy and me. Joy was never much of a drinker. I had only seen her try hard liquor once, and she only rarely had a glass or two of wine with a meal. But she didn't hesitate now, and she waved me off when I went to add water to her drink. She took the glass I handed her and poured most of the whiskey into her mouth. She coughed and gagged a little, then made a face, but it did seem to help her. She finished, handed the glass back to me, and said, "More."

I refilled her glass, and topped mine off. I had only had time to take one small sip of mine.

"I've fallen into a fairy tale," Joy mumbled while I was pouring her second drink.

"Sort of," I said, returning her glass.

"With strange creatures, evil witches, and all that?"

"Enough strange creatures, I suppose. No witches, but there are wizards, some good, some not. That kind of magic is gender-specific." The way Parthet put it was a lot earthier. *"The only woman with the balls for magic is the Great Earth Mother,"* he told me when I asked him about witches, *"and she is far beyond mere magic."*

"My Uncle Parker—his real name is Parthet, by the way—is a wizard."

"That funny old man?" She hesitated a bit, took a more controlled drink of her whiskey, then said, "I guess he does look a little like the phony wizard in *The Wizard of Oz.*"

"Well, Parthet may not be the most talented wizard around, but he *is* for real. So are the dragons, trolls, evil elflords, and all the rest."

"Oh, shit," Joy said. She took another long drink, coming close to the bottom of the glass again. I took a fair-sized drink myself. I had never heard her use the word *shit* before. She was starting to pick up one of my bad habits.

"You ready for the fifty-cent tour of Castle Cayenne?" I asked.

Her smile was weak, but she was trying. "Might as well," she said. We both emptied our drinks first.

"We're closer to the top than the bottom, so I guess we start there," I said, leading her to the stairs.

Castle Cayenne was more than a thousand years old. At least some parts of the original were still in use, though the castle had been rebuilt, repaired, and renovated several times in that millennium. Even I had made some changes to the place in the three years since King Pregel presented it to me as my "local" residence. The biggest change was the water supply. We now had a fifteen-hundred-gallon water tank on the roof and a three-inch fire hose running from it to a small stream several hundred yards from the castle. I didn't have a pump, but Uncle Parthet had come up with a dandy spell to make water run uphill—or up the hose at least—to keep the tank full, so I had running water in the castle. I even had hot water, during the day and for a few hours after sunset, on days when the sun shone. I didn't have the most efficient solar system, but at least I could take a bath without freezing or having servants haul buckets of hot water up from the kitchen. Castle Cayenne also had a rudimentary septic tank and drainfield installed outside to help get rid of waste, along with the accompanying odors and health hazards that go with the lack of modern sewer systems. Maybe I couldn't give Cayenne all of the modern conveniences, but when I moved in I was determined to go as far as I could.

Cayenne doesn't even pretend at being fancy. It's just a simple circular tower, sixty-five feet high and fifty in diameter, with crenelated parapets. There's no outer wall, no gatehouse, outbuildings, moat, or little turrets sticking up at corners. It's just a single naked tower. Cayenne was built in a region of Varay that had little to fear from outside invasion. The rationale was that it would help control bandits in the area—the foothills of the Titan Mountains—and there was little trouble with bandits any longer.

Joy and I climbed to the roof to start our tour of the castle. The roof has my water tank, a small shelter for a sentry (though I had never bothered to post a sentry since I took over the place), racks of spears and bins of arrows, and a small stack of stones for hurling down at attackers who had never come. I wouldn't be at all surprised to learn that some of those stones had been sitting there since the castle was first built.

The time difference between Chicago and Varay meant that it was still light out when Joy and I climbed to the top of Cayenne. Sunset was nearly a half hour off and we had a good view of the surrounding countryside—forest and low, rolling hills, with the mountains off in the distance, to the south.

"It's not Kansas, not even Chicago," I said. Joy nodded and tightened her grip on my arm. "To the south, those are the Titan Mountains, supposedly an impassable barrier with nothing beyond them." I pointed. "Everything else you can see is southern Varay."

"If the mountains weren't so high, it might almost be Kentucky or Tennessee, maybe even the Ozarks," Joy said softly. Her voice still sounded shaky, but not as bad as before.

"Pretty much," I agreed. "The mountains are much

higher, though, even higher than the Rockies. Maybe even up close to the Himalayas. But they are mountains. Maybe that's why I like this part of the country." Well, the terrain and the fact that it was about as far from the Isthmus of Xayber as I could get in Varay. According to Parthet and everyone else I consulted, the power of an elflord diminished in some kind of strict proportion to the distance from Fairy and his demesne.

The sixth floor of Cayenne, the first one below the roof, holds living quarters for the small live-in staff and my "retinue," Lesh, Harkane, and Timon. The fifth floor holds my private apartments—bedroom, sitting room, bathroom. The fourth floor has a small office, but most of the level is set aside for weapons practice; call it a gymnasium. The third floor is Cayenne's version of a great hall—not particularly great, but it takes up the entire level. The second floor has the scullery, larders, and various supply closets. The ground level is mostly a stable. The outer door is thick wood sheathed with metal, inside and out. Two wooden bars the size of railroad ties slide into metal brackets to lock the door. Other wooden bars could be propped against the door to give extra support, and outside there was a slight ramp leading down to grade, making it that much more difficult for attackers to batter down the door. A lockable wrought-iron gate across the bottom of the ramp was the final touch. There was no way to tell if the defenses were really adequate. They had never been fully tested.

Joy and I didn't go all the way down to the ground floor, though. We stopped in the great hall. It was suppertime. I don't have a large staff, but Lesh had obviously passed the word that I had returned.

"I'm starving," Joy said when we smelled the food and saw the first trays being hauled up from the kitchen. I thought an appetite was a good sign.

"Oh, yes," I said, and then I laughed. "That's something else about this place. You eat and eat and can't possibly get fat. It's a literal impossibility."

Joy giggled, and it sounded healthy rather than hysterical. I tried to hold back a sigh of relief.

"Now, *that's* what I call a proper fairy-tale world," she said.

We sat at the table and Timon rushed about to serve

both of us. Joy was as upset at that kind of attention as I was when I first came to Varay, but I told her she would get used to it . . . . even though I had never really gotten comfortable with it myself and I usually told Timon to knock it off when we were "at home." I didn't permit any of the nonsense—two tables, servants eat "below the salt" or wait until afterward—at Cayenne that held most places in the buffer zone either. The cooks came out, and the two lads who helped Timon with the serving, Harkane, Lesh, and the six men-at-arms under Lesh's command all sat at the table and we ate together. I introduced Joy to everyone.

And everyone dug right into the food. I ate with my customary abandon, but I kept watching Joy put away food at the same time. She *never* ate much. She was short and thin and she always told me that she intended to stay thin. But she didn't show any diet control at all during her first meal in Varay. She put away food, wine, and coffee—especially a lot of food. It is probably an exaggeration to say that she ate as much in that one meal as she had in the year and odd months that I had known her, but it is a tempting exaggeration.

Timon loaded up our plates at the start of the meal, and whenever he happened to notice one of us getting low on anything, he tried to get around to replace it, but I kept waving him back to his seat. Even after three years, he couldn't get it into his head that I really didn't appreciate that kind of service at home. It might be socially required at Basil or elsewhere, but I didn't want it in my own little place with no visiting big shots.

Cayenne is a compact little community. My two cooks and most of the others who work in the castle live in the small village that sits alongside the creek a few hundred yards downstream from the castle. The guards are the only locals who come close to living in the castle, and three of them have families in the village. Cayenne village was founded to supply the castle and it was still doing that after more than a thousand years.

The current population of Cayenne village was seventy-three.

I was just getting to the point where I was almost full when Parthet came barging in—clomping down the stairs from the passage to Castle Basil. I started to invite him to sit down and eat, but he didn't give me a chance.

"Something extraordinary has happened," he said, short of breath. "You'd better come along to Basil right now."

"Slow down, have a beer," I said. It was unlike Parthet to pass up any opportunity to eat, no matter what the crisis.

"No time. Come on, lad. This is urgent." He appeared to notice Joy then. He smiled and winked at her. "Glad to see you finally made it here, my dear," he said. Then he turned to me again. "What are you waiting for?"

"Hang on. What's this all about?" I had *never* seen Parthet refuse a beer before.

"He says his name is Aaron."

4

Aaron

"Aaron?" I said. Beside me, Joy stopped eating and looked up at Parthet too. "What's this all about?" I asked again.

Parthet chuckled and shook his head. "I think you'd best see for yourself, lad. You wouldn't believe me if I told you."

"Come on, Uncle. After three years of this place, even the Cheshire Cat wouldn't surprise me." I made a face. "Your timing could sure use some work." Then I turned to Joy. "You want to wait here or come along?"

"Come along to where?" Joy asked.

"To Castle Basil, the capital."

"Through another one of those spooky doors?"

"I'm afraid so. You don't have to come if you don't want to. You can wait here and get settled in if you prefer. I shouldn't be gone too long. Right, Uncle?" I looked over at Parthet again.

"Probably not, lad, probably not." He was still chuckling. Whoever Aaron was, he sure had Parthet tickled.

Very quietly, Joy said, "I don't think I'm up to being left behind yet."

I gave her hand a squeeze. "It won't be so bad, now that you know what's coming. We'll go along and see what's got Uncle Parthet smirking so, then we'll come back. Pretty soon you won't think any more about using the magic doors than you would about an elevator."

"I'm not sure about that. This is too much like 'Beam me up, Scotty.' "

I laughed and we got up from the table. "I never even thought of that," I said.

"Must be a flaw in your education."

"Did you get enough to eat?" I asked, glancing sideways so I'd be sure to catch her reaction as we followed Parthet to the stairs.

"I've never eaten so much in my life," Joy said. "It was as if I was starving to death. I hope you weren't lying about not gaining any weight."

I chuckled. "I've been eating like that for more than three years and I weigh exactly what I did before I came here."

We stopped for my swords before we popped through to Basil. The swords bothered Joy until I explained. "It's a formality. Tradition says that the Hero of Varay *must* be armed at all times in public." That worked until I strapped on both of the claymores, one sword diagonally over each shoulder. Then I had to explain the superstition that an abandoned elf sword would work to a person's disadvantage. That's the word I used. Joy nodded, but she was obviously unsatisfied with my explanation. I didn't strap on my regular broadsword, the blade I had practiced with as a teenager, the one I had used until I "inherited" my first long elf sword, Dragon's Death. My belt only held my dagger, and Joy didn't say anything about that. Since we were just going to Castle Basil, there was no need to carry anything else in the way of weapons, no bow and quiver of arrows, for instance, and I didn't bother to put on armor.

The doorway leading to my bathroom in Cayenne opens into my bedroom at Castle Basil.

"I see you've got yourself a real setup here," Joy whispered to me after we went through. "You can hop from bed to bed without even putting your pants back on."

"The only bed I'm interested in is the one you're in," I whispered back. It's nice to find the right thing to say once in a while—especially when it's the truth.

There was a crowd in the great hall of Castle Basil, but more organized than usual. As we crossed the room from the doorway, it looked as if everyone but the king was present. The focus of all the attention was the head of the lower table. The crowd was so thick that I couldn't see who, or what, they were all staring at.

As we crossed the room, Parthet whistled shrilly to get folks' attention. A few looked, then a few more. They saw Parthet. They saw me. There was some whispering.

Most Varayans were more impressed with a Hero of Varay than I was. Half the time I still had to check to make sure that people weren't staring at me because my fly was open. A path opened in the crowd. People backed off to make room for us.

And I got my first glimpse of Aaron.

He was eating, but someone tapped him on the shoulder, then pointed when he looked up. Aaron looked our way, then stood up.

Aaron was black, extremely dark-skinned. I had known only one black guy that dark before, and he used to brag about it. ''Ain't no honky skeletons in *my* family closet.'' He never sounded convincing when he tried to talk like that. An honors student at Northwestern, from a well-to-do family. Barry had never had much contact with what one of our English professors called Standard Black American English.

Aaron was thin, with close-cropped hair, dressed in blue jeans, print shirt, and Adidas sneakers. All of his clothing looked new. The jeans were rolled up into exaggerated cuffs.

Parthet moved a little ahead of Joy and me.

''Aaron, this is Gil Tyner,'' Parthet said.

Aaron looked up at me without blinking. ''You the Man?'' he asked. Aaron didn't sound comfortable talking like that either.

I smiled. ''I studied computer science at Northwestern University, Aaron,'' I said. ''And this is Joy Bennett. She just graduated from Northwestern.''

''I know where that is,'' Aaron said. ''I'm from Joliet.''

''How old are you, Aaron?'' I asked.

''Eight, almost nine.''

''What's your full name?''

''Aaron Wesley Carpenter. I'm supposed to start fourth grade this year.''

It was easy to see that Aaron was scared, but he was trying to hide it. At least he didn't seem to be as panic-stricken as Joy had been. Maybe being a kid has some real advantages.

''You get enough to eat?'' I asked.

''I *never* get enough to eat,'' Aaron said, very earnestly. It got a laugh. Apparently, his appetite had drawn comment back home.

"Well, why don't you sit back down and keep eating. We can talk while you eat, if you don't mind."

"You gonna tell me how to get home? My gramma's gonna be worried."

Aaron and I sat down. Joy stood right behind me, her hands on my back—although she almost got tangled up in my swords first. Aaron looked at the sword hilts sticking up over my shoulders.

"Are those real?" he asked, pointing with a chunk of bread.

"The swords?" I asked. He nodded, then I did. "They're real."

Aaron looked around at all the people who were still staring at him. Now that he was at least a little less hungry than before, the crowd was beginning to bother him. I could understand that. I'm not at all that fond of crowds myself.

"Uncle, can you . . ." I gestured around. Parthet caught my meaning and, with Baron Kardeen's help, shooed off most of the gawkers.

"You want to tell me what happened to you, Aaron?" I asked after we had some clear space around us. Joy sat at my other side after the guards who had been there slid down the bench with their mugs of beer.

"Don't know what happened," Aaron said.

"Just tell me what you remember."

"*He-Man* was on TV. Gramma lets me watch that."

"Don't your parents let you watch it?"

He shrugged. "They both work."

"Okay, go on, Aaron," I urged. "What happened? You were watching *He-Man*."

"News came on, right in the middle. The man said a ship got blowed up. Gramma screamed and started crying. I got scared and something went *poof*, and I wasn't there no more."

"Why did your grandmother scream?" I asked, even though I could make a decent guess at the answer without much trouble.

"Mom and Dad went on the boat." He stopped eating then and started crying. Tears ran down his face. He didn't sob or make any noise. The tears just flowed.

"He appeared in the town," Parthet said softly, behind Joy and me. "I mean that just the way it sounds. He just popped up suddenly, out in front of the Bald Rock. There were several witnesses. The boy was scared and the townspeople brought him straight up here. I've never heard of anything like this happening before."

"You heard about the *Coral Lady,* I take it," I said, very softly, turning away from Aaron.

Parthet nodded. "We heard. That's why we all came back here so fast. Your mother wanted to wait until we could make sure that you had made it through, but I, uh, overruled her."

I couldn't hold back a smile. *That* was a scene I would have liked to see. Even Dad had trouble overruling Mother on anything, and Parthet wasn't a particularly assertive sort.

"I made a quick jump to Louisville to check on you after I found the swords on my bed," I said.

"You wear them well."

"Yeah, well, I'd better not come up with any more of these things. I feel like a complete jackass wearing two of them."

"Just think of the legends you're spawning," Parthet said, chuckling broadly. "It's something rare for a mortal to be able to claim even one elf sword. You've got two of them."

"Until Xayber sends another hotshot after me, maybe two or three of them together next time."

All this time, Aaron Carpenter sat at the table crying silently. He wasn't paying any visible attention to us, but I tried to keep an eye on him. When he started wiping at his eyes with his sleeves, I turned back to face him head on.

"Your parents were on vacation?" I asked.

He shook his head. "They're doctors."

That stopped me flat for a minute. "They had a meeting on the boat?" I asked finally. It was the only thing I could think of. Aaron nodded.

"You were staying at your grandmother's house when you went poof?" I asked, and Aaron nodded again. I asked him for the address and he rattled it right off without any hesitation or doubt.

"You gonna take me home?" Aaron asked.

My automatic affirmative was stopped when Parthet jabbed me in the shoulder. I turned to look at him and he shook his head vigorously.

"Hang on a minute, Aaron," I said. "I'll be right back." I got up and went off with Parthet, pulling him along by the sleeve of his Louisville Cardinals sweatshirt. Joy slid along the bench to where I had been sitting and started talking to Aaron.

"What the hell's got into you?" I asked Parthet when we were far enough away that Aaron wouldn't hear us.

"You can't take him home," Parthet said.

"Why not? His grandmother is probably going crazy if she saw him disappear like that. Even if she didn't actually see it."

"His parents are dead. They were on the *Coral Lady.*"

"I figured that out. What difference does it make? He's still got family."

"You're going to find a way to convince his grandmother that she isn't crazy?"

"It can be done," I said. "Just what's got into you?"

Parthet hesitated a beat before he answered. "You remember that I told you that I would know when it was time for me to start training an apprentice? Well, it's time. Nothing like this has ever happened. It's the clearest message I could have. Aaron is here to be my apprentice."

"He's just a kid!"

"That's the best time to start training him. The only time, as a matter of fact."

"Isn't eight years old a bit young to ask somebody to give up any hope of ever having children of his own?" I asked. I hadn't forgotten about *that* consequence of becoming a wizard.

"That comes with initiation, not with apprenticeship," Parthet said.

"It's beside the point anyway," I said.

"You still don't realize how singular an event this is, do you?" Parthet asked.

"I guess not. And it doesn't really matter."

Parthet shuffled from one foot to the other while he stared at me. "It has never happened before, anywhere, anytime. People don't blink in and out like that, not even in the buffer zone. That lad has a stronger touch for the craft than I've *ever* seen, even in someone out of Fairy. He must be a natural."

"I'm going to see if I can get in touch with his grandmother," I said slowly. "You have no right to keep him here."

Parthet really wasn't ready to give up the argument, but I turned and went back to the table, and Parthet followed.

"You have any brothers or sisters, Aaron?" I asked.

He shook his head.

"You want to go back to your grandmother's house now, or would you like to look around here first? If you want to look around the castle for a while, I'll go tell your grandmother that you're okay, that she doesn't have to worry."

"You'll tell her?"

"Sure. There's a lot to see here. It's a pretty neat castle." I waited a moment wishing that Lesh had come through to Basil with us. I had a feeling that if I turned Aaron over to Parthet, the youngster might not get much of a free choice. Parthet wanted to keep Aaron in Varay more than I had ever seen him want anything. There was only one possible out.

"You see that tall guy over there?" I asked Aaron. I pointed across the table. "That's Baron Kardeen. He's the king's right-hand man. He knows everything there is to know about this castle, and I'm sure he'd be happy to show you around the whole place." I looked up at Kardeen. So did Aaron. The chamberlain smiled and nodded. We went around the table. I took Kardeen aside and told him to keep Parthet away from Aaron until I could make arrangements to get him home. And I told him why.

"Leave it to me," Kardeen said. I left Aaron with him and went back to Parthet.

"I do have something to ask you, Uncle," I said. "Mother said that new rings are your job. I need a set for Joy. Any problem with that?"

He was scowling, but he shook his head. "A minor magic, new rings. I have molds." He glanced her way. "Small hands, right?"

"Her ring fingers are smaller than my little fingers,"

I said, holding out my hands. "You need an exact ring size?"

He shook his head again. "I think I can come up with the proper size. I've seen her hands." At least I didn't get any excuses about his not being able to see any more. I made sure that he got his eyes checked and got new glasses every year, whether he wanted to take the time or not. He didn't complain too much about that after seeing how much better he could see.

I went back to the table for Joy and then we stepped back to my apartment in Chicago, directly from Castle Basil. It was Joy's third time through a doorway, so she hardly blinked.

"You have these gizmos set up everywhere?" she asked.

"I'm afraid not. But I wish I had clued you in before we took that plane from Louisville to Chicago. If I had known what kind of mess was going to meet us at O'Hare, I think I would have."

"What do we do this trip?"

"Get hold of Aaron's grandmother, if she hasn't gone completely bananas." Then I remembered something I should have thought of before. "I didn't ask Aaron what her name is. I don't know if she's his paternal grandmother or maternal grandmother. I guess that rules out the telephone. We'll have to drive to Joliet."

"Her name is Emma Carpenter," Joy said. "I asked him."

I kissed her. "You get a phone number?"

"No, but with the name and address, you can get it from information."

Of course. I got the number and dialed. There was no answer. I let the phone ring on and on, just in case she was already in bed. It was after eleven o'clock. Joy went to the television to find out what the latest news on the *Coral Lady* was. The stories didn't seem much different from what they'd been earlier—a little more detail, such as the fact that there had been a medical conference taking place on the Coral Lady, a blend of work and vacation. News was still slow in being collected. Rescue teams were being assembled and flown in from military bases and from places where they were accustomed to dealing with radioactive materials, arsenals and nuclear power plants. Navy and Coast Guard ships were on the way to the area. Getting everything organized and on the move was providing monumental confusion. Streams of refugees were fleeing the area, choking all the roads. But there had been no additional blasts, and the diplomatic scene remained peaceful if not quiet.

"You've been on that phone for ten minutes," Joy observed. "If she hasn't answered by now, she isn't going to."

Still, I let it ring a few more times before I hung up.

"You think she might be at a relative's?" I asked.

"If she is, there's no way we can hope to find her," Joy said. "But if she got *really* terrified when Aaron disappeared . . ."

"A hospital?"

"Or worse. She could have had a heart attack or something. Two big shocks one right after the other like that."

"She might not be very old for a grandmother," I suggested. "She may just be in her late forties or early fifties."

"And maybe not," Joy replied. "How many hospitals you think there are in Joliet?"

"I don't have any idea. I don't think I've ever been there," I said. Joy started to say something, but I beat her to it. "I know. Call information."

I did. There were two of them, Silver Cross and St. Joseph's. St. Joseph's just gave me a polite "We have no one listed by that name here." The woman I talked to at Silver Cross was different.

"Are you a relative of Mrs. Carpenter?"

"Not exactly, but her grandson wandered off after he heard the news about his parents and ended up with my uncle. I figured that Mrs. Carpenter would be worried about the youngster, and there was no answer when I called her house."

"I see. Would you hold the line for a moment, please?" There was a click as I was put on hold. The wait was maybe thirty seconds long.

"Hello. Social Services, may I help you?"

I had to repeat the entire story. It didn't come out any more coherently the second time. There was a silence on the other end of the line when I finished.

"What is your name, please?"

A long-distance call could be traced easily in any case, so I gave my real name.

"Is the grandson with you now?"

"No, he's with my uncle. I said that. What about Mrs. Carpenter?"

"Mrs. Carpenter was brought in this evening. Cardiac arrest. I'm afraid she didn't make it."

"Do you know of any other relatives in the area? I know that Aaron's parents were both doctors, but not much else."

"I'll check with our chief of medical services. He may know. The Carpenters were both on staff here. If you'd care to bring the boy in here, sir, we can take care of getting him to relatives or to the county's family services people if there are no relatives."

"Fine. Is the morning soon enough? I imagine Aaron's asleep by now, and he's had enough of a shock for one day."

There was another long silence. I guessed that the woman I was talking with had to check with somebody else. "It's irregular, but I think you're right."

"He is in good hands for the night, and we'll get him there to the hospital first thing in the morning," I said.

I gave her my name again as well as my address and phone number. Then I explained that my uncle didn't have a phone and so forth. At least the woman in Family Services—or whoever she was getting instructions from—seemed to know enough about Chicago to realize that my address was a damn good one. And I got off the phone before anyone thought to ask what I was doing calling from forty miles away.

When I hung up, I looked to Joy and shrugged.

"We take him back in the morning?" she asked. I nodded.

"If we can pry him away from Uncle Parthet," I said. "He thinks that Aaron should stay in Varay and be his apprentice."

"You have to take him back. You gave them your name and address."

I nodded and smiled. "If I don't show up with Aaron Wesley Carpenter in the morning, the police will come looking for him, and for me. That's why I did it that way. I think that is strong enough to make even Uncle Parthet pay attention. If he won't, Kardeen will, or Grandfather if he's up to anything. Family honor is a big deal in Varay."

"Do we go back now?" Joy asked.

"Unless you want to stay here. It looks like it's going to be safe, for the moment at least. I won't force you to go back to Varay if you don't want to."

"But that place won't just go away though, will it?"

I shook my head. "I'll tell you the whole story when we get a chance, but Varay is as much my home as this world."

"Then I'll have to find a way to get used to it." She took a deep breath, then got up from the sofa and came to me. We hugged. "It still scares me. I can't help worrying that I've gone completely out of my mind."

"That's normal. That's how I felt when I found out about it. Uncle Parthet is going to make you a set of rings like mine. They're the keys to the doors. I'll show you how to use them and where all the doors are and where they go. Then you'll have as much freedom as anyone has."

"You mean anyone can use them?"

"Not exactly. It's a family magic."

"I'm not part of your family."

"You are in the important way." I put my mouth right up against her ear and told her just why she would be able to use the doorways.

"Aren't you afraid I'll run out and make a lot of other guys part of the family?"

"I don't think secondhand works."

"But we'd better make sure about me. It's been so long. Maybe it wore off." She started nibbling at my ear.

"We'll take care of that soon enough. You ready to go back to Basil?"

She sighed. "As ready as I'm going to get, I guess."

This time, I explained just what I was doing at the doors and showed her how the rings had to touch the silver tracing. Back at Castle Basil, I told her where the silver came from, that it was damn hard to get any, and about some of the connections that had been put in.

I asked around and found that Aaron's tour was still going on. Baron Kardeen had taken Aaron up to the battlements of the keep. I didn't feel like climbing all that distance, so I went after Uncle Parthet. He was in the great hall, drinking with a few other people. The other people were talking and drinking. Parthet was just drinking.

"The grandmother's dead," I told him. "Aaron goes back in the morning. The people at the hospital have my name and my Chicago address. He has to go back."

"Dead?" Parthet asked. I nodded. "Then he has no family at all there now, right?"

"I don't know that. The people at the hospital will check. His parents were both doctors there."

Parthet shook his head. "You had to go and mess in things."

"I had to," I conceded. "You know that."

"You don't understand." His voice was more morose than angry now.

"You keep saying that," I told him.

"Think about it. You have a major disruption in your world. Thousands of people are killed by terrorists. A nuclear bomb goes off. Then a little black kid just goes poof in your world and turns up in downtown Basil. Coincidence? Horseshit. We haven't seen the last of the trouble yet. That bomb has to have repercussions here, and in Fairy. It will—it *has* to—make the elflords stronger. And when they get stronger, they spill over into the seven kingdoms. Mark my words, lad. Things are going to get stranger yet."

He stopped for a minute, stared at me, then shook his head and drained his beer.

"I told you that I would know when it was time for me to start training an apprentice, and then you get in the way when the time finally comes."

I still didn't respond. His anger wasn't far from the surface yet, and I wasn't going to give him any new fuel.

"Just watch the trend, boy. Things have to get worse here, soon!"

5

Dragon Eggs

Joy and I took Aaron to Castle Cayenne with us. Even if I hadn't been concerned about what Parthet might do if left to his temptations, I think I would have taken Aaron with me. Since I had given my name to the people at the hospital, I was responsible for Aaron's well-being until I got him home, and we would be leaving very early in the morning.

Aaron's tour of Basil had given him plenty to get excited about. He managed to suppress any emotion about the loss of his parents for the moment, and the instantaneous teleportation to Varay didn't seem to bother him at all. *Poof* was explanation enough for him. It was getting quite late when we took the doorway to Cayenne, and I figured that Aaron would be ready to sleep soon. I sent Timon to put together a bedtime snack for both of them, and to find a place for our guest to sleep.

"It's going to be a short night for us, I'm afraid," I told Joy when we were finally alone in my Cayenne bedroom. "With the time difference between here and Chicago. . . . I want to get Aaron to Joliet as early as possible. The sooner we get him turned over to the people at the hospital, the better."

Joy sat on the bed and bounced a couple of times, checking to see how comfortable the mattress was. "I suppose that means that you're just going to want to sleep tonight."

I gave her my best Groucho Marx leer and said, "I don't know about that."

"Your stitches!" Joy said, as if she had just remembered that I had gone through an operation less than four days before.

"All the more reason to find out." I had almost forgotten myself. I hadn't felt a twinge in hours—really, not since hearing about the *Coral Lady.* Worrying about that hadn't given me any time to think about my wound.

"We can always catch a nap after we get back in the morning," I told Joy. I had already stripped off my weapons. "An hour to drive to Joliet, an hour back. With any luck at all we can be in and out of the hospital in fifteen minutes."

"You didn't ask Aaron if he has any other relatives around."

"I know. I didn't want to start him thinking about home yet. He might wonder about his grandmother, and I don't want to be the one to tell him about her. Especially not tonight."

Joy nodded. Then she was quiet for a moment before she said, "All I need now is a hot bath."

"It's kind of late for hot water here. We can both catch a shower in Chicago in the morning."

"Primitive," Joy said.

"Yep, and so am I."

"I hope so," Joy said, starting to undress.

I extinguished the two oil lamps in the bedroom. There was a torch burning out in the hall by the stairs, and the door has a narrow transom above it, so the bedroom wasn't totally dark. We finished stripping in silence and met at the center of the seven-foot-wide bed.

Joy's mouth was warm and active. Her nipples were peaked and hard when we came together. We had been without each other for a long time. One fix wasn't enough for either of us, even though we knew that it was going to be a short night.

After we finished our second go of the night, we lay close together under the big feather comforter, facing each other, tangled together. Joy's head was on my left arm. Our bodies touched here and there, though Joy had carefully shifted away when she happened to brush against the bandage across the cut on my abdomen. The stitches hadn't interfered at all, and there had been no pain from the wound. A Hero of Varay heals quickly, especially when he gets the chance to heal in peace without adding new injuries to old.

While Joy's breathing slowed and steadied as she slid toward the rhythms of sleep, I continued to caress her softly with my free hand, letting my fingers glide lightly over her side and around her buttock. I could see her smile in the faint light. Half asleep, she snuggled closer to me. My hand came to rest on her hip, and I slept too.

I woke because I had to go to the bathroom. My bladder felt ready to burst. I staggered naked to the john and took care of business. It was chilly. Nights can be like that even in the middle of a Varayan summer. The luminous bands on the wind-up clock in the bedroom said that it was nearly three o'clock, so it was almost six in Chicago—too late for me to go back to bed and hope for more sleep.

Joy was snoring lightly. I put on a bathrobe and slippers and left Joy to sleep a little longer while I climbed up to the battlements to look around.

I've always loved castles. When I was just a little kid—I couldn't have been more than five or six that Christmas—my parents, aka Santa Claus, gave me a toy castle with a bunch of plastic knights and so forth. The last time I looked, that castle, somewhat battered and beaten, with many of the plastic men missing, was still in the basement back in Louisville, packed away in a box with a lot of other toys and games that I had outgrown or forgotten along the way. But there had been other castles, even before I learned about Varay—a lamp with a square wooden tower and drawbridge, a sandstone sculpture, jigsaw puzzles, calendars, posters, and what-have-you. *Now,* I realize that my affection for castles was carefully cultivated by my parents, like the "combat" sports that Dad involved me in from the time I was six years old. Up to the time that I went off to college, there was a book on the shelf in my room that showed how castles were built, by someone named Macauley or something like that. And one autumn, when I was nine or ten, I even got the chance to build a castle of my own in the backyard. Dad had ordered a truckload of concrete blocks. I forget what he had planned to build, a shed or workshop, something like that. But then he came home badly hurt after one of his "business trips" and announced that he would have to put off his construction until the next spring. There wouldn't be enough time to finish it before winter brought snow and ice to Louisville. I asked if I could build a castle until then and he said yes, so I had my very own castle for nearly five months. I moved and lifted those concrete blocks all by myself, spending as much time as I could building and then playing in my castle. It was almost ten feet high, and sturdy enough for kids to play on, with plywood floors supported by two-by-fours so we could get up to the "battlements." For almost five months, that castle made me the king of the neighborhood.

I enjoyed standing on the battlements of Cayenne or Basil alone, day or night. It wasn't just that I was still a kid inside, though that is probably part of the answer. The surroundings are perfect for thinking, for meditating, even for brooding. That night, I was uneasy about a lot of things. The nuking of the *Coral Lady* was still a frightening topic. No nuclear weapon had been used against people anywhere in the world since the end of World War Two. That wasn't just before I was born, it was before my *father* was born, if only by a few weeks. Then there was Aaron's mysterious appearance to ponder, Parthet's uncommon anger over being forced to turn him loose, and his prediction that things would get worse in a hurry. Even the talking head of the dead elf would be enough to haunt anyone's night, awake or asleep.

I hadn't forgotten the dead elf.

Soon, very soon, I was going to have to broach that issue back at Castle Basil. We had to do something permanent with the dead elf. Maybe Uncle Parthet thought he had a new toy to play with, keeping the head of the elf in a vat of alcohol, but I wouldn't rest easy until the son of the Elflord of Xayber was put out for the birds, or buried, or something. If the head could talk to Parthet, it could probably also talk to the elflord, his father, and we didn't need a spy of that nature around. Xayber would be after me again soon enough without the head of his dead son urging revenge.

The stars moved overhead, the constellations of the buffer zone—the Cooper, the Warlord, the Twin Horses, others that I didn't recognize right off yet. The groupings of stars were different from any I knew from Earth. I would have been delighted to see at least one familiar constellation, Orion the Hunter, for example, but he didn't hunt the skies over the seven kingdoms.

I started shivering after just a few minutes up on the

battlements, and I decided that I wasn't dressed for a long session of brooding. Besides, it was time to wake Joy and Aaron and get started toward Joliet. It had to be near dawn in Illinois.

Joy had rolled over on her side and stopped snoring. I lit one of the oil lamps in the bedroom and started to get dressed before I called her name. She moaned something unintelligible and rolled over again, but she woke instantly the second time I called her. She sat straight up, eyes open wide. I guess she had just remembered where she was.

"It wasn't a dream," were her first words.

I went to her and kissed her before I said, "Varay? No, it's not a dream. And it's time to get up."

She looked at the window. It was still pitch-black outside.

"It's the middle of the night!" she said.

"It is here, almost three-thirty," I said. "But that makes it about six-thirty in Chicago. There's a time difference."

"Where is this place then, Iceland?"

"You've got your zones moving in the wrong direction," I said.

"I don't mean that, I mean the temperature."

"It's not *that* cold," I said.

"Cold?" She dropped the blanket she had been holding around her. She had goose bumps all over. "It is too that cold." She pulled the blanket back up.

"Time to get dressed, dear," I said, holding back a laugh. "Which suitcase do you need?"

"Both of them."

That figures, I thought. I got the two bags and set them up on the bed close to her. One held underwear, sweaters, and blouses. The other held skirts, slacks and jeans, and two extra pairs of shoes. Joy started to dress warm.

"It's probably hotter than hell in Chicago," I warned as she pulled on a heavy sweater.

"Then I'll change at your apartment. I've still got some things there. I'm worried about freezing before we get there."

"I'll get Aaron," I said, turning away so Joy wouldn't see me grin.

My mention of Aaron slowed Joy down for a moment. "I feel so sorry for him," she said.

"Me too. But we've got to get him back to whatever family he has left before Parthet gets too possessive."

"Is your uncle always like that?"

"That's hard to say." I stopped and stared vaguely at Joy for a moment. "*I've* never seen him like that before, but 'always' covers something over twelve hundred years in his case."

"You're kidding." Joy came out from under the blanket long enough to slip on panties and blue jeans—quickly, then heavy socks and tennis shoes.

"I don't think so," I said. "He was only admitting to a thousand when I first came here, but one time I caught him talking about Charlemagne's court as though he had actually been there and he admitted it. That takes him back to A.D. 800 or thereabouts, and he claims to have known Merlin and Camelot, so that drags it back even farther."

Joy stared at me, all thought of the cold shoved aside for a bit. "You're serious," she said. She turned to sit on the edge of the bed. "You're really serious."

"I am. Get him talking about history sometime. You'll see."

Joy stood up, raised the sweater to pull the jeans up where they belonged, snapped and zipped, then rearranged the sweater. I wished that we had more time. I would have liked to watch her take everything off again.

"It's part of being a wizard," I said. "They live virtually forever unless something violent happens to them. But the price is sterility—no kids, no way, no how. And Parthet wants to initiate Aaron. I told him that Aaron's too young to make that kind of decision."

"I certainly hope you told him. But . . . your uncle is really that old?"

"He's probably a lot older than that even." I took a deep breath. There was something I hadn't planned on mentioning to Joy just yet, but . . . "Down below the cellar of Basil Castle, there is a crypt with the remains of all the kings and heroes of Varay. But there aren't any wizards buried there, not a one. The other tombs go back a couple of thousand years beyond what Parthet admits."

"You think he's been around that long?"

"I don't know. He never gives me a straight answer, and nobody else around here is old enough to remember a time when he didn't look the way he does now. The king is only one hundred and twenty-eight."

"Only?" Joy got up and we shared a too-brief kiss.

"Only. I'll go get Aaron," I said again. "We can have breakfast back in Illinois."

Joy sat on the edge of the bed again to wait until I got Aaron. Aaron was still sleeping, so I just picked him up and carried him down from the sixth floor. Timon woke, but he's always been a light sleeper, afraid I'll want something and he won't hear me call the first time. Aaron didn't make a sound. I needed both hands to open the doorway to Chicago, but Joy held Aaron for the few seconds that took. Aaron was quite a load for her, though.

As soon as we were through the passage, I took Aaron back. He still didn't wake. I laid him on my bed in Chicago. Joy beat me to the bathroom in the master suite, so I went out and used the other bathroom for a quick shower. Joy hadn't come out yet when I finished, so I turned on the television in the living room, volume low, to check out the morning news before we got too far away from the escape hatches to Varay.

The *Coral Lady* was obviously still the main topic, and the damage done to western Florida. Main topic? It was the *only* story anyone was talking about. It was the traditional off-season for tourists in Florida, but traditional seasons don't mean as much in Florida as they used to. With the Disney complex not all that far away at Orlando, tourism wasn't nearly as seasonal as it had once been. There were still so many visitors around that it might be weeks before anyone could make an even half-way accurate estimate of onshore casualties. The Air Force had a lot of planes in the air checking radioactivity levels and the direction of drift of the radioactivity. Two full divisions of the Army had been moved to the perimeter of the affected area to deal with refugees, to try to cut down on looting, and generally to try to restore order. Many of the medical people who had gone to Chernobyl a few years before were gathering to help in Florida—except for one doctor who had been on the *Coral Lady*. Casualties were being airlifted to hospitals as far away as San Antonio and Baltimore for treatment.

The press were getting frustrated at their inability to get camera crews into the area on the ground, and most of their aerial footage had to be shot from a distance as well. But there was finally some tape of the devastation: the missing span of the Sunshine Skyway Bridge, the wreckage of the remainder, the ruins and ashes ashore. Fires were still burning out of control around much of the perimeter of Tampa Bay. The "conservative" estimates predicted a minimum of sixty-five hundred dead, fifteen thousand injured or exposed to *immediately* dangerous levels of radiation, perhaps millions facing long-term health problems as a result, and two and a half million people displaced, either permanently or temporarily. The monetary cost had only the vaguest estimates yet, but they started at fifty billion dollars and climbed to over a trillion.

"That wasn't a dream either," Joy whispered. I hadn't heard her come into the room.

"No, no dream. It's going to take forever to clean up after this one."

Joy put her hands on my shoulders. "This world will never be the same." I think she was talking about the nuclear bomb, but maybe she was thinking about her introduction to Varay too.

"I'm afraid that the *Coral Lady* won't be the only case like this," I said. "The genie's out of the bottle and we may not be able to get him back in." Like when car bombs become so faddish. "It's a miracle it's taken this long. You remember that A-bomb they found in New York a few years ago?"

"I remember."

"It may have been the same batch of terrorists. Or different people with the same idea. There's tons of uranium and plutonium unaccounted for."

Joy shook her head. "The sooner we get started, the sooner we get back," she said.

I nodded. I was ready to change the subject too.

"I just hope Eddie kept my car going the last three months." Eddie was the day man down in the building's garage. I paid him to run the car a couple of times a week while I was "traveling" to keep the battery charged.

* * *

It was still too early for Eddie to be on duty, but my LeBaron started right off, so I knew that he had been doing his job. The odometer reading hadn't changed, but the low-fuel light started blinking as soon as I turned the key in the ignition. Aaron finally woke up while I was backing out of my parking space.

"Where are we?" he asked, his voice still sleepy.

"We're in Chicago, Aaron," I said. "We're on our way to Joliet now."

"I'm going home?" I couldn't tell what he was feeling, disappointment, sadness, or a mixture of both.

"Yes, you're going home," I said, and I had to be careful to keep any emotion out of my voice. But Aaron curled up as best he could under the seat belt in the backseat and he went to sleep again.

We had got an early enough start to stay ahead of the worst of the rush-hour traffic downtown. I took Lake Shore Drive down to the Stevenson Expressway and got on that for the straight run out to Joliet. Traffic never got completely insane that morning, and even the inbound traffic across the median seemed a lot lighter than usual. I suspected that a lot of people had decided that it was a good day to play hooky from work, to keep up with the latest news . . . or just in case there was any more trouble like the bombing in Florida.

Joy found Silver Cross Hospital marked on the map in my glove compartment, but I still had to stop and ask directions when we got to Joliet. The main entrance to the hospital was just opening up as we arrived.

Aaron had slept the whole way out. I had to wake him when we reached the hospital. I didn't want to carry him inside and maybe cause misunderstandings.

I hated every second of the hospital ordeal. A volunteer at the front desk directed us to Family Services. There were people waiting for us there—hospital people, a police officer, and a couple who introduced themselves as Aaron's aunt and uncle. Aaron went to them and started carrying on about the wonderful things that had happened to him, while it was all the aunt and uncle could manage to keep from bawling from their grief and their anxiety over Aaron. The uncle thanked me for bringing Aaron in and for taking care of him. When he asked where we had found him, I repeated the story I had told on the telephone. The cop stopped frowning. I was worried that he would ask a lot of uncomfortable official questions, but he started listening to Aaron's tale of knights and castles and a funny old wizard and he forgot all about Joy and me. We were able to slip away like the Lone Ranger and Tonto, and we got out of the hospital almost as quickly as I had hoped to.

Once we were out of the parking lot and on our way back to the Interstate, I breathed a lot easier.

"They'll assume that his story is just a reaction to the shock of losing his parents," I said. "What else *could* they think?" When Joy didn't reply, I looked her way. She was just staring straight forward. Tears were running down her cheek.

"He'll be okay, Joy. He'll do fine."

She nodded a little at that, but she still didn't speak, so I turned on the radio and we listened to the still-continuous coverage of the *Coral Lady* disaster.

The drive back to Chicago went a little slower than the ride out, but traffic still wasn't up to its usual rush-hour madness. Joy and I said virtually nothing the entire drive. She wasn't quite up to breakfast yet, so we went straight back to my place. Food could wait a little while. We pulled into the garage under my apartment building before nine-thirty.

In the elevator going up to thirty-eight, Joy clung to me and I held her. She still wasn't talking.

"We've still got time to make breakfast at Castle Basil," I said when we got inside the apartment. She just nodded.

Before we left for Varay, I went through the place twice, making sure that I didn't leave anything turned on, making sure that I wasn't forgetting anything I might really want in Varay. It was almost as if I was leaving the place for good. That realization hit me, and I stopped abruptly in the living room. I forced myself to look around the room, almost casually. I *did* feel as though I might never see the apartment again, even though it was only a doorway away from Cayenne, Basil, or Louisville. I didn't say anything about the feeling to Joy, but it made me very uneasy. It wasn't *exactly* like a warning from my danger sense, but after the *Coral Lady*, I didn't need much to set me on edge.

I was shaking my head when Joy and I stepped through to Cayenne. I needed to stop there before we went on to Basil.

Since we had been gone for a while, I went to the door leading out to the hall and stairs, planning to go downstairs to check in, so to speak. But Lesh was waiting just outside the door.

"I knocked before, lord," he said. "When you didn't answer, I figured you weren't back from taking the boy home."

"We got him safely delivered," I said.

"You told me to remind you about Harkane and Timon."

I nodded. That was something that had come up during the goodwill tour. Timon was old enough to move up from page to squire. Harkane would become a full-fledged man-at-arms, ready to be knighted as soon as he proved himself in the interim capacity. Both would remain in my service, as my retinue continued to grow. But Timon's promotion meant that I needed a new page to take his place.

"I'll speak to Baron Kardeen about them today if I get the chance," I said. "Joy and I are going through to Basil for breakfast. You want to come along, or is there enough to eat here?"

Lesh grinned. "We'll manage, especially since you two'll be gone."

I grinned back at him. Getting Lesh to loosen up had been difficult. He was still more impressed with my position than I was, but at least he was willing to open up a little now and then.

"I'll send Timon right up for you," he said.

I started to object, but quickly changed my mind. I had to have a page at Basil, probably two of them now that Joy was with me. Protocol. Tradition. Varay was basically feudal in nature, and anyone with any kind of social status had to have servants. "Then maybe he can help choose his own replacement," I said, and Lesh nodded.

"What was all that about?" Joy asked after Lesh clomped down the stairs. I explained the basics as quickly as I could.

"They put a lot of stock in formalities and rank and

such here,'' I said. ''I knighted Lesh three years ago. Sometimes I think he's still not comfortable with it—any more than I'm really comfortable with all the nonsense that goes with my titles.''

Timon came racing up the stairs so soon after Lesh went down that he must have been waiting for the summons. Timon was grinning all the way up the stairs. It was a big day for him, like making the move from grade school to high school, I guess—something like it anyway.

Joy, Timon, and I stepped through to Castle Basil and made our way down to the great hall just as the sun was making itself visible for the day. I wore my knife and both elf swords, and Joy's arm was linked through mine. Timon stepped out in front as we reached the great hall to announce us.

But I didn't hear one word he said. I glanced toward the head table and received one of the biggest shocks of my life.

Aaron was sitting up there next to Parthet.

Parthet stood up quickly when I started hurrying across the great hall. He held up a hand like a traffic cop trying to get cars to stop.

''I didn't do anything,'' he said before I got halfway to him.

''What happened?'' I asked, slowing down only a little. I could hear Joy hurrying to catch up with me. We went around to the head table. Two places were set for us.

''Just what happened before, it looks like,'' Parthet said. ''This time, he appeared right here in the great hall.''

''Where were you when you went poof this time, Aaron?'' I asked.

''Right there where you left me,'' he said. His voice sounded shaky. He had apparently been crying. He looked around, then looked up at me again. ''Right after you left, Uncle Jake told me that Gramma was dead. I said no, she couldn't be. Then my head felt real funny and I was here again.''

''How many people were there with you?'' I asked.

''Uncle Jake and Aunt Sue. The policeman and two ladies from the hospital.'' He held up his hand and extended a finger for each of them. "Five people." That many shocks in twenty-four hours, I'd probably have to count on my fingers too. It was more than any child should ever have to suffer.

"Do you need any more proof that he belongs here?" Parthet asked softly. Family—they're the people who never show any hesitation at saying, "I told you so."

"I won't argue the point right this minute," I said. "But that also doesn't mean that I've changed my mind. I've got to think on it first."

Servants had already started to bring in breakfast, so the discussion was easily postponed. Parthet is hard to distract at mealtime, even when it's something that's really got him hopped up. Joy and I took our seats and Timon did his best to keep our plates and mugs full. He really didn't have much trouble. Joy started slowly, though before long she was shoveling the food in almost as rapidly as anyone else in the hall.

Not even deep thought can slow me down much during a Castle Basil meal. I can think and eat at the same time without any difficulty at all. And I had a lot to think about. Besides the panic in my world over the *Coral Lady,* there was the way that Aaron Wesley Carpenter kept popping up in Varay and the talking elf head that Parthet still had. And King Pregel was still sick.

Of course, Pregel seemed to be sick as often as not. His health was precarious. He would get over one thing and be fine for a week or a month—even for three or four months running—and then he would get sick again. When my great-grandfather got sick, seriously ill, Mother would tear off to our world and bring Doc McCreary back for a long-distance castle call. Doc McCreary would do what he could without any of the equipment available in a modern hospital, and leave the day-to-day nursing to Mother and a few local women Mother had been training. The king would recover and the level of tension in Castle Basil would decline.

By the time breakfast started to wind down, I had some ideas on precautions to take after Parthet's warning that there had to be trouble ahead for Varay and the rest of the buffer zone, but I still didn't have real answers. I asked Parthet if there had been any weird manifestations other than Aaron's two sudden appearances.

"None that I've heard of," he said. "But there are bound to be more. The disruptions are just too great for there *not* to be more." Then he pulled a small leather bag out of some recess in his clothing. "Here, I got these done last night. I couldn't sleep." I opened the bag and found a set of rings like the two I wear. I gave the new rings to Joy.

"The eagle always goes on your left hand, the signet on the right," I told her. She slipped them on and they fit perfectly. That's not the kind of thing that Uncle Parthet was likely to make a mistake about.

"These are the rings that open those doorways?" Joy whispered.

"Yes, and they identify you as part of the royal family as well."

"But I'm not, really."

"You are in every way that matters. We can take care of the formalities any time you're ready. I'll have to ask the chamberlain. I don't even know how marriages are done here."

"Was that a proposal?" We were both whispering by then.

I smiled. "I guess it was. What do you say?"

She blinked, but that was the extent of her hesitation. "I say that I think we've come too far to back out now."

I grinned at her before I turned back to Parthet. There was still business to talk about.

"I think I need to make a fast tour of the border castles to see if anything's happened, and to warn them to be careful," I told Parthet. "Find out if there's any unusual trouble with Xayber or warlords out of Dorthin." Parthet nodded around a mouthful of ham. I snorted. "Find out if there are any other kids like Aaron popping up around Varay." That caught Parthet's attention. He stopped chewing to stare at me, but Joy was at me from the other side.

"How long will you be gone?" Joy asked.

"Well, let's see," I said as I turned again. "There are five border castles in the north and east, four more in the west. That makes nine castellans to talk to in Varay, and Duke Dieth over in Dorthin. I don't think I could possibly finish in less than three or four hours."

Joy seemed to miss a beat on that. Then she swatted

my shoulder. "I thought you were going to say three or four weeks."

I smiled. "There's no reason why you can't come along," I said. Before she could respond to that, I said, "Let's go find Baron Kardeen."

I had already looked around to see that nobody was still shoveling the food in so fast that he would be devastated to have breakfast end. That was another tradition that I had tried without success to end—the tradition that the meal was over as soon as the ranking member of the royal family or court left the table.

Kardeen was in his office, hard at work already, a large platter of food holding down one edge of the scroll he was writing on.

"Two problems for your expert attention," I told Kardeen after we got past the hellos and so forth. I told him about my personnel situation. He said that he would send Timon to the Master of Pages with instructions and he would make the necessary entry in the records of the two "promotions." Any ceremony was up to me, whatever I wanted to make of it.

"What's next?" Kardeen asked then.

"What's the procedure for getting married around here?"

He waved a finger back and forth between Joy and me and raised an eyebrow. I nodded.

"We're really not big on formalities here," Kardeen said, directing that mostly at Joy. "There are the rings, of course." He looked back and forth between us, and Joy held up her hands to show him the rings.

"Mostly, it's just a matter of entering the marriage agreement in the court records and having it announced by the magistrates around the kingdom," Kardeen continued. He hesitated then and looked at me. "There is one bit of ceremony you might want to consider. It's hardly old tradition." He shrugged. "Your parents did it when they got married."

"What kind of ceremony?" I asked.

"They met in front of the king and me, faced each other, and linked their fingers together so the rings were touching." He demonstrated. With two people doing it, it would look like finger-wrestling, a painful little sport I hadn't tried since I was a freshman in high school.

"How is the king?" I asked. He hadn't met Joy yet. That was something we had to correct before there was any ceremony anyway.

"Pretty much confined to bed yet," Kardeen said. He made a helpless gesture with his arms. "It's hard to tell. You know that. He's been worse before, I suppose. Your mother is upstairs with him now, probably feeding him breakfast. You can go up and see." This latest downturn had happened after he heard that I had been wounded by the elf warrior in the Bald Rock.

The baron led the way upstairs, walking quickly as he always did. My great-grandfather was sitting up in bed, propped up by a dozen thick pillows. He wasn't reading now though, the way he had been the last time I had seen him. Mother was sitting on the edge of the bed, holding a tray of food on her lap and feeding the king.

"Hello, lad," Pregel said. Both his voice and his smile were weak.

"Grandfather, this is Joy Bennett. We'd like to get married." The king didn't like to have anyone talking about his health in front of him, no "How do you feel" or anything like that, especially when he wasn't feeling well.

His smile got a little broader. "Come over here then, children," he said. He scooted himself up a little higher. Mother set the breakfast tray on a small nightstand, then stood up and moved out of the way.

"I've heard about you, young lady," Pregel said, reaching out to take her hand. *His* hand was shaking rather badly. Joy clasped it in both of hers. "And yes, you are lovely."

"Thank you," Joy said, stuttering a little before she added, "Your Majesty."

"Don't worry so much about the formalities, dear," the king said. "I quit worrying about them decades ago. Now, how are you bearing up?"

Joy shot me a quick look. "He knows that you had never been here before yesterday," I told her.

"I still wonder if I'm going crazy, sir," she said, obviously uncomfortable.

"Healthy sign, they tell me." Pregel laughed softly and reclaimed his hand. "So, when do you two want to do this?"

"We haven't really talked about timing," I said. "Is there anything wrong with right now?" I aimed that question more to Joy than to the king.

Joy smiled. "I don't see anything at all wrong with now," she said.

"Nothing like the rush of young love," Pregel said, and he laughed again. "I don't see anything wrong with now either." He looked at Mother, then at Kardeen. Neither of them contradicted him.

There really wasn't much to the ceremony. Joy and I stood facing each other, right there next to the bed. Grandfather, Mother, and Baron Kardeen were the only witnesses. Too late, I thought to warn Joy what might happen when we completed a circuit with the rings. There just wasn't time to say anything. When we linked our fingers, I could feel the familiar electricity—and I saw Joy's eyes get wide. The exchange of vows was impromptu—obviously. I don't remember exactly what either of us said, though Joy probably does. I said something about promising her my undying love and she said pretty much the same thing. We broke the circuit of the rings, accepted congratulations, and left the room.

"What the blazes was the shock?" Joy asked when we were in the hallway alone.

"I didn't think about it until it was too late. It's some sort of side effect of the magic of the rings."

"It felt like my hair all stood on end."

"It didn't," I assured her.

"I don't mean on my head," Joy whispered, looking around to make sure that we were really alone.

I started laughing, very loudly, and Joy's face got red. She started pounding on my nearest shoulder, until she missed and hit the guard on one of my elf swords.

"Do you have to wear those things all the time?"

"The Hero of Varay must be armed," I said. "I think I'm even breaking tradition by taking them off to bathe and sleep."

We started right out on my tour of the border castles. I let Joy operate the doors each time we made a hop. It's not that the doors take practice, but I thought that it might make her feel a little more confident of using them if I didn't happen to be around. The full tour ended up taking a lot more than three or four hours. We spent the entire day making the circuit, and it could easily have taken even longer. I introduced Joy around. We sat and chatted with the various castellans, gave them the warning, asked for news, and looked around a little at each place.

Baron Resler was still in charge at Arrowroot. He was civil but not overly warm. But then, that was his normal style. Baron Hambert ran things at Coriander. He was a lot warmer, and he made a point of telling Joy that he owed his barony to me. I cut him off when I thought he was about to start telling her about the Battle of Thyme. I didn't want to lay that story on Joy yet.

Although proximity had nothing to do with the speed of using the magic doorways, we went from Coriander over to Carsol, the capital of Dorthin, to talk with Dieth. He was as ebullient as ever, carrying on about the work of holding that kingdom together. It was an adventure rather than a pain in the butt to him. I got Joy out of Carsol before Dieth could get too deep in details as well.

Castle Thyme was being renovated, as were the other two small castles to the south of it. I had insisted on that. Even though Dorthin was no longer a threat, I knew we couldn't count on that always being the case. One of the first things I had insisted on after the Battle of Thyme was that we had to have doorways into all of the border castles, ways to avoid the sort of ambush that had cost my father his life.

Then we hopped over to the western border. Varay hadn't had trouble over there for ages. Castle Curry, the major fortress on our border with Belorz, was as peaceful as ever. Baron Veter was still a minor, only a couple of years older than Aaron. The castellan was his guardian, Sir Compil, an elderly knight who liked to tell me stories about the grandparents I had never known. They had died back in what would be the early 1940s in the other world. When World War Two had our world in an uproar, Fairy and the buffer zone were in similar chaos. Varay had lost four Heroes in as many years.

All in all, it was a pretty good tour. No one had any hard evidence of really weird happenings, although you can always get a few strange tales in a place like Varay. There were no indications of invasion from any of our neighbors. There were rumors, but there are always rumors. At both Arrowroot and Coriander, the word was that the Elflord of Xayber was on the verge of a successful end to his civil war, perhaps within weeks or even days of overthrowing the Elfking and taking his place . . . or at least obtaining a favorable truce that would leave him free to pursue "other interests," like getting even with me. At Carsol, Duke Dieth mentioned a rumor that the blind wizard of the late Etevar of Dorthin was now working in Mauroc, the kingdom east of Dorthin, the farthest east of the seven kingdoms. The rumor was that the wizard had somehow regained at least partial use of his eyes. *Something* was plainly going on in Mauroc. There were refugees fleeing west, crossing Dorthin to settle in Varay or to go even farther west.

If the Elflord of Xayber was about to finish his war inside Fairy, he would certainly look south at Varay, particularly since his son was there. And trouble in Mauroc could easily spill westward, particularly if Parthet's apprehensions were justified. I would have to discuss both sets of rumors with Kardeen and Parthet, but I decided that it could wait until the next morning. This was my wedding day, after all. Joy and I stopped back at Castle Basil just long enough to collect Timon and our two new pages, boys named Jaffa and Rodi.

I wasn't too interested in new pages at the moment, or in the supper we rushed through when we got back to Cayenne. As soon as we could, Joy and I left everyone in the great hall and retired upstairs to our bedroom.

It was a beautiful night, all either of us could have asked for. It didn't matter that we were off in something like Never-Never Land for real. That night was our own fairy tale.

But we were wakened at dawn by Uncle Parthet pounding on the bedroom door. And by his screaming. I pulled on a robe and went to the door, ready to commit mayhem. I opened the door and Parthet almost fell into the bedroom.

"The kitchen at Basil is full of dragon eggs!" he shouted.

6

The Sot

If Parthet hadn't been in such an obvious panic, I would have sniffed his breath, then asked him to walk a straight line. But running around like a chicken with its head cut off took too much energy for Parthet to be simply drunk. He carried on for a couple of minutes and I waited for him to run out of a little steam.

"Calm down," I said then, a brilliant choice of words, naturally. "You're not making any sense."

He stopped his frenetic pacing and jabbering and stared right up at me. "The kitchen at Basil is full of dragon eggs," he said, very calmly. "You do remember dragons, don't you?"

"I remember." As perhaps the only mortal in Varayan history to ever kill one, let alone *two,* dragons and survive, I wasn't likely to ever forget dragons.

"Where did the dragon eggs come from?" I asked.

"From the chicken coop."

Before I could jump on that statement, Joy came up behind me and asked, "What's the matter?"

"Uncle Parthet says that the kitchen at Basil is full of dragon eggs."

Then, very softly, Joy whispered, "Is he sober?" right close to my ear. But there was nothing wrong with Parthet's ears, even if he was virtually blind without his thick glasses.

"I'm sober, young lady," he said. "Dragon eggs just make me a trifle nervous."

Joy swung the door open wider. She had slipped into a bathrobe. "I'm sorry," she said. "It just sounds so . . . so *bizarre.*"

"It *is* bizarre," Parthet said. "That's why I'm upset."

"Okay, there are dragon eggs in the kitchen at Basil,"

I said. "What do you want me to do, dice them all up nicely with Dragon's Death?"

Parthet did everything but make steam come out of his ears—and *that* wouldn't have surprised me. His face got so red that I thought he was going to blow a gasket.

"Calm down, Uncle," I said. "Let's go see your dragons. Give me a minute to get dressed."

Joy was already getting clothes out for me.

"You want to come along?" I asked her.

"I think I'll pass this time."

"They'll have breakfast ready downstairs any minute, I imagine," I said. "You go ahead and start eating. I'll try to get right back, but if I'm not here soon, I'll get something to eat over at Basil. If there's anything but dragon omelet." I whispered the last as quietly as I could. The door to the hallway was shut and Parthet was on the other side, but I didn't want to take any chance at all of him overhearing and getting angrier than he already was. Dragon eggs in the kitchen? Even if Parthet was right, I didn't see what the big deal was.

Parthet didn't have anything to say as we stepped through to Basil and hurried on to the huge kitchen area behind and below the great hall. The cooks weren't around. The kitchen was deserted but for two men-at-arms who held their halberds aimed more or less at a huge cast-iron kettle near one of the fireplaces.

Eggs at Castle Basil are generally served scrambled, cooked by the gross in kettles that are large enough for boiled missionary, stirred constantly with spoons the size of canoe paddles. I saw two large egg crates, the kettle in the center, and a small collection of eggshells on the floor to one side.

"The cooks had started preparing breakfast," Parthet said. He pointed at the kettle and gestured for me to precede him. I nodded and went up to the kettle and looked down.

There were some normal eggs in the bottom, yolks and so forth, but there were also a couple of tiny dragon forms—fetuses, I guess I would have to call them. They appeared perfectly formed, so I assumed that they were close to being big enough to hatch. I reached over to the nearest egg crate, took an egg out, cracked it on the edge of the kettle, and dumped in a regular egg. The second one was normal too, but the third I tried had another of the little dragons.

Altogether, I cracked a dozen eggs and got four dragons.

"Are these regular dragons or those small scavengers that run around the woods?" I asked.

"I haven't the faintest idea," Parthet said. "At this point, dragons are dragons, as far as I'm concerned."

"Is that what their eggs normally look like?" It didn't seem right. I thought reptile eggs were usually leathery.

"No. These are chicken eggs. They came out from under chickens—yesterday it would have been."

"You're the wizard. What does it mean?"

"I wish I knew," Parthet said. There was no trace of his earlier anger in his voice or face now. "It may just be part of the increased weirdness I warned you about, but I'm afraid that there may be a lot more to it. It seems that it must be some kind of omen."

"Not a good one, I take it."

"No. Kardeen and his clerk are already searching old manuscripts, trying to find references. I need to get busy doing the same thing. The answer must be around here somewhere. I hope."

"What do you want me to do?"

"Right now, it may be enough just to lend your presence. This has a lot of the working folks scared. We'll get men to load all these eggs up on a cart, take them out to the forest, dump them, crush them. But nobody will handle the eggs without a Hero around to bail them out in case a mama dragon comes around or something."

"What about tomorrow's eggs, and the next day's?" I asked. "I can't see doing this kind of thing every day."

Parthet shrugged. "Until we know what's going on, we can do little more." He scowled down at the eggs. Then he shook his head. "I'm sure that news of this has already started to spread. We'll have all kinds of bizarre reactions. Some farmers will likely kill all their chickens. Maybe more will just bury the eggs. I don't know. We'll have to keep watch. But I'll bet that scrambled eggs are going to be hard to come by for a while."

"Is this happening at any of the other castles, or is it just here?"

"I haven't checked yet," Parthet said. "That's something else on the list."

So I rode shotgun for the garbage detail. It wasn't the most glamorous of assignments, but I wish that all Hero jobs were that simple. None of the fetuses made a move, or even a sound. No full-grown dragons came to dispute what we were doing. By the time I left the keep for my detail, Kardeen and Parthet were getting a grip on the rest of the morning's needs. The cooks were shooed back into the kitchen. Breakfast being late at Castle Basil was scandalous. Parthet was getting ready to hop around the kingdom to check on the eggs elsewhere, and to send riders to outlying areas that didn't have family doorways handy. Baron Kardeen was arranging to send riders to the villages around Basil.

Meanwhile, I shepherded more than a hundred dozen eggs to a pit outside the town and watched while two of King Pregel's stalwarts smashed eggs with paving stones, poured lamp oil over the mess, and set fire to all of the eggs, good and bad. We stood around and watched while the super omelet cooked and burned, and when the fire died out, the soldiers shoveled in dirt and more rocks to bury the mess. Then we rode back to the castle.

When I walked back into the great hall of Basil, nearly two hours after I left, I spotted Joy and Aaron up at the head table. Breakfast, the *late* breakfast, was just starting to wind down. There was less table talk than usual, and what I could hear was all about the mysterious eggs. "Who's attacking our food?" one soldier asked me as I passed. All I could do was shake my head. In the buffer zone, an attack on the food supply could be catastrophic.

I kissed Joy as I sat next to her. "I didn't think you were coming over," I said to her before I turned to Aaron. "Hello, Aaron. How you doing?" I asked while a platter of breakfast was filled in front of me.

"Pretty good," Aaron said, grinning. "You guys eat like this all the time?"

"All the time." I smiled back at him, then turned to get a start on my own belated breakfast. Smelling that dragon omelet cook had given me a real appetite.

"I think maybe there's a problem," Joy said after I had a few minutes to take the edge off. "A farmer came to the castle gate, back at Cayenne, and said that there's a dragon on his farm. Lesh talked to him. He said that the farmer was scared out of his wits. Were there really dragon eggs here?"

"Tiny dragons in chicken eggs," I said. "We've burned and buried them." And now a full-sized dragon, I thought. Just what I needed.

"I suppose the farmer said that his dragon was as big as a mountain," I said.

"He said it was big. It was scaring his family and his livestock."

"A real dragon?" Aaron asked, excited.

"It could be," I told him. "There *are* real dragons around here."

"Can I go see it?"

"I don't think so, sport." I grinned. "Dragons can be dangerous."

"You gonna kill it?"

"That's what everyone expects of me. Maybe after it's dead you can have a look. I'll have to check with Parthet first." Parthet and I really hadn't finished our argument over Aaron's future, but for the moment at least, the wizard had claimed guardianship over Aaron. After our previous go-rounds, I didn't want to haul Aaron off anywhere without checking with Parthet first. Although I hadn't admitted it to myself yet, I guess I had already given in to Parthet's arguments.

"Did Lesh come through with you?" I asked Joy.

"No. He was still trying to calm the farmer when I left."

I had been wolfing down the food as quickly as I could. The platters were getting low. I got down a little more before I resumed the conversation.

"I'd better go see what's up. Why don't you stay here with Aaron? When Parthet gets back from *his* running around, let him know where I've gone. I'll get back as soon as I can."

I started to get up, but Joy put her hand on my arm. "You think there really is a dragon?" she asked.

I hesitated, then nodded. "The way things are going the last couple of days, there probably is."

"Be careful, Gil."

My smile may have flashed and vanished too quickly,

but I assured her that I would be careful—as careful as possible. That was a major qualifier.

I stepped through to Cayenne and went down to the great hall. Lesh and Harkane were waiting for me there, all duded up for combat. Timon was down in the ground-floor stable with the horses. For the first time, *he* was dressed for fighting too, ready to claim his new status as my squire. I grinned at him, tousled his hair, and let him help me put my armor on—chain mail over a padded leather tunic, and a steel and leather helmet with a long, curved strip of iron that comes down over my nose. I hate that helmet. Most times, I prefer to substitute a Cubs cap for it, but I was riding out to do battle with a dragon—possibly—and dragons aren't to be trifled with. With my luck, I'd run into one that rooted for the Cardinals.

After more than three years of Varay, I no longer felt quite as foolish riding out to do battle as I had at first. I had my two elf swords, a dagger with a foot-long blade, a compound bow with a full quiver of razor-headed arrows, and a .458 magnum big-game rifle. Dragons are the biggest game there is. The remaining major snag is that firearms only seem to work about one-third of the time in the buffer zone, less often than that when things are really critical. I had bought the rifle after my first two encounters with dragons, but I had never had a chance to test it on a live dragon. Believe me, I never even considered going out *looking* for a dragon just so I could test-fire the weapon. A Hero doesn't get to be an *old* Hero by looking for trouble he doesn't absolutely, positively have to face.

"How far are we going, Lesh?" I asked.

"About an hour's ride, lord," he said. He pointed off into the foothills, toward the higher ridges of the Titans beyond.

"What did you make of this farmer's story?"

"He's seen a dragon, right enough, lord, close enough for details. He gave me a good description," Lesh said.

"How big did he say it was?"

"Said when it put out it wings it covered his whole farm."

"I hope he was exaggerating."

"I'm sure he was, lord," Lesh said. But, like as not, the dragon was still large enough to be a major pain.

I tried not to show it—putting on a brave front is essential PR for a certified Hero—but, to phrase it as concisely as the language permits, I was scared shitless. The traditional lore in Varay was that no mortal could slay a dragon and live through the experience. I had killed two of them, though the first really didn't count, since an elf warrior had done at least ninety percent of the job first. But the elf was about to crap out permanently, and he told me to take his sword and finish the job. I did, and got to keep the sword to boot. That was how I got Dragon's Death. The second dragon came during the Battle of Thyme. That dragon was a weapon controlled by the wizard of the Etevar of Dorthin, brought in to try to get rid of me and scare off the Varayan army so that the Dorthinis could conquer Varay. That dragon was pretty much my own kill, though the fight was too close for me to do any gloating over it, so the *new and improved* "traditional" wisdom was that only a mortal who *had* killed a dragon *could* kill one. But if the next dragon I met had me for brunch, the Varayans would simply move on to "Release 3.0" of the new and improved traditional wisdom to cover the situation, maybe something like "Three dragons and you're out," or something equally half-witty. I was pushing the odds so far out of shape that even Lloyd's of London wouldn't cover my kind of risk.

There isn't much level ground in the region surrounding Castle Cayenne. "Flat land" is the top of a hill or the narrow valley between two ridges. The roads, such as they are, tend to follow the valleys—when the many spring-fed streams in the area leave room for paths or trails. In the spring, when snowmelt from the mountains is added to the normal flow of water, the hills can be more like chains of islands scattered around like bead necklaces. But even at the flood, the waters rarely get dangerously deep. Just pesky.

The farmers of Varay are good at land conservation, though. They follow the contours of the terrain to minimize erosion. Back home, even with all the scientists working on agriculture and soil retention, some farmers don't bother with such elementary steps. And even though Varay remains technologically in the early Middle Ages, the farmers get almost modern yields from their fields. To feed us all as much as we need to eat in the buffer zone, the farms *have* to be extraordinarily productive. Part of it, according to Parthet, is simply the magical nature of the seven kingdoms, but I'm never willing to slight the importance of the people out working the fields nine or ten months a year. They do the visible magic.

We stopped a couple of times to talk to farmers who were out working. I asked if they had seen this new dragon in the region. One was sure that he hadn't. "I'd sure a-known if I had." The other wasn't certain, but he thought that maybe he had seen a dragon flying in the distance the day before.

The sky was clear, with just a few wispy cirrus clouds off in the west, and it wasn't all that hot yet as we rode out. The breeze was from the north and still carried a faint hint of the cool it picked up over the Mist, hundreds of miles away. Wearing twenty-five pounds of armor and padding makes a person very sensitive to temperature. With the sun out, wearing armor does for you about what a wrapping of aluminum foil does for the potato you throw in with the coals on your barbecue.

"We're getting close," Lesh said about the time I was wondering how much farther we had to go. I didn't do so much horseback riding that I was really comfortable with it. I rarely went anywhere in Varay that I couldn't get to through one of our magic doorways. I had done enough riding for the year on my tour of our western neighbors. I wasn't eager for another marathon ride.

I had been watching the sky since we left Cayenne. Dragons aren't forced to stay anywhere they don't want to stay. The two I had close experience with hadn't come near the ground except to attack. On a few other occasions I had seen dragons flying high. Those hadn't even bothered to attack.

What I *didn't* expect to find was a dragon squatting on the ground building a nest.

Something about this dragon didn't look quite right. I thought that it was just some trick of perspective at first, but then I realized that the "problem" was simply that the dragon was relatively small—*far* smaller than the two dragons I had killed. It had used its claws to scrape a shallow depression in the top of the next hill, but the dragon was still only fifty or sixty feet long, a midget compared to the other dragons I had met up close and personal.

"A runt!" Lesh said. He sounded as relieved as I felt.

I chuckled. "You want to handle this one?" I asked.

He looked to see if I was serious and decided that I wasn't. Oh well, it was worth a try.

"There's something nobody has ever said anything to me about," I said. "Nobody ever said anything about dragons building their nests right here in Varay. It's always *They come in from the Mist,* or *They come in from the Titans.*"

"I don't go lookin' for them!" Lesh said.

"Very wise attitude," I said. "But what do we do with this thing?"

"You have your gun," Lesh reminded me.

If it decides to work, I thought. I wasn't optimistic . . . and I wasn't sure that a gun would make the slightest impression on a dragon if it *did* work. It might just make the damn thing mad.

I estimated the distance to the dragon at about three hundred yards. I would probably have to get a lot closer if I wanted to have any hope that the gun would be sufficiently effective. Using an elephant gun on a sixty-foot dragon *might* be as useful as plinking at an elephant with a .22. And *closer* would give me a poor angle for the shot through an eye toward the middle of the back of the head, the only target that seemed to have any chance of dropping any dragon.

I dismounted, and my companions did likewise. Timon took the reins of all four horses and moved them back a few paces. Harkane held both the rifle and my bow, waiting for me to make my choice. Maybe I should have a golf bag, add a couple of wedges.

"You suppose it's the sporting thing to do, shoot the damn thing while it's just sitting there?" I asked. It was a rhetorical question, I suppose. I sure as hell wasn't going to walk over, give it the finger, and make rude noises to get it mad. The dragon knew that we were there. It kept its eyes on us. but it wasn't making any threatening gestures. It was just watching, the way any wild animal might, as long as you stay outside its flight distance.

"Well, I might prefer the dragon to be sleeping, myself,'' Lesh said. ''But don't count the teeth on a free horse.''

''Yeah.'' I realized that I was stalling. The other times I had faced dragons, I didn't have much choice in the matter, especially the second time. The dragon in question was looking to use me for chewing exercise. But this dragon was just sitting there in its nest—getting ready to lay eggs with baby chickens in them for all I knew.

''Give me the rifle,'' I said.

The rifle was a Mannlicher bolt-action with a four-shot magazine. I took it, ran the bolt to get a shell into the firing chamber, and took aim. The telescopic sight brought the dragon's face right up close. There was no way I could miss. I could look right into that bloodshot amber eye and see the blood vessels along the surface. The dragon didn't even blink.

I moved forward a half-dozen paces, a little lower on the slope. When I started to lose my angle on the dragon's head, I stopped and lifted the rifle again. I aimed, took a breath, held it, and squeezed the trigger. Nothing happened, just a click. I ran the bolt and tried again and got a popping sound like somebody stepping on a paper cup. There was no recoil, but when I ejected that round, all that came out was the cartridge case. Lesh bent down and picked up the slug, maybe eight inches in front of the muzzle.

''Your father never had much luck with guns here either,'' Harkane said. ''Except once when he used a rifle as a club.''

I left the bolt open while I looked down the barrel. Light glinted off my thumbnail, so I knew that the barrel wasn't blocked, so I tried one more shot. This time I got a slightly louder plop and just a hint of recoil.

''I saw the bullet fall,'' Harkane said. ''It went about three horse lengths.''

I handed him the rifle. ''I guess I have to go over there and do it the hard way,'' I said. Harkane handed me my bow. I was going to have to get a lot closer to the dragon to do any good with it, though. And I didn't have any hope at all of actually *killing* a dragon with an arrow. All I could hope for was to weaken it a bit, blind it with a little luck. Then I would have to finish the job with Dragon's Death.

We all made the trek except Timon. I told him to stay with the horses and watch from our hilltop.

Going up the opposite slope, I tried a couple of arrows, but I was at the wrong angle to have a good shot at either of the dragon's eyes. I hit its snout once, and then it waddled backward, out of sight. I gave the bow to Harkane and drew Dragon's Death. As I continued up the hill, the sword's eerie battle tune started winding its way up out of my throat as usual.

Harkane notched an arrow to the bow. Lesh had his spear extended, ready to use that. But all that either of them might be able to do was distract the dragon while I did the important work with my six-foot cleaver.

The dragon was up on all four feet when I could see him-her-it again, still backing away, groaning mightily. I pulled my other elf sword and rattled the two blades together, then went back to just Dragon's Death. I couldn't see trying to fight with both of those oversized steak knives at the same time.

Finally, the dragon quit backing up and hurled itself forward. I brought my sword up and braced myself, ready to meet the charge, but the dragon flapped its wings desperately and flung itself into the sky, clearing my head by a good ten feet, well beyond the range of Dragon's Death. The dragon climbed, circled once, then flapped away toward the south and the higher peaks of the Titan Mountains.

I took a deep breath and sat down.

"I never heard of anybody scaring off a dragon afore," Lesh commented while we watched the beast flap its way off into the distance. The dragon looked awkward in flight from our vantage. "It's like it knowed you're a dragon killer."

"You missed your true calling, Lesh," I said. "You should be working on Madison Avenue, hawking deodorant and cereal and stuff like that."

"Lord?"

"Nothing, Lesh. Here, help me up." I raised an arm, and Lesh helped me to my feet. With all the armor, it's impossible to look graceful getting up off the ground. The dragon finally faded from our view, angling off behind one of the nearer peaks, quite a few miles away. I walked a little higher on the slope. There were no eggs in the depression that the dragon had scooped out.

"Let's go home," I said as I turned and started back down the hill. We started walking back toward our horses. Timon met us in the valley between the hills. We mounted up and started back to Castle Cayenne, a lot more relaxed than we were riding out.

I left my armor and leather padding at Cayenne and stepped through to Basil. Life appeared to be getting back to normal in the great hall there. No one was bitching about calamities lurking in the victuals for lunch, and the smells of cooking food made it out of the kitchen to tempt appetites—not that they needed blandishments. I asked around and learned that Parthet had returned. He and Kardeen were closeted somewhere still trying to figure out what dragons in chicken eggs might mean. Joy and Aaron were chatting at the head table, either *still* or *again*. Joy always gets on well with kids, better than I do. I stopped off with them for a couple of minutes, long enough to kiss Joy and to tell Aaron that there was no dead dragon for him to see, before I wandered off on my own again.

At first, I did just wander. I had no conscious goal in mind when I left Joy and Aaron. Parthet and Kardeen would keep for a while. But when I found myself near the stairs that lead down to the cellar and crypt, I decided to stop in to have a few words with Dad. That may sound crazy, but whenever I feel lonely, or just feel a need to talk out a problem, I tend to go down under Castle Basil to the room where all the Kings and Heroes of Varay are buried. I can stand there by the end of Dad's niche and tell him what I've been up to, or whatever is bothering me. Sometimes I even chat with Vara, the first King and Hero of Varay.

Do I believe in ghosts? Do I think that they really hear me? I'm not sure how to answer that. Before I came to Varay, the answer would have been an easy *no*. But when things got rough, just before and during the Battle of Thyme, I found doubt. Two nights before the battle, I had a dream or a vision—I'm still not sure which it was. In this whatever-it-was experience, I found myself in the crypt. All of the dead Heroes were sitting around a table, waiting for me to join them. Vara told me that he had vowed that no Hero of Varay would ever die alone again, the way he had. When my time came, and Vara indicated that my time had indeed come, the whole Congregation of Heroes would be there to welcome me.

A dream? A vision? I don't know. But getting things off my chest down in the crypt always seems to help.

The catacombs are deep under Castle Basil, down in the solid rock on which the castle sits—not all that far above the level of Basil Town. Torches are kept burning on every landing along the stairs, replaced by the duty guards. There are two cellar levels that are used for larders and wine cellars and the like, then one more level, smaller and considerably below the others. That was where I headed.

I heard noises coming from the catacombs as I descended the stairs—barely audible at first, but slowly becoming quite distinct. I stopped for a moment and checked my reach to the swords slung over my shoulder. The elf swords are in what are, in effect, speed rigs. There are no scabbards that have to be cleared. Each sword is held in place by two spring-loaded C-clamps. If I had to pull five feet of blade out of a scabbard before I could use it, I'd never finish a draw.

Usually, I have complete privacy when I go down to the burial chamber. No one else has ever seemed interested in my sort of routine pilgrimage—people don't lay flowers for the dead or anything like that in Varay—and since only kings and official Heroes are buried there, funerals are rare. But someone was down there now, maybe more than one someone.

The stairway was six feet wide, against a wall on one side, but without even a banister on the other. I moved as softly as I could on the stairs. The noises were real, and they were definitely coming from inside the burial chamber.

I had been stabbed too recently to take anything for granted, even in Basil's crypt. Dragon's Death was the first thing I stuck into the room. I moved in quickly behind the sword, and stopped just inside the doorway, ready for anything.

There were two workmen inside, preparing a new burial niche at the kings' end of the room. One worker noticed me and dropped his chisel. It clattered off the stone. The other worker turned to look. Neither had heard me coming.

"What happened?" I demanded.

"This is supposed to be secret, Your Highness," one worker said, his voice quaking. He couldn't take his eyes off my drawn sword. I put it back over my shoulder.

"Has the king died?" It didn't compute. Lunch had been starting as normal upstairs, and the atmosphere would have been much different if the king had just died.

"No, Highness," the same worker said, bobbing his head low—over and over. "But the Lord Chamberlain set us to working himself. He fears the worst, he said. A secret. It was to be a secret."

I didn't bother to ask anything else. I just turned and started running up the stairs. I had more than a passing interest in King Pregel's health. It wasn't just that he was my great-grandfather or that I was extremely fond of him. I was also his heir designate, and I certainly wasn't ready to become King of Varay. Frankly, I didn't care if I *ever* inherited that job.

There are 108 steps between the catacombs and the level of the great hall. The steps are low, but too deep to take them two at a time. My legs ached by the time I finished climbing them. Kardeen wasn't at lunch in the great hall—he rarely ate there—so I had to go on to his office. I went right past his clerk without stopping.

Kardeen and Parthet were at the chamberlain's desk. They had old scrolls scattered all over the desk and floor. Kardeen was a stickler for order. His desk was always neat. I had never seen the office in such a mess.

"I've just come up from the crypt," I said when Kardeen looked up. "What's going on?"

"His Majesty's health has worsened dramatically this morning," Kardeen said, very softly. "You mother is with him. She doesn't think he can make it back this time."

"He has to," I said, but I wasn't talking to Kardeen and Parthet any longer. I was already on my way out the door.

"Come to my workroom after you see the king," Parthet shouted after me. I nodded, but I don't know if he saw the gesture.

I ran all the way upstairs and pulled up short just outside the door to the king's bedroom so I could catch my breath before I opened the door and went in. There wasn't much light in the chamber—just an oil lamp burning on a table near the side of grandfather's bed, and it was turned down low. Mother was sitting in a straight chair next to the head of the bed. She turned when she heard me come in and held a finger to her mouth so I would be quiet. As if I might come in shouting dirty jokes or something. Mother took a close look at the king, then got up and came across the room to me.

"Let's go out in the hall," she whispered.

"What happened?" I asked when the door was closed between the king and us.

"He's been doing poorly. You know that," Mother said. "This morning, he heard the commotion downstairs and somebody told him about the dragon eggs. It seemed to take all the fight out of him. All his vitals are getting bad."

"Why don't we get him to a real hospital then? Get Doc McCreary to take care of him there."

"It wouldn't help. The King of Varay is tied too tightly to the magic of this place. Leaving Varay now would almost certainly kill him."

"And if we *don't* move him?"

Mother shook her head. "I'm even afraid to leave him long enough to go for Hank McCreary," she said. "Anyway, by the time he could get here . . ."

I don't think I completely managed to suppress the growl that was my reaction to that kind of dead-end thinking.

"Why don't you take a break?" I suggested, as evenly as possible. "Powder your nose or stretch your legs, or something. Give me a few minutes alone with him."

Mother wanted to argue, I could see that in her eyes, but she shut her mouth before the first word of protest could get out. I was relieved when she nodded and started for the stairs. If she hadn't gone on her own, I would have carried her off, and I'm fairly certain that she realized that. I know it sounds horrible, and maybe it was, but I had to have some time alone with Pregel and—as Hero and heir—I had that right. And Mother . . . well, I'll leave it at this: I still hadn't forgotten that she and

Dad had completely concealed Varay and my heritage from me until I was twenty-one and Dad was in trouble, already dead, actually. They had programmed me to take over as Hero from the time I was a baby. After living their lie for twenty-one years, my patience with my mother could get ragged in a hurry.

I went back inside the bedroom, lengthened the wick on the oil lamp that was burning, lit a second, then pulled the drapes open on the window to let some daylight in. Mother had the room so gloomy that it might already have been the king's lying-in-state.

"Grandfather?" I walked up along the side of the bed nearest to him. His face was pasty white, his cheeks unshaven for several days. His thin hair was disheveled. He didn't open his eyes or move. I sat on the edge of the bed and laid my hand on his chest, lightly, feeling the slight movement as he breathed, the even fainter pulse.

"Grandfather. It's Gil." His eyelids flickered a little. There was a little movement at the edges of his mouth. He seemed to breathe just a little deeper.

"I've got good news," I said. I figured that it was good news anyhow. If the story about the dragon eggs had sapped him, maybe I could give him back a little vigor. "A dragon was sitting out near Cayenne this morning. They called me to take care of it. I went out there and scared the dragon off. I went 'shoo' and it skedaddled."

He opened his eyes and stared up at me.

"Truth," I said. Well, it was *close* to the truth. "The last we saw of the dragon, it was hightailing it into the Titan Mountains. Lesh, Harkane, and Timon were with me."

He may have smiled a little.

"Of course, it wasn't the biggest dragon ever, but it was big enough, and it turned tail and ran."

I was sure of the smile then. It was weak, but clearly visible.

"You'd better hurry and perk up here, Grandfather. I've got work enough of my own to do without worrying about doing your job as well."

The smile got a little wider as his eyes slid closed. I held my hand on his chest for another minute or so. He was still alive. I thought maybe he was doing a little better. I couldn't be sure.

Parthet had two rooms in the castle, one over the other, in the northeast tower. The lower room was his workshop or laboratory. The other was a bedroom. He still had his cottage in the forest, but it seemed that the only time he used it anymore was when he just wanted to get completely away from everybody else. That wasn't too often. His social instincts were strong. And since I had made him keep glasses with a current prescription, he was in more demand for his wizardry.

I let Mother back into Pregel's room—she was just coming back down the hallway when I opened the door—and then I went on to Parthet's shop. The chamberlain was there with him. They were still going through scrolls and books.

Parthet's tower was narrower than the tower that held Kardeen's offices. Parthet's rooms were only about fifteen feet in diameter, and the lower one was in the state of disarray that I always associated with my uncle. The only thing I spotted in the room that was new since my last visit was a large glass vat—about five gallons large—sitting in the center of Parthet's work table. The elf head was in the vat, eyes closed, long hair floating toward the top of the alcohol that came to within an inch of the lid. Like seaweed.

"When are you going to get rid of that damn thing?" I snapped, pointing at the head.

"When he can't do us any more good," Parthet snapped back.

"It's sick. Maybe you can make him talk to you, but I bet his father has even less trouble hearing him. I'd just as soon the Elflord of Xayber didn't have a pressing reason to turn his attention to us again."

"We may be damn lucky to have Junior there with us," Parthet said.

Kardeen cleared his throat and cut off any reply I might have made to Parthet. "We heard that you were off chasing a dragon."

I nodded and gave them the capsule summary.

"That sounds encouraging," Kardeen said, glancing at Parthet.

"It's about time *something* sounded encouraging," the wizard growled. "Look. We've gone through so many musty old tomes this morning that I've just now stopped sneezing from all the dust. Some of the ancient books of lore are maddeningly vague or ambiguous, but as near as I can gather, things like chickens laying dragon eggs are among the signs of the End of Everything, or the complete domination of Fairy over all three realms, or your choice of total, top-of-the-heap, major-league disasters.

"You don't know which?" I asked, as if it made a difference.

"Hard to tell for sure, but it looks like the complete scrambling of everything, even the lords of Fairy, at the very least. Not much solace in that." He looked at the severed head.

"Is there any way to reverse the trend?" I asked. "Any way to stave off the collapse or whatever?"

"The ancient treatises make a point of saying that there is a cure for any ill. The problem is that we can't find out what the cure is, or exactly what we have to cure. But *he* might know." Parthet pointed at the head again.

"Okay, but what have you got to trade?" I asked.

"What do you mean?" Parthet asked, letting his arm drop.

"He's dead. He's an elf. I doubt that even your truth spells will be very effective on him now. You'll have to do a deal, and what can a dead elf want?"

Parthet looked at the elf's head, then back at me. "Okay, what?"

I shrugged. "I didn't say that I knew the answer, just the question. Why don't you ask him?"

Parthet went to the glass vat, took off the lid, and set it aside. He started mumbling one of his obscure, incoherent chants as he reached in and grabbed a handful of hair. He lifted the elf's head out of the raw alcohol and held it over the vat while the whiskey dripped off the head.

The eyelids opened and madly bloodshot eyes—in a head that didn't have a drop of blood left—started to look around. The elf looked at Parthet, at me, and at as much of the room as he could see. Baron Kardeen was behind the elf, out of sight.

The son of Xayber opened his mouth. The first sound out was a monstrous, drunken belch, followed by a badly slurred, "Where's the rest of me?"

7

Two Heads

I almost choked myself cutting off a laugh, but I guess that none of the others were familiar with that line. People in Varay might recognize the name Ronald Reagan, but I doubt that anyone (with the possible exception of my mother) had seen any of his movies; there are no movie theaters or television in Varay. And the question didn't sound nearly as funny the second time the elf asked it.

"Where's the rest of me?"

"We have some questions for you," Parthet said, throwing in a few totally incomprehensible words of magic for good measure.

"Where is my body?"

"Tell him," I said, even though I realized that we might be throwing away a bargaining chip.

"It's safe," Parthet said, turning the head so they could look at each other eye to eye. "It's here in the castle." I thought that was a nice compromise. Tell the elf but don't tell him all of it.

The elf started a singsong chant. I felt his sword getting warm on my back and I could see Parthet's face getting red. The wizard went back to his own chanting.

"Enough, dammit!" I shouted. I whipped the hot sword off my back and touched the tip of the blade to the elf's upper lip.

"You recognize this?" I asked.

"I know my own," he replied.

"You know who I am and why I'm wearing *your* sword?"

"I know."

"You came here disguised and tried to kill me. You lost and I killed you," I reminded him. "I took your head straight off, in case you missed the details. It wasn't even a difficult stroke. Your head bounced off the table and then it just sat there and couldn't believe what had happened. Now, either you help us or we bury you in pieces with a day's worth of shit.'' I was starting to get as touchy as Uncle Parthet.

The detached face lost its belligerent look, but slowly. After we both had a moment to cool off, I started to tell him about all of the crazy things that were happening, in the mortal world and in the buffer zone, and my guess that they had to be reflected in Fairy, that *his* death might even have been part of the weirdness. He took the news about the dragon eggs very seriously, but without any of the histrionics that Parthet had displayed.

''What do I get for my help?'' the elf asked, as I had known he would. ''A negative thing is not enough.''

''You know what has to be done to stop this madness?'' I asked.

''I know. I'll even tell you the nature of the solution, and then we can bargain for my hire. Simply knowing the solution won't help you. And maybe I won't bother to tell you how to achieve the solution even. It can mean no difference to me now what happens.''

''Okay, how do we stop whatever it is that's happening?'' I asked.

''You merely have to find the balls of the Great Earth Mother and bring them together.''

It took a couple of seconds for my brains to catch up with my instincts. The elf wasn't being a smartass. Uncle Parthet had told me the story once, the creation legend that was accepted as gospel in the seven kingdoms.

Back in the chaos before creation, the Great Earth Mother wandered around (and the legends aren't specific about *where* she was wandering, since nothing had been created for her to wander around on), looking for a mate (and where *he* came from was glossed over as completely as where Cain and Abel found *their* wives). After looking around ''from before infinity to beyond infinity'' and getting hornier all the time (except that time hadn't started to run yet), the Great Earth Mother found her stud and got laid so that the world and heavens could all be created. Then, sometime after it was over, the Great Earth Mother decided that she liked the universe they had created together but she couldn't stand the mate who had helped make it possible, so she did a black-widow number on him, but kept his gonads for souvenirs, just in case.

And the son of the Elflord of Xayber was telling us that we had to find these family jewels in order to keep the whole shebang from coming to an end . . . the End of Everything, to give the phrase the same inflection that Parthet had used.

"You have any idea where we can find these . . . balls?" I asked.

"I know precisely where they are. But they will cost you more than you ever expected to pay for anything."

I waited for the other shoe to drop, but the elf was waiting too, and he had more time than I did.

"What do you want?" I asked eventually.

"I would shrug if I had shoulders to command," he said, letting his eyes wander for a few seconds. "What can you offer that makes it worth my while?"

I hesitated for a long moment before I answered. "I can see that you are properly laid out, head and body, so you can find whatever peace there is for your kind." Parthet started to protest, but I held up a hand to silence him. "I will give you my personal promise of that, the vow of the Hero of Varay." After that, there was nothing Parthet *could* say—if the elf accepted the deal.

"It's not enough," the elf told me though.

"Just what are we supposed to do with these family jewels once we get them?" I asked—a distraction, something to give me a little extra time to try to think of a cheap way to sweeten the pot.

"Now, that would be giving away too much," the elf said. "I need something to hold back as a guarantee."

"As a guarantee for what?" I asked.

"Ah, I just figured that out. My price is that you—you personally, Hero of Varay—take me home to my father. All of me, head and body."

"No!" Parthet said, preempting any reply from me. "That is an impossible request. This is the heir to Varay."

"As I was heir to Xayber?" the elf said. "Very well. You've made your decision. And I have made mine. There is no other price."

Parthet threw the head across the room, off a wall. The

head rebounded with a soft squish and fell almost straight down. I went over and picked the head up, by the hair, just the way Parthet had held it. I wanted to puke but didn't. Couldn't. I thought to say something, but I couldn't decide what to say, so I just returned the head to its vat of alcohol and put the cover on.

Parthet and Kardeen followed me out of the work-room. I rubbed my hand on my jeans, trying to get rid of the memory of even holding that head.

"Unless you've got another way to locate these relics, if they exist, then he has us over the proverbial barrel," I said once we were well away from the room.

"But we may have all we need from him," Parthet said. "He told us what the cure is. All we have to do is find the pieces."

"That seems to be a big enough job," I said.

"Maybe not. We might have references here that will help. In fact, even without looking I think I can narrow the search down. The family jewels of the Great Earth Mother will be found in two of her shrines—two different ones, some distance apart," Parthet said.

"But you don't know which shrines," I said.

"Not yet, but I may be able to find out, or at least narrow the possibilities to a manageable number."

"How many shrines are there?"

Kardeen answered that. "There must be hundreds, more likely thousands, scattered throughout all three realms.

"All *three* realms? I don't remember coming across any in my world," I said.

"Few of those are in decent condition," Parthet said, distracted. "Most are passed off as ancient archaeological sites and plundered. Avedell, your mother, could likely pinpoint at least a score of them. She made quite a study of it when you were a child. The ring of stones at Stonehenge was one such shrine, once upon a time."

"Then if one of the jewels was in that world, it might have been carted off to a museum, or lost, or something."

"Possible, but unlikely," Parthet said. "They must be the most powerful magic artifacts in creation. Their presence would cause things to happen. And the Great Mother

Earth is unlikely to have left them without suitable protection.''

''Like what?''

''I may know more after I do my research,'' Parthet said, sidestepping the question neatly. ''And now, I really must get at that. I don't know how much time we have before things get too bad to stop.''

Parthet turned and headed back to his workroom. Kardeen walked on with me.

''So these things really exist?'' I asked.

''If you mean has anyone actually seen them and reported seeing them, the answer is no, not in any of the records that I have seen,'' Kardeen said. He shook his head. ''But I would not disbelieve the story. There is *something*, there has to be.''

''You know that we're going to have to deal with Xayber's son before this is over,'' I said.

Kardeen didn't answer immediately. I glanced at him. He looked lost in thought.

''The king would never consent to the deal the elf demands,'' he said finally. ''The Elflord of Xayber has too bitter a grudge against you, and he isn't likely to forget the reckoning.''

''None of that matters if things come down to a choice of risking me or the possibility of losing everything, which includes me. There won't be any choice, any at all. The End of Everything sounds awfully final, while I *might* survive a close encounter with Xayber. I have before, and I know a little more of what's going on now than I did then. There's at least some chance in that option.'' I wasn't overly confident, but even in a worst-case scenario, it was still the only way. If we somehow managed to latch on to this pair of perhaps mythical family jewels and figured out how to use them to keep Armageddon or whatever from happening.

''Something can be worked out with the elf,'' Kardeen said, but he didn't sound overly confident either.

''What are you going to do, offer him a new pair of suspenders?'' I asked. I was usually very careful not to be sarcastic with Kardeen. The chamberlain was a good guy, organized, efficient, indispensable—and a good friend—but this time, it just slipped out of me. ''He wants me to take him home to Daddy,'' I said, trying to sound a little more serious. "I guess part of that is concern for being laid out proper, but I imagine that it's more because his daddy sent him to kill me and this is his only way of getting the job done. Maybe . . ." I stopped talking and almost stopped walking.

"Maybe?" Kardeen asked blandly, slowing down to match my reduced pace.

The idea that had popped into my head wasn't fully formed, so I didn't want to spring it on anyone until I had a chance to turn it over in my mind a few more times. "Look, if it comes down to actually making a deal with the elf, let me do the making, all right? I've got a few ideas of my own on this."

Kardeen made a formal nod of agreement. "It's your neck on the line," he observed, and I nodded back.

"By the way, I think you'll be able to pull the workmen out of the crypt for a while. I don't think that grandfather will need it quite yet."

"Prophecy, or a gift of healing?" he asked.

I started to treat his remark as a joke until I recognized that he wasn't making a joke, he was serious. "There's something in the legends about the Heroes of Varay being able to do that?" I asked. In turn, my question was also serious. I was still learning about the magic that went with my job the hard way, falling into one bit of it after another.

"Vara was said to be a healer at special times."

"But Vara was also supposed to be of Fairy blood," I reminded him. In the three years and odd months since I fell into the job of Hero of Varay, I had read every word that existed of Vara and his time, and I had heard the much more extensive legends that were handed down and embellished from generation to generation. Vara was something like the Prodigal Son, but he didn't go crawling home in shame. He set up the buffer zone to cut his father and older brother off from the mortal realm, which they had been using for their personal sport—and some of *those* tales sounded straight out of Bulfinch and Homer . . . or vice versa.

"We all have something of the blood of Fairy," Kardeen said. "It's what makes the seven kingdoms so special. We come from both worlds. And in your family, the line is direct."

"How long do you figure Parthet will need to find out where these . . . relics are, or to find out that he can't find them?"

"He'll keep at it until he exhausts all of his sources—and until I've exhausted mine. It may be a couple of days, probably not much longer."

"A couple of days of everybody going into a panic at anything the least bit out of the ordinary?" Somehow, that didn't come out too well. I had visions of Chicken Little.

"You don't seem to take any of this very seriously," Kardeen said, the closest he had ever come to scolding me about anything.

"I take the deaths of thousands of people back home very seriously," I told him. "I just haven't seen anything to convince me that dragon eggs have anything to do with nuclear bombs or the End of Everything or anything else."

"You'd prefer to think that it's a coincidence?" Kardeen asked.

"I'd prefer to think that it was all a bad dream. Since I know it's not, I don't know what to make of it, but I'm not ready to jump all the way to doomsday conclusions."

Parthet was busy, every minute, keeping at his work. Kardeen had loads of work to do, all of his regular work and this extra quest for information—however he planned to fit *that* in. One way or another, there would be plenty of work for me coming up, but at that moment there really wasn't anything I could do to speed things up. I went back to the great hall. Joy was sitting by herself.

"Where's Aaron?" I asked.

"He's off with one of the boys from here in the castle," Joy said. "I guess he's exploring. Are we ready to leave?"

"Not yet, I'm afraid. It won't be long, though." I got a mug of beer and hung around long enough to drink it. "I've just got a little more to do here. I'll be back in a few minutes and then we can go."

I went back up to the king's bedroom to check in with Mother. Pregel was awake and seemed measurably stronger than he had just a little while before. His smile was encouraging.

"You look better," I told him, despite his long-standing aversion to talking about his health.

"I feel better," he replied. Mother shrugged and nodded.

I sat with them for a few minutes, then went back to the great hall to collect Joy.

"There's something I never thought to ask you," I said as I plopped down on the chair next to her. "Have you ever done any horseback riding?"

"You mean on real, live horses?" she asked. I nodded, and Joy shook her head. "I don't even ride on merry-go-rounds. They make me dizzy."

"Well, a real horse doesn't go in circles like that normally," I said, ruling out any wisecracks about dizziness. "Unless it's on a racecourse."

"I haven't seen any cars here," Joy noted, figuring out where I was leading.

"No internal combustion engines of any sort. They don't work. Besides the doorways, there are just two ways to get anywhere, foot and horse. The doors don't go everywhere, and feet will only take a body so far."

"I think you're telling me that I'm going to have to learn how to ride."

"It's not that bad, really. A good horsc is as comfortable as a rocking chair." And then, because I couldn't let the opportunity pass, I added, "Mostly, learning to ride is simple arithmetic."

"What do you mean?"

"You just have to get back up in the saddle one more time than you fall off." I laughed and ducked as she took a light swing at my shoulder.

"You stinker," she said. Then she started laughing too. "When does all this falling off start?"

"Pretty soon, I think. I'll talk with Lesh, have him give you lessons."

"Why not you?"

"Something I read once said that spouses should never try to teach each other anything, that it just makes reasons to fight. And besides, you'd clobber me the first time I laughed at you falling."

"Darn right I would. I may clobber you just for thinking about it."

"We'll have to see about getting you a horse here. We

don't keep a lot of spares at Cayenne.'' The light mood seemed to evaporate from me then. There was no special reason that I could see, but I sort of slumped a little and felt the smile leave my face.

''You mean I've got to ride home?'' Joy asked, not catching the change at once. ''How far is it?''

''No, you don't have to ride home, though it would be a nice jaunt if we wanted to take a week or so to ourselves. I don't think we can afford the time right now, though. But there's a good stable here and we'll be able to find a horse that's just right for you.'' The conversation was suddenly an effort, and I had to really push myself to continue it. I'm still not certain what happened to me sitting there.

''Who's going to pick out my horse?'' Joy asked.

''Well, you obviously don't know enough about horses to do it.'' I held up a hand to keep her from saying anything about my charge. I wasn't looking for another swat even a playful one. I quickly added, ''I don't know a hel of a lot more. All I know is that you open their mouths and look at their teeth, and I don't know *why* you're supposed to do that. So I guess we'll just do what I usually do, let Baron Kardeen take care of it. That's pretty much a guarantee that you'll get the best horse for you that can be found in the kingdom.''

''Really?''

''He's the glue that holds Varay together,'' I said.

''How old is he?''

''About twenty years older than your father,'' I said and then I realized that Joy had finally noticed the change in my mood. She was trying to bring me out of my sudden funk. I almost told her not to bother. Instead, I took a deep breath, held it for a moment, then let it out. managed to paste a smile across my face then. Maybe Joy knew what she was doing after all. I took her hand and stood up. ''Let's go home.''

''Home?''

''Cayenne,'' I said. Joy didn't look particularly elated—there was no way she could consider my castle her home yet—but she didn't complain.

Joy and I stepped through the doorway to Cayenne and went up to the battlements to be alone for a while. *I* had never found it necessary to station a sentry about Castl

Cayenne, but I knew that Lesh put his men on rotation whenever I wasn't "in residence," when the place was his responsibility—or even when we were both gone. The countryside was generally peaceful, and I had the special danger sense of the Hero of Varay to protect me, so Lesh had, grudgingly, decided that maybe sentries weren't essential when I was around. My "establishment" wasn't so large that I had to find work for the people I did have.

I boosted myself up into one of the crenels and sat sideways in it, back against one side, feet against the other, swords skewed around so I didn't have to worry about slicing my back. Joy leaned against me and pulled my arm around her. We stayed like that for a few minutes, then Joy turned around in my arms and stared me straight in the eye.

"What's wrong?" she asked.

"What do you mean?"

"You know what I mean. What's going on around here? Something is wrong, it has to be, maybe something as big as what happened to the *Coral Lady.*"

"There are no nuclear weapons here. I don't think they would work." But I knew what she was driving at. I closed my eyes to avoid the look Joy gave me.

"The trouble seems to be spilling over here," I said when I opened my eyes again. "That means work for me, Hero-work."

"Dangerous work?"

"By definition," I admitted. "And this time, if Parthet is right, the stakes are as high as they can get."

"Can't you get out of it?"

All I could do was shake my head.

8

Death Vow

"You do what you have to do."

I heard that piece of advice many times while I was growing up. Dad tossed that one out anytime I had to make a difficult or painful choice. I don't know when the first time was, but the first time that really sticks in my mind came when I was fifteen and we were deer hunting in the Rockies. I shot a handsome stag but didn't kill it. The animal was badly wounded but managed to get away. *You do what you have to do.* In that case, it meant four hours of dangerous tracking through rough country to find the stag and finish the job. Of course, Dad didn't send me off to do the job alone—though he might have a year later. Still, either or both of us could have been killed or badly injured tracking that wounded stag down into a canyon and through a stretch of frigid white water. And then we couldn't get the whole carcass back out. We skinned it, saved the horns, hide, and as much meat as we could, and then hiked and climbed back to our camp. It was totally dark by the time we got there. We were both freezing and wet, and it's amazing that we didn't both get sick.

The price the elf demanded for his help was high—potentially as high as it could get for me—but I didn't have much choice, and the elf knew it. It was my duty, and *you do what you have to do.*

Duty. That led me to thoughts of Annick and her warped sense of duty. She thought it was her *duty* to spend as much of her life as it took to find and murder her father, the elf warrior who had raped her mother and sired her. In the process, Annick attacked anything and anyone out of Fairy who came within reach. I hadn't seen her myself since the day of the Battle of Thyme, but I had certainly *heard* about her and her exploits often enough. Annick was a few months younger than Joy, but while Joy had been in college, Annick had been making one foray after another north into the Isthmus of Xayber, ambushing soldiers of the elflord, setting fire to houses, laying traps of one sort or another to cause trouble even when she wasn't around. Back in my world, she would have been a terrorist, planting bombs or whatever—creating mayhem, maybe even incidents like the *Coral Lady.* The most charitable thing I could think about Annick was that it was a waste. At times I pitied her. At times I thought she was no better than a mad dog. She was so consumed by her hatred that there wasn't room for anything else in her life. She called it duty. I called it obsession, insanity. There was no rational excuse for what she did, no way to justify it, even in the buffer zone. Annick would keep up with her madness until it killed her. And one of these days it would. I was surprised that she had lasted as long as she had already.

Up on the battlements of Cayenne, I held Joy for several minutes, until we were both feeling a little better. Then we went down to the main hall for dinner. Hunger in Varay gives very little way to any competition. Afterward, while Joy went to the kitchen to compliment the cooks, I went over a few things with Lesh.

"I don't want anyone filling Joy's head with all the horrors we've been through," I told Lesh. "She's shaky enough without hearing about all the injuries and so forth. I'll tell her myself, in time." Lesh just nodded and waited. "She'll worry enough when we're off on this next business."

"I understand, lord," Lesh said, and I was sure that he did. Lesh—*Sir* Lesh to give him his proper title—was my right-hand man. He served as chamberlain, steward, majordomo for Castle Cayenne. He was my representative to the village, and he was my companion on all of my Hero-work. He had also become my closest friend, and not just in the buffer zone.

"We'll be off soon?" Lesh asked when I didn't continue.

"Probably within the next few days," I told him. Then I reported what I knew so far and what was left to learn.

"Oh, something else for when we have time," I said

when I got through the essentials. "Joy doesn't know how to ride. You think you can teach her?"

"Aye, lord. What horse did you have in mind for her?"

"I'll have Baron Kardeen find one at Basil. We really don't have one here that would be right for her, do we?"

"Well, perhaps she could take a lesson or two on Timon's Gheffy."

"No real hurry, Lesh. Things may be hectic for a time."

"More dragon eggs?" he asked, in the same way he might have asked if I thought it would rain in the morning.

"This and that," I said. "Parthet's in a panic about all the omens."

"It's a wizard's job to know about such things," Lesh reminded me.

I shrugged. "Whatever comes, it's likely to mean work for us."

"Aye, that's for sure." Joy was coming back. Lesh spotted her before I did. "I'll take care of the riding lessons, lord."

If I could just cut down the number of "lords" to one or two a month, it would be perfect. But Lesh's sense of Varayan propriety was just too strong.

Joy started talking about the methods the cooks used and how much she had liked food that she had never tasted before. All the way up to our rooms, she carried on about the kitchen and the problems of fixing such large meals for a crowd. I let her talk and just nodded or grunted as needed to keep her going.

"There's not much light for reading in here," Joy said when we got to the bedroom. "Those kerosene lanterns and oil lamps just aren't enough."

"We can fix that. I've just never bothered. I've always treated the three places as one big apartment. When I want to read, I just go through to the other room." I hesitated, suddenly recalling the way I had felt when we left Chicago the last time, as if I might never see the place again. "I don't suppose there's any real reason to stop, especially since the plumbing is a lot better in Chicago."

"You don't sound very happy about it though."

"Just nerves, I suspect."

"Because of that ship?"

"That's part of it. But things are also stranger than usual around here, what with the dragons in the eggs and all." I was being vaguer than necessary. While I still didn't know precisely what all the strange omens were leading up to, I could be relatively sure that it would mean acute Hero-work before long. But Joy still wasn't all that comfortable just *being* in Varay. I hoped to let her *gradually* learn just how much my "job" entailed.

"You have to stick around?" she asked.

"Well, I shouldn't be out of touch for long, but Parthet and Mother both know how to get hold of me if I'm back in our world." I shook my head. "There was something else, just before we left Chicago the last time. Part of the magic of being Hero of Varay is a special awareness of danger. You remember the way I *knew* something was wrong before we heard about the *Coral Lady?*" I waited for her to nod before I continued. "Well, that danger sense was kicking up when we left the apartment in Chicago. I had a feeling that I might never see the place again."

"That settles it. Let's go right this minute and put that fear to rest."

I chuckled. "I forgot that you minored in psychology."

"Phooey. It's just common sense."

"I know, like getting back on the horse right away when you fall off," I said.

"Did you have to bring that up?"

"Yep, I had to. Okay, let's give Chicago a try, but cautiously. Stay behind me while I open the way."

"You really believe this stuff, don't you?"

I shook my head, as emphatically as I could. "I've had my face rubbed in it too many times for *any* of it to be a question of belief. The rules are different here. Each of my two elf swords came from a dead elf warrior. Parthet has the head of the second one in his workroom, in a tub of booze. He's cooked up some magic that lets the elf talk to us. And the danger sense has been keeping me alive for more than three years. It's all real, Joy, whether anyone believes in it or not. Like gravity."

Joy's face got a little pale.

"It takes time to sink in, I know," I said, softer. "But

this isn't Wonderland or Never-Never Land. This is as real as the *Coral Lady* or lung cancer."

"And just as dangerous?"

"At times. But there's danger everywhere. You just have to know how to deal with the particular dangers of the place you are. Like street smarts, knowing how to stay out of trouble in a city back home. Chicago is probably a lot more dangerous than Varay. You just have to get used to a different set of dangers."

Joy nodded, very slowly.

"There's something else maybe we should talk about," I said. "Your parents. Your brother and his family."

"What about them?"

"There are no telephone lines or mail deliveries between St. Louis and Varay, for one thing. For another, if things keep getting weird, this may be the only safe place left. Relatively safe. At least there are no nuclear bombs or crazy terrorists willing to kill thousands of innocent people to get their names or beliefs mentioned on the news." No, terrorism in the buffer zone was retail rather than wholesale.

"How can I tell anyone back home about this place? I'm not sure that *I* believe it yet."

"I know the problem," I reminded her. "Look, we don't have to do it right this minute, maybe, but you should be thinking about it. Maybe the next target will be the Gateway Arch or one of the riverboats on the Mississippi."

"If you're trying to scare me, you're doing a darn good job."

I sat on the bed and shook my head, slowly this time. "I'm not *trying* to scare you, Joy. This *Coral Lady* bombing and all the strange things that have happened here—I don't know how to handle it all myself yet. And I don't know how much more of this roller-coaster up-and-down we'll have. This world has dangers. It has elflords and dragons, and evil wizards. It has sicknesses that our world hasn't seen in ages, but not as much as you might think. It's primitive and it can be uncomfortable for anyone who's only known the comforts of modern civilization back home. But it doesn't have as many wholesale dangers as what I used to call the 'real' world."

"And this is where you belong." No question. Joy looked out the bedroom window, then came over to the bed. "So this is where I belong too. I'll get used to it." Her smile was weak, but she sat next to me and put her head on my shoulder.

"I will get used to it," she repeated.

"I know you will," I said. "Come on. Let's go get some lights and whatever else we need. I've got a pair of good camping lanterns with fairly fresh batteries back in Chicago."

"No hurry. I don't think I'll be doing much reading tonight. Besides, I just thought of something else. Aaron disappeared from Joliet again. They may come looking for you."

"It's possible," I agreed. "But if he simply disappeared out of a room filled with people, after we left, they're going to be pretty confused to start with." I started to laugh, then stopped quickly. "It's really not funny," I said. "I feel sorry for them, especially the aunt and uncle. They had enough shocks to deal with already."

I stood and stretched. "You were right about the psychology, though. Let's visit Chicago anyhow. See what's on the news. It's been more than forty-eight hours since the *Coral Lady* explosion. There ought to be something fresh about it on the airwaves."

"You're sure you want to go?"

"Yeah. Just remember what I said about when I open the doorway. Stay behind me. If there's big danger close, I'll know."

Joy nodded, and we kissed before we went to the doorway.

I hesitated before I touched the silver tracing, though, thinking. Danger can come in a variety of guises. At the moment, a crowd of police uniforms in my Chicago apartment would be almost as dangerous as a raging elf warrior, especially if they saw my entrance and the elf swords I had slung back over my shoulders. Even though I wasn't around when Aaron Wesley Carpenter disappeared from a room filled with people, there would certainly be questions for me. There was a damn good chance that my connection to him might make me a fugitive in my native world. I sure as hell couldn't explain the way he vanished so that Illinois bureaucrats would buy it. Partly, that was why I wore the elf swords even though we were going back to the other world. Mostly, it was because I was more used to blades than guns by this time. A sword can't misfire, and it never runs out of ammunition. But it would sure add to the confusion if police saw me appear out of nowhere with those blades over my shoulders.

Finally, I touched the silver tracing, ready to back off and break the connection if I had to. But there were no uniforms visible, no flood of danger signals pouring through the passage. Joy and I stepped through and I made a quick tour of the apartment to make sure that there were no surprises.

"Perfectly safe," Joy said. I don't know if that was for my benefit or her own. She stayed close to me through the entire inspection.

"Looks like," I agreed. "But if there's a knock at the front door, we bail out the nearest exit. I'm not ready to stand around and answer questions." I showed her where all of the magic doorways were and told her where each one led.

"What time is it?" Joy asked.

I shrugged, then headed into the bedroom, where the nearest clock was.

"Ten-fifty," I said, even though Joy was still at my side and could read the clock as easily as I could. "Too late for the regular news. *Nightline* should still be on, though, and then we can switch over to CNN." We headed for the living room.

"I'm going to call home, since we're here," Joy said. I nodded and turned on the television. I was only moderately surprised when a quick scan of the channels showed that there was still coverage of the disaster on all three regular networks. It took a few minutes to find out that the shows were just long special reports. The continuous coverage had finally ended, earlier that day.

I tuned in during the middle of a piece from the State Department. There had been strident complaints and threats out of Teheran, Beirut, and Tripoli. The complaint was that the United States had strafed, bombed, and firebombed a city in North Africa, totally destroying it and killing as many as fifteen thousand civilians. The threats were of massive retaliation against American citizens and installations around the world. The Pentagon, the State Department, and the President acknowledged that we had attacked a training camp for terrorists in the Libyan desert and suggested that the total number of casualties, killed and wounded, had to be considerably below five hundred.

While Joy was on the telephone talking to her mother, I kept the volume low on the television, just loud enough so I could hear it. And although I was listening to the news, I couldn't help overhearing parts of Joy's conversation, which got more agitated as it went on and Joy heard more of the news, from her mother and from the TV.

"Gil and I got married yesterday. I think it was just yesterday," Joy said after nearly ten minutes of other talk. I nodded. It *had* been just the day before.

"Well, it was a spur-of-the-moment decision," Joy said. "You know we talked about it before Gil went off on his business trip, and we just decided that the time was right, you know, after that bombing."

Close enough, I thought.

"*No,* I am *not* pregnant."

Then the conversation got interesting.

"We got married in a castle. . . . No, we're not in Europe. I'm calling from Chicago. . . . Well, I can't really explain where the castle is over the phone, but I can *show* you if you and Daddy come up here to visit."

By that time, Joy and I had seen film of the bombing runs made against the terrorist school in retaliation for the *Coral Lady.* The TV in the living room has a forty-five-inch screen. It's almost like being at the theater. Joy was staring at it while she talked on the phone. The only way that fifteen thousand people could have been in the few buildings we saw in the film was if they were already dead and stacked up like firewood.

Then reporters covered another string of threats against the United States and all things American.

"Why don't you come up over the weekend?" Joy said on the phone. "Get Danny and his family and all of you come. . . . It is? You're sure today is Friday? . . . I guess it is. Well then, *next* weekend. That gives you a whole week to get hold of Danny and make arrangements. . . .

You have the address here. We're right on the lake. . . . That's right, not too far from Wrigley Field. . . . No, I don't know who's playing next weekend. I don't think Gil does either."

I shook my head. I didn't even know if they were in town. I hadn't been out to a Cubs game since April, the first week of the season, just before I started my goodwill tour of the buffer zone.

"No, he says he doesn't know. We'll check and let you know. . . . Okay, next week, Saturday morning. Bye, Mom." Joy hung up and came over to sit next to me on the sofa. Close. She seemed drained by the call.

"They're coming?" I asked.

"Mom and Dad, for sure. I don't know about Danny and his family. Mom thinks I'm on drugs or something, talking about castles. She wants to see the castle, and she wants to see a marriage certificate."

I laughed. "You knew it wouldn't be easy."

"We don't have a marriage certificate."

"I'll have Baron Kardeen draw one up. Real parchment. That should impress your mother."

"Once we convince her that's it legal."

The network anchorman on the television was drawing in comments from a half-dozen correspondents stationed around the world now, with the predictable reactions of diplomats in the capitals of our allies and others.

"It is going to get worse here, isn't it?" Joy asked.

"Probably," I said. "That's why you decided to get your family here, isn't it? To take them to Varay?"

Joy nodded. "I guess. I'm still not sure how we're going to manage it, though. Can we find room for them?"

"No problem," I assured her. No problem except, maybe, time. Eight days was long enough for a lot of varieties of hell to break out. But it wouldn't help to worry Joy about that too quickly.

"I may be busy by then," I added, "but you've got the rings, so you can make the transfer. Get my mother to help if you have to. She knows both worlds. If I'm away, just don't spend too much time here."

"Where are you going?"

"I don't know yet." I know I had just finished telling Lesh that I didn't want anyone scaring Joy with stories of my "exploits," but I couldn't keep Joy completely in the dark. I just had to try to ease her into it gently. "It depends on what Parthet and Kardeen find out about the dragon eggs and all the other crazy things going on. I'm the official Hero. When things get rough, there's plenty of work for the Hero." And then, because Joy had a right to know what I was getting into, I started to tell her about the interview with the dead son of the Elflord of Xayber, about the family jewels of the Great Earth Mother and the quest I would have to begin as soon as Parthet could point me in the right direction—until a new item on the television stopped me.

"Perhaps understandably," the anchorman said, "there has been a dramatic increase in the number of UFO sightings since the bombing of the *Coral Lady.* But tonight, we have the following videotape recorded by a news cameramen from our affiliate in Chattanooga, Tennessee, during the station's eleven-P.M. newscast."

The beginning of the sequence showed the full moon in a clear sky over the city. The network anchorman continued to talk over the footage.

"This scene was being shown live as a backdrop for the weather segment on the local news. Viewers in the Chattanooga area saw this just as you're seeing it now, except that the day's weather statistics were superimposed."

And then a large silhouette crossed, and almost totally eclipsed, the full moon.

"This is exactly how the television viewers in Chattanooga saw it live," the network anchorman repeated.

Then there was another tape, obviously a recording of the newscast itself. One of the local news anchors introduced the station's "certified meteorologist," who went right into his opening spiel as the day's high and low temperatures and the other weather statistics appeared on the screen over the full moon and night sky. The weatherman was into his third overlay before he noticed something on his monitor off to the side.

"Everybody wants to get into the act," the meteorologist joked after doing a double take. "We seem to have a star-struck bat or something angling in for a close-up." He moved a step toward the side of the frame, closer to his monitor.

"I've never seen a . . ." He stopped, then looked off

past the camera in the studio. ''Can we get a better shot on this, Dave?'' he asked. There was a delay, and then a zoom just before the creature left the moon behind.

''That doesn't look much like any bat I've ever seen,'' the weatherman said. ''I think we've got something interesting here, folks. Maybe our technical people can go back and get us more detail.'' He recovered then and hurried through the rest of the weather report.

The scene shifted back to the network anchor, who had one eyebrow arched.

''This is what the station's video technicians came up with.''

I really didn't need the grainy enlargements, the series of stop-frames. I had recognized the creature the first time.

''That is a dragon,'' I said, and Joy clutched at my arm.

''How?'' she asked. Good question.

''I guess it's just part of the general disruption,'' I said. The *trend* that Parthet told me to watch.

''. . . The Air Force has refused any comment at all concerning this sighting, but civilian air traffic controllers at Chattanooga did report an unidentified radar echo crossing their air space at the same time as the videotape was being filmed. Naturally, we'll have any further information for you as soon as it becomes available.'' The network anchorman smiled and shook his head. ''Frankly, I don't have any more idea what that could be than you do.''

He cleared his throat and moved on to the next segment, a panel of security experts who gave viewers tips for protecting themselves against terrorists. I switched channels and saw part of the videotape of the dragon again.

''A dragon,'' Joy said softly. ''How much damage can one of those things do?''

''A lot, I suppose, but I don't think it will last long in this world. They're carnivorous, vicious, and big, but they can be killed. The Air Force should be able to bring it down.''

''How big?''

''The biggest ones can get to be a lot bigger than a 747.''

"Do they breathe fire?"

"I don't think so. They don't need to. The second one I killed, I could have ridden my horse right into its mouth, down as far as its tonsils." If it had tonsils. I didn't know. The finer points of draconic anatomy held little interest for me. "And my horse is bigger than the Budweiser Clydesdales."

"What do we do now?" Joy asked.

"Go home, get some sleep. I'll get the lanterns. That's what we came for."

"I'm going to raid your library too," Joy said, almost dreamily—as if she were suddenly half asleep. "If you're going to be off on another trip, I'm going to need something to read."

I was tired too. Coming back from my goodwill tour of the western kingdoms, I had looked forward to catching up on my sleep and just resting for a long time, and I had been busier than ever. Once I got out of the hospital. That seemed like ages ago, not just a few days. I didn't have the slightest pain left from the stabbing or from the surgery . . . stabbing of another kind. I was almost completely healed from both. In fact, I could almost forget it all except when I was naked and saw where they had shaved me before my surgery, or felt the hard ridge of new scars still in the angry, raw stage.

There are some disadvantages to living in Varay—no music from home, no movies or television. What hurt most was that I mostly had to do without music in Varay. The occasional minstrel who stopped by Castle Basil was no replacement for MTV. I had tried taking a portable stereo back, in my early days there, but it didn't work. All the radio picked up in Varay was static. There were no stations in the buffer zone, or anywhere close enough to penetrate. Going through the passages to Varay erased all of my tapes, and the batteries wore down incredibly fast when I tried it with compact discs. The battery lanterns we were taking along so Joy could read would have the same problem. If there was time, we'd have to do some shopping and pick up a few extra Coleman kerosene lanterns and a good supply of fuel for them. Or we would be doing most of our reading in the daylight.

Joy and I spent about twenty minutes collecting stuff to take along. This time I piled up a lot of things that I might never need but wouldn't want to miss if something happened. I just piled things by the doorway. I planned to let Joy hold the passage open while I carried and pushed it all through.

"Are you planning on moving everything you own?" Joy asked.

I stopped and looked at what I had already stacked up. "It looks that way, doesn't it?" I shrugged. "I keep thinking that I ought to take the stuff through while I can."

"If you really think it's going to get that bad, maybe we should make a list and buy up everything we can think of tomorrow."

I nodded. "Good idea. You make up the list. Be as extravagant as you want to be. Money's no problem." That led me to think of something else. I went to my safe and took out a small locked drawer.

"If things get really bad here, this may be all scrap paper, but I must have something in the neighborhood of six or seven million dollars lying around this world."

"Lying around? Six or seven *million* dollars?" Joy actually looked impressed. We had never really discussed money. She knew that I had enough to do just about anything we wanted to do together. One time she had remarked that I never asked how much when either of us saw something we wanted.

"Mutual funds, certificates of deposit, bank accounts, a little real estate. My accountant sends me a monthly statement. They pay me good money for the work I do." And beyond that, I was due to be the next King of Varay—if I stayed alive long enough to inherit the throne. If I ever did run short of cash I had reserves I could draw on back in the buffer zone . . . but I had never come close to running short. My tastes aren't *that* extravagant. "All the papers are in here." I put the locked drawer on top of the stack of things to go to Varay.

I had the same feeling as the last time I left the apartment, that I might never see the place again. The first time I had been wrong. Who could tell about the second? Repeated often enough, there's always a chance of being right eventually with a prediction like that. The thought that I might be cut off from Chicago, from this entire world—maybe forever—was depressing. Varay would be much less inviting without the opportunity to take time out from it whenever I needed a break.

And then I just had to sit down and look away from the stack.

"Are you all right?" Joy asked.

"Yeah, I'm okay. Just tired, I guess."

"Then let's go home and get some sleep. We can haul this stuff over in the morning."

"No, we'd better get as much as we can now. You open the doorway. I'll start humping everything through."

I did get the entire stack moved through, but I had a rotten night afterward. I slept poorly, waking with rapidly disappearing nightmares, dreams that I couldn't hold on to long enough to know what they were about. I never used to have trouble with nightmares. That started with my introduction to the Congregation of Heroes, just before the Battle of Thyme. Nightmares had been a periodic nuisance ever since.

I tossed and turned so badly that I woke Joy several times. Finally, I got dressed and went up to the battlements to pace.

Maybe that was a bad idea. It usually is, especially in the middle of the night. I mean, the times when I really feel like prowling around up there, I'm usually already feeling down and the scenery just makes it worse. I still think it all stems from *Hamlet.* I first read that when I was nine or ten and had to look up a lot of the old words. Coming to Varay the way I did, hoping to rescue my parents in a world I had never heard of, fixed the *Hamlet* idea firmly in my head, and I'd never been able to shake it.

Sleep was what I needed, and I wasn't likely to get much sleep walking back and forth atop Castle Cayenne. I searched the skies, looking for some evidence of the general way things were falling apart. A herd of dragons wouldn't have surprised me in the least. Neither would a flock of ICBMs, or little green men from Mars or someplace else. I had more than three years of living in Varay, but I still suffered the occasional reality crisis. And *knowing* the problem didn't seem to help solve it.

The full moon was about ready to set in the west.

The full moon was rising in the east.

I didn't stop to list all of the ways that it was impossible. In Varay, that doesn't seem as vital as it would be back in the "real" world. But it was still wrong. It was yet another impossibility, like dragon fetuses in chicken eggs.

This time, I didn't even stop to put on a weapon. I ran downstairs and through the portal to Castle Basil and went looking for Parthet. He was in his workroom, candles and lanterns burning all over the place. He looked up slowly when I came barging in. He was obviously about one yawn short of falling asleep.

"What is it?" he asked.

"Come up top, quick," I said. I almost picked him up out of his chair and half-dragged him to the stairs.

"What is it?" he asked again while we climbed stairs. His voice sounded more alert now, and a little angry, but I didn't say anything until we came out onto the tower's battlements.

"Look at the moon," I said. I pointed west, then east, turning Parthet. He started trembling.

"We're running out of time," he said.

"Have you found out where I have to go to find those balls?" I asked.

"Yes, in a general sense, but not in a more exact sense."

"Tell me."

"One is located in a shrine somewhere in the Titan Mountains, *'at the limit to which mortals may aspire,'* is how the oldest texts put it. The other is in a shrine on an island *'lost in the Sea of Fairy that none may find or leave.'* That's as close as I've been able to narrow it down."

"It's more than I expected," I said.

"There's worse," Parthet said. I waited, but he seemed reluctant to provide the rest.

"It might not help if I could tell you exactly which shrines the jewels are in." He paused again before he laid it on me. "According to the sources I've been able to find, it takes someone *'of the blood of Fairy, whole and pure,'* to find the jewels of the Great Earth Mother.'"

"So we're back to Junior," I said.

"We can't do it his way."

"Look at the sky again, Uncle. Two full moons in the

sky. And there's a dragon flying over Tennessee back in my world. You're the one who said we're running out of time. Just let me do the deal with our elf."

"He's looking for a death vow."

"If that's what it takes," I said.

My hands shook for a moment, but when I got back to Castle Cayenne, I was finally able to sleep.

9

The Rock

No one disturbed Joy and me when morning came. Sunrise was a couple of hours gone when I finally woke. Strangely, I felt more rested and relaxed than I had in a long time even though I was still several days short on sleep. Lying in bed when I woke, I remained motionless for long, luxurious minutes experiencing an unusual tranquil glow, a warm floating sensation. At first, my thoughts were limited to a passive awareness of my body and how good I felt. My perceptions broadened only very slowly. I became conscious of Joy at my side and I turned my head so I could see her—and I saw her as I never had before.

Joy. Emotions coursed madly through me, racing, overlying each other, blending in new ways, an exhilarating kaleidoscope—not just the intense passion she usually aroused, something more powerful and complex. She was still asleep. Her face seemed totally relaxed. There were scarcely visible freckles across her nose, tiny lines at the corners of her eyes. She breathed quietly through barely parted, full lips. Her hair was draped across one cheek in a riot of shadings of blond and light brown over lightly tanned skin. Thin neck, soft shoulders. I felt a love that I really didn't understand, love that I had never completely recognized before, and something more, a deep empathy, a sense of being part of a greater whole.

It was a perfect moment.

I reached out slowly to touch her cheek, to brush the hair away from the corner of her mouth, and she opened her eyes before I touched her. She smiled and made a contented sigh. Her cheek was warm, her hair as soft as ever.

We kissed.

"I love you," I whispered, and Joy echoed it.

I propped myself up on one elbow and peeled the blanket and sheet off of us. Joy lay motionless while I stared at her and tried to memorize every soft contour of her body. I looked, and then I leaned over and kissed each nipple. When I laid my hand on her stomach, Joy seemed to catch fire. She pulled me over on top of her and we shared a long, deep kiss—tender and passionate by turns, and then we shifted into more urgent foreplay. Everything seemed to be deliciously protracted, as if time had slowed to stretch the moment for us. There was no frenzied abandon to our lovemaking that morning. Each instant expanded to let us savor it fully—sex as symphony, the way it is in dreams but rarely in life. We reached a blinding orgasm together, but I didn't lose my erection, and as soon as the waves of the first climax ebbed, we started moving toward a second, rolling over on our sides together. For a time, it felt almost as if we were melting together, becoming one person. I slid my arms around Joy and held her. And our second climax was as wild as the first.

After that, we both needed time to get our breathing and heart rates back in order, time to come down from the dizzying heights. Our bodies remained tangled together while I slowly deflated. The deep blush faded from Joy's face and the pale skin of her breasts. I stroked her cheek and told her again that I loved her. I may have dropped a tear or two into the pillows when I realized how totally I was committed to her . . . and how likely it was to come to an end, all too soon. I had to go off and be a Hero again, and if I survived the first quest, then I would have to go into the den of my most powerful enemy to return the body of his son, the son I had killed. I didn't look forward to another confrontation with the Elflord of Xayber, especially not where his power was greatest.

To keep my thoughts from wandering farther in that direction and spoiling the morning, I had to get out of bed. I went into the bathroom and started to fill the huge oval tub that had been carved from a block of granite and polished until it sparkled. The sun had been out long enough to give us hot water for a bath.

Joy was still in bed, lying spread-eagled like a pose for a men's magazine—and lovely enough to grace the best of them. I picked her up and carried her into the bathroom. While we waited for the tub to fill, we made love again. We started standing up, me holding her, her legs wrapped around my hips, and ended with me sitting on the side of the tub, still holding her, moving her against me until everything went all dark and light and crazy for us again. Somehow, I managed to get us turned around and lowered into the tub without disengaging or falling. We sat in body-temperature water and washed each other slowly, lovingly, not separating until we had to.

The morning was half gone before we dressed.

"I'll probably be leaving on this job tomorrow morning," I told Joy when I couldn't postpone it any longer. "And I'll probably be busy getting ready for the trip most of this afternoon."

Joy nodded. "I figured that it had to be that soon." She hesitated, then said, "It's going to be very dangerous, isn't it?" The form was a question, but the tone wasn't.

It was my turn to nod. I might not have volunteered that information, but I wouldn't lie to her about it. "I have to locate a couple of relics that might not exist, from unknown places that no one has ever been to, and figure out how to use them to keep everything from continuing to unravel." Piling impossibility on impossibility—but it still sounded mundane and simple when I put it into words like that.

"You won't go alone, will you?" This time it was a real question.

"I doubt it. I'm the crown prince or whatever here. I'm supposed to have a proper retinue at times like this. Lesh, Harkane, and Timon will all go with me, maybe even Uncle Parthet. He can come up with useful bits of magic now and then." I didn't plan to mention the elf's head that we would need for a guide.

"How long will you be gone?"

"I don't have any idea yet. Actually, this may turn into three separate trips, one right after the other. Depends. The first place is somewhere in the Titan Mountains to the south, the second is an island somewhere out in the Mist—the Sea of Fairy—north of Varay, and the third is the stronghold of the Elflord of Xayber in Fairy. I may be able to sneak back here between trips. Maybe."

"Do you really have to go?" That was the ultimate question, I guess. The answer was unavoidable, though.

"I have to go. It's the only hope of straightening everything out again, the only chance to get life back to normal, here and back in our world." After three years, I still made the distinction. Joy had only had a couple of days to see the differences.

"But why you?" she asked, passing by any question about grandiose delusions, Messiah complexes, or any of the other things most people might be tempted to ask.

I snorted, maybe added a bitter laugh. "Because I'm Gil Tyner, Prince and Hero of Varay. It would have been my father's job if it had happened before he was killed. Now it's my job."

"And we can't just go back to Chicago and forget it all, let them find another Hero?"

"No, we can't." I was quiet for a moment before I continued. "I didn't really choose this Hero job. My parents trained me for it without telling me what it was all about. Then, when my father died, I had the job dropped on me before I really had any understanding of what was going on. Still, I can't just walk away. It's a matter of family, if nothing else." I put an arm around her, and we walked to the window. It was a bright, warm day, right at the start of August. The grass and trees were green, the grain fields turning color, nearly ready to harvest. In southern Varay, the wheat comes in at the end of July or early August.

"You'll do okay here while I'm gone. You'll have the rest of the staff to take care of things, treat you like royalty. You can always pop through to Basil for company. My mother will be there. Kardeen too. And you'll have your folks here this time next week."

"And they're going to expect *you* here," she said. "How am I going to explain the fact that you're off gallivanting so soon after our wedding?"

I just looked at her for a moment while I fought back the urge to bust out laughing. "Don't you think you'll have enough to explain to them?" I asked. "They won't even notice that I'm gone."

Then we both started laughing.

"I guess I'll manage," Joy said when we got it under control. "I'll be waiting when you get back."

There wasn't much more we could say just then. We went downstairs to put in an appearance. I had to talk to Lesh and the others, tell them what we had to face and give them the option of staying put. No one took it. I was certain that no one would. Joy went to the kitchen to get us something to eat—and to avoid listening to the shop talk, I guess. We had missed breakfast and it was still a little early for lunch, but there were always sandwich fixings and whatnot to tide people over at Cayenne, like most places in the buffer zone.

Joy brought back a plate with huge ham sandwiches and the Varayan answer to potato chips and french fries—half-inch-thick slices of potato fried so that they were crunchy on the outside and soft inside.

"The choice of drinks seems to be beer, wine, or coffee," Joy said.

"That's usually the choice, unless I pick up a case of Pepsi and bring it over."

"Maybe I'll go get some this afternoon while you're busy."

The idea of her going off alone like that made me nervous, but I finally nodded. "You'll probably find it easier to go through Louisville," I said. I reminded her which doorways to take, told her where my mother kept the spare keys to her van. We had to go back upstairs to get a set of house keys for her. I also gave her one of my bank cards and the code number to use it and told her how to find the bank machine and then the supermarket. "It's in a big shopping center. If you think of anything else we need, go ahead and get it."

"In that case, I could use someone to help carry things."

I thought about it for a second. "Lesh and Harkane will both be busy, but go ahead and take Timon. He's been there a few times and he knows enough English to get by."

"What do you mean? He speaks perfect English. Everyone here does."

I laughed. "You mean you haven't noticed?" I asked.

"Noticed what?"

"Watch people's lips when they talk. The only people

in Varay who speak English fluently are you, me, my mother, and Uncle Parthet. Lesh is pretty good at it, but he slips into Varayan quite frequently. Harkane's almost as good as Lesh, and he tries harder. The rest of the people here speak no English at all, except for Timon."

Joy got a bewildered look on her face.

"You ever see a foreign movie dubbed in English?" I asked. "Seen the way words and lip movements don't match?" She nodded. "It's like that here." I switched into Varayan for the last sentence and Joy's eyes got wider.

"And everybody sees me like that?" she asked.

"Except for the people who speak English well enough to avoid having the translation magic kick in. Part of the magic of this place lets everyone hear his own language, no matter what language a speaker uses. You get used to it in time."

"I think I'd rather learn to speak Varayan."

"You can't, not here. The translation magic makes it impossible for anyone to learn a foreign language in the buffer zone. I had to take my lessons back in our world, and that's where I taught Lesh, Harkane, and Timon what they know of English. Well, Harkane knew some English before. He was my father's last squire."

For a time, I knew that Joy would be staring at people's lips whenever they spoke. I went through that too.

"Ah, you'll find that Timon's English is pretty sports-oriented," I said. "I've taken him to see all the Chicago teams in action. But he can get by around food too." Timon loved football and hockey most of all, hard contact sports. Soccer and basketball were lower on his list, and baseball still confused him a little. His proposed remedy for a called third strike was for the batter to take off the umpire's head with his dandy warclub. I could see the temptation of that myself.

"Just remember," I said, getting more serious. "Keep an ear on the news and don't waste time there. If I get the mess straightened out here, maybe we won't have to worry so much about what might happen in the other world, but I haven't started yet."

I waited around to see Joy and Timon off through the doorway. Timon had changed to blue jeans and a Chicago Bears jersey, number 50, Mike Singletary's number. Timon liked Singletary's approach to the game. "He looks like he's ready to bite their heads off," Timon said one Monday night while we were watching the Bears play on television. The networks always liked to show a close-up of Singletary looking out over the line.

After Joy and Timon left, Lesh and I went to Castle Basil to get going on our work.

"Since we'll probably be going to the mountains first, we're going to need a lot of rope, as much as you can lay your hands on," I told Lesh as we walked from the doorway toward Basil's great hall. "A couple of grappling hooks if you can find them." I had done a little climbing with Dad—we had sampled a little of almost everything, it seems—but not a lot. I tried to describe pitons and some of the other climbing gear I thought we might be able to fake. I didn't know of anywhere in either Chicago or Louisville where I could just walk in and buy climbing equipment off the shelf, and I was positive that we wouldn't have time to do any traveling or to wait for the items to be delivered by mail order. If the place we had to reach in the Titan Mountains was really at the very limit to which people could climb, we were going to have to leave our horses behind at some point and finish on foot, which also meant that there was a limit to how much gear we would be able to take along.

"Don't worry, I'll get it all fixed up," Lesh said, and I knew he would. Within his own limits, Lesh was as efficient as Baron Kardeen.

We parted at the entrance to the great hall. Lesh went off toward the courtyard and I went into the hall. This trip, I was properly accoutered for public display, blades hanging off of me like icicles from a Christmas tree. As usual, there were a few people lounging around the great hall, and others who were working. But neither Parthet nor Kardeen was in evidence, so I went on to Parthet's workroom.

Parthet wasn't there either, but Aaron was sitting at the wizard's desk, reading. It *was* Aaron, no doubt of that, since he was the only black in the seven kingdoms, but he looked so different that he was almost unrecognizable. It wasn't until he stood up that I realized why.

"You look like you've grown six inches since yesterday," I said.

"Yes, sir, all of that." He grinned very briefly, but it was a happy grin, not self-conscious. His voice was different too, with an adolescent harshness to it. To all appearances he had put on five or six years of age overnight.

"Has Parthet been conjuring over you?" I asked—sharply, I suppose.

"No, sir. He was surprised too this morning."

"You're taking it pretty good."

"Ain't *that* much fun being a little kid." It was just another adventure to him, no worries about the impossibility of all the things that had happened to him. In a way, I envied him.

"Where's Parthet?"

"Upstairs, sleeping, I think. He was up all night."

"I know. What are you reading?" I gestured at the scroll he had been going through.

"It's about some dude named Vara. You know about him?"

"I know. When Parthet gets some free time, ask him to take you downstairs to show you where Vara is buried."

"He was for real?"

"He was for real, but I don't know how much of that stuff he really did," I said, pointing at the scroll again. "Things get exaggerated over the years."

I went out and climbed the tower stairs to Parthet's other room. He *was* sleeping. I could hear his snoring even through the six-inch-thick wooden door. I opened the door and hit him with a screeching whistle. Parthet woke immediately and popped up to a sitting position.

"Is that any way to treat an old man?" he demanded.

"What happened to Aaron?" I asked.

"Not my doing. His parents died, his grandmother died, he suddenly appeared in Varay—twice. Why should the fact that he's growing up overnight be any different than the rest?"

"Let's just say that I'm suspicious of wizards who want apprentices."

"If you'll think back, I didn't want an apprentice, but I recognized the signs when he showed up here." Parthet cleared his throat, coughed a couple of times, and got out of bed. He had slept in his clothes.

"What time is it?" he asked.

"After noon."

"It worries me in a way," Parthet said, his voice lower, almost somber. "The fact that he's growing up so quickly may mean that he will be needed before he could grow up naturally. I'm old, but I had planned on getting a lot older."

"Maybe it's just part of the general weirdness, like two full moons in the sky at the same time, or the dragon eggs."

"Perhaps." Parthet shrugged. "Anyhow, the lad's a positive genius. I worried that he might not be able to understand some of the texts he'll have to master to become a wizard. The translation magic can't reduce complex formulas into language so simple that someone who doesn't have the vocabulary can understand. I mean, how would you explain calculus to someone who had no concept of numbers? But the lad reads. He comprehends. He asks more intelligent questions than you do sometimes."

"Okay, he's smart. Have you come up with any way we can do this other thing without the elf?"

"No." Just the single word, without any futile protest against what I was going to have to do. But Parthet had undoubtedly stayed at his work all night making absolutely certain that there was no other way. And then he had slept because there was nothing else he could do about it. The way I had slept after I finally made my decision to meet the elf's terms.

"Have you figured out what I've got to do with the family jewels once I've got them?"

This time he shook his head. "Possession alone *may* be enough, though I doubt that. Possession may impart the knowledge, the instinct to use them. Or the elf may have some idea. If nothing else, I may be able to conjure up the answer once you bring them back here."

"I'll do the talking to the elf," I reminded him. "You've decided that you're not going along on this caper?"

"I could never climb the Titans. It's all I can do to climb the stairs here in the castle. I keep wishing that I had used some of that last sea-silver you collected to connect the different floors here, like an elevator.''

''Next time,'' I said with a smile. ''I'll try to pick some up on my way back from Xayber.''

''You do that. You going to talk to Xayber's son now?''

''Not yet. I've got to talk to Kardeen and do a couple of other things first. Maybe an hour or two.''

''He'll wait,'' Parthet said.

''I know.''

I left Parthet and headed for the chamberlain's office. I told Kardeen what I thought we would need and that I had started Lesh off at collecting the gear.

''There have been a few climbers here,'' Kardeen said. ''Some of our young soldiers like the challenge of trying something that's supposed to be impossible. Not all of them make it back, but most give up before it's too late.'' He gave me an apologetic look with that.

''So?'' I asked, managing a smile. ''That just means that most of the young soldiers are smarter than I am. And they had the choice. But I've done a little climbing. I won't be a total novice when we get to the difficult bits.''

''I'm tempted to join you myself on this one,'' Kardeen said, grinning self consciously. ''I did some climbing along the nearer heights of the Titans when I was young. Before I got married and inherited this job.'' Kardeen rarely talked about his past or his family unless I asked a direct question. That was his sense of place, I guess, something that I came up against almost every day in Varay. I had been in Varay nearly six months before I learned that the young clerk who was always in Kardeen's outer office was his son, Maldeen.

''I'd welcome you in a minute, you know that, but I think you've got more important work here. If I manage to complete this first trek, I'm going to need a boat stocked for a voyage and people willing to dare sailing out of sight on land into the Mist.''

''And that's not the easiest task,'' Kardeen said. ''But I think we can manage. Finding a vessel safe enough for long-distance work is harder than finding the men to sail it.''

''Then it might keep you busy for a day or two?'' More

than once I had joked with Kardeen about the way he seemed to get everything done immediately.

"At least." He smiled. "What are your immediate plans?"

"I have to do the deal with our elf first, but unless he comes up with new demands, we'll probably leave tomorrow morning. As soon as I know where we have to enter the Titans, we'll use a doorway to the nearest point and ride from there." I told him that it would be just me, my three people, and the elf's head.

"You'll probably need at least two extra horses to carry supplies and equipment," Kardeen said.

"Lesh is probably in the mews choosing them now."

When I left the baron's office, I headed for the crypt again. My last visit there had been cut off when I found the workmen fixing a place for my great-grandfather. I still wanted a few minutes down there to think, and talk. Sure, the conversations were one-sided, but talking a problem out there sometimes helped me get a better perspective.

I walked slowly down the steps, thinking about Parthet's idea of installing magic doorways as elevators. The idea felt better all the time.

This time, there were no sounds of workmen to distract me on the way down. And they had cleaned up their mess in the burial chamber. But there was a stranger there now, or most of him. I had never asked what had been done with the elf's body. Somehow, it had ended up in the burial crypt, which probably wouldn't have gone over very well with the permanent residents. The body was laid out on a simple stretcher, on the floor. It didn't look as if anything had been done to the body, but it didn't seem any worse for the time it had lain around without its head. There was no puddle of blood, no odor of decay.

"There goes the neighborhood," I said loudly. I had to make some kind of joke. A body lying out in the open is different from a room full of headstones.

"At least you're not likely to be hotheaded down here, even if you had your head with you," I said, looking down at the body. The crypt was deep inside the rock on which Castle Basil stands. It was cool in the room no matter how hot or cold it was outside, like being in a cave. I think they say it's always fifty-eight degrees in caves back home—Mammoth or Carlsbad, or any other cave system. You get underground and you have a constant temperature. The torches burning in the crypt and on the stairs couldn't warm it up all that much.

Deep in the heart of a rock bigger than the Great Pyramid, in a room used for the same purpose, to bury kings and heroes, I walked away from the elf's body and over to the end of Dad's burial niche.

"Have you met your new roomie?" I asked, laying my hand on the capstone. "He came to Varay to kill me and I killed him instead. He's dead, but he's still trying to get me. And I don't have any choice. I have to walk right into his trap."

Dad didn't answer. I doubt that I could have handled the situation if he had. After meeting the Congregation of Heroes in that room once, I'm spooked easily by ghosts.

"I don't know if you're somehow aware of all the crazy things going on here," I said. "Maybe you are. There's so much that's improbable about this place, maybe you *are* aware of it all. And maybe you're watching what I do. The dead elf is the son of the Elflord of Xayber. He thinks that he has me trapped and trussed up ready to send to his father. If I make it that far, though, maybe I can come up with a few surprises. I hope so."

I was silent for a moment, listening, not so much for an answer as for any sound of someone coming down the stairs. I would hate to get caught making a soliloquy in the catacombs. That kind of thing could start rumors.

"It all starts tomorrow, I expect. It looks like we have to go to the ends of this world on this one—both ends, up the unscalable mountains and out across the uncrossable sea. How can an angry elflord hope to compete with that?

"Oh, by the way, Joy and I got married. I know you haven't met her, but I'm sure you'd like her. She's here in Varay with me now. Someday, if we get that kind of someday, I'll bring her down, but not yet, not when I'm getting ready to leave on a crazy mission like this one."

I stood there for another few minutes, then climbed back to the livelier levels of the castle. Lesh was waiting at the top of the stairs. I guess he knew my habits better than I thought.

"Are we all set?" I asked.

"It's coming good," he said. "We got people working on everything. I'll have to check it out later, but it's good for now."

"Well, if everything's cracking nicely here, what would you say to a tall mug or two down at the Bald Rock?"

Lesh grinned. "It is a right hot day."

We took the magic doorway down to the Bald Rock in the town of Basil. I hadn't been back to the inn since the night I was attacked—not all that long before. The landlord remembered that too. He came right over, full of noisy apologies and exaggerated bows. He was mortified, he was distressed, he hadn't been able to sleep or eat right since it happened, worrying about me . . . and on and on. But he also claimed to be "right proud" of the way I had handled the outlander. I tried to reassure Old Baldy that I didn't hold any of it against him, but he insisted that the drinks were on him that afternoon. I didn't argue. After all, Lesh and I didn't have time for more than one or two beers apiece.

"This is going to be a rough one, Lesh," I said when we started our second, after I had stopped the innkeeper from having his boys set up a full keg for us.

"Gots to be better than dragon eggs for breakfast," Lesh said.

"You may not think so before it's over."

"Be that as it will. Do we have time for another?" He finished his mug in a long draft.

"Best not. We've still got work to do. We get really going here, we may never get back up there. And after all, there's plenty of beer up on the rock."

"Aye, there is," Lesh agreed.

We walked up the rock to the castle. That was one way to get a little exercise and sweat out some of the beer. The Rock. One of the old legends I kept hearing said that the stone that Castle Basil was built on was the hub around which all three realms rotated, the center of the universe. I wouldn't be surprised if the people of the other six kingdoms in the buffer zone had the same sort of legends about their own local landmarks. But Basil's rock *was* some sort of anomaly, a huge block of homogeneous stone just out in the middle of nowhere, geologically. It wasn't part of any mountain chain, fault zone, or anything else. According to Kardeen, there wasn't any stone like it in any of the mountains of the buffer zone. It was unique.

Two beers wasn't nearly enough preparation for the confrontation with our guide. I got Parthet and Kardeen to witness the deal after I cautioned them again to let me do all the negotiating.

"You want to get home and I want to get the balls of the Great Earth Mother so I can stop all the strange happenings," I said when Parthet pulled the head out of the alcohol.

"You know my terms. I'll tell you where they are if you will take me home to my father—all of me."

I shook my head. "Telling isn't enough. You'll have to go along to identify them. Once I get them back here, I'll make sure that you get back to your father."

"You personally must take me home."

"I'll take you back under truce with your father."

"You take me back or there's no deal."

"I'll discuss the details directly with him. We have talked before. But without your help, I can't start and you have absolutely no hope of ever getting home. We'll bury you with the dragon eggs."

"If you don't get the jewels, it won't matter what you do with me."

"Perhaps." I was careful to avoid showing any reaction to his first admission that he had a stake in the success of my mission. "Or perhaps we can get the information elsewhere. The Elfking himself might be interested, or one of the other elflords."

"Go ahead. Try."

It had been an empty bluff, and the elf had called it.

"I'll get you home to your father," I said.

"Bring my body up here."

Parthet was against it, but I nodded and Kardeen went to get men to haul the body up from the crypt. The elf remained silent until his body was carried into the room.

"Stand me up there." The soldiers lifted the body onto its feet and it stood without further support from them.

"Set my head back on my shoulders."

"I think not," I said. "Not now. Once we get back with the jewels of the Great Earth Mother."

"You'll take me home to my father? You, yourself?"

"I will."

"Then let's shake hands on our bargain."

I nodded and the elf's right arm came up, hand extended. I stepped closer, shook hands with the headless body, and felt the cold crawl up my arm. The pact was made.

10

Nushur

"Where do we enter the Titan Mountains?" I asked after I had wiped my hand on my trousers.

"As far east of here as possible," the elf said.

"Near the border with Dorthin?" I asked.

He considered that for a few seconds. "It will do."

"We'll leave tomorrow morning then," I said. "Portal to Thyme, and ride south from there." There were gates closer to the Titans along that border, but the doorways there weren't situated to make it easy for horses, and we would strain the resources of either of the small castles south of Thyme if we took enough for our expedition.

"You do realize, of course, that for you to get back to your father, you'll have to do whatever you can to make sure that we succeed and get back here," I told the elf. "If I don't make it back, you don't get home."

"There is always that risk," he said. "And there is one detail you might consider. Floating around in that alcohol fogs my mind. It isn't necessary. I will remain as I am until I get home."

"Not on the basis of my spell," Parthet said. "I didn't try a preservative, just a communications magic."

"*No,* certainly not on the basis of *your* puny magic," the elf sneered. "But you let me talk and I have talked."

"If you don't need the alcohol, we'll find another temporary home for you," I said. "That pot would have been awkward on the road anyway." I wanted to ask who else he had been talking to, but I didn't want to give him the satisfaction of the question.

"Take good care of my body while we're gone," the elf said, turning his eyes toward Parthet. "It is part of the bargain this *Hero* has made."

"It is," I agreed.

"I will know if it is disturbed, and if it is, my cooperation ends at that moment,'' the elf said. ''I hope that is thoroughly understood.''

I stared at Parthet, and he nodded. Behind him, so did Baron Kardeen.

''It will be properly cared for,'' Kardeen said.

''You can't get a better promise than that,'' I told the elf. ''In fact, I think we should get the body back into storage right now.'' I didn't want to leave head and body together in the same room. The elf had seemed much too anxious to have us set his head back on his shoulders. Maybe he couldn't put himself back together without help, but then, maybe he could. He *had* controlled his arm and hand at a distance.

Kardeen called the two soldiers back in. They laid the body back on its stretcher and carried it from the room. Parthet looked at the head he was holding.

''If the alcohol is out, we'll have to find something else for you here then,'' Parthet muttered. ''Don't want you just rolling away and getting lost.'' He stared over the head at the wall for a moment, then turned to me.

''I think I have just the thing. Gil, would you go upstairs to my room? On the shelf, next to the window. You'll see what I want.''

I nodded and hurried up the steps. As soon as I opened the door of his upper chamber, I saw what he wanted—a wicker birdcage. I laughed almost all the way back down to the workroom, but I was careful to put on a straight face before I went inside.

''I assume this is what you were talking about?'' I said.

''The very item,'' Parthet said. ''The bottom unclips there.''

I took the bottom of the cage off and set it on Parthet's work table. He set the elf's head on it, clipped the cage over its bottom, and dried his hands.

''It might not be the most dignified setting, and I do apologize for that,'' Parthet told the head. ''But it keeps you out of the alcohol and leaves you free to speak whenever you need to. And it will be easier to transport you like this than in the pot.''

The elf didn't say a word, but I thought that he must be fairly burned up at the idea. I think *I* would have been, despite Parthet's apologies. The rest of us left the room quickly.

"Aren't you afraid that he'll conjure up some mischief in there?" I asked Parthet.

"No more now than he might have before," Parthet said, shrugging as we walked toward the great hall. "I have certain strong protections, especially in my shop. While they might not completely baffle our guest, they will at least make any mischief harder to accomplish and easier to detect. My magic may be infinitely weaker than his, but I've been in business a long time, and I have done a lot of my work in that room. The influence builds."

"I think we ought to put his body behind the strongest locks around, and keep a guard over it until we're out of here," I said. "I have the notion that if he puts head and body together he won't need us to get home to his father."

"You may be right," Parthet said. "That handshake of his was impressive."

"My hand is still freezing."

"I'll take care of security for him," Kardeen said. When we reached the great hall, he called out to two of the soldiers who were lounging around and got them busy.

Lesh got up from the table, drained a tankard, and came to meet me.

"Everything's ready, 'cept for what we'll need to fetch from Cayenne in the morning, our weapons and such, and a case of those magic dinners you got stored." *Magic dinners*—I had a big stock of freeze-dried meals. They take a lot less room to pack than real food.

"That's good," I said. "We'll be going to Thyme by portal and ride south from there."

"Into Dorthin?" Lesh asked.

"Not if we can avoid it." Yes, Dorthin was technically mine, and Dieth was ruling the country as duke in my name, but Dorthin wasn't entirely tame, and many of the warlords in the marcher territories of Dorthin were particularly independent . . . and hostile to me and to Varay.

The afternoon was just about shot, so Lesh and I headed back to Cayenne for supper. It would be a night for heroic pigging out, for eating far beyond the point of satiation. The four of us who were going on the road in the morning would all try to fill ourselves to the bursting point against the inevitable light rations of the next few weeks—or months. In the height of summer, it might not be as bad as it would be at other seasons. Lesh and Harkane were sure to know which wild fruits and vegetables would be ripe and edible, and we could figure on occasionally supplementing our stores through the benefices of some unsuspecting wild animal along the way, but there was simply no possible way to mount a lengthy expedition in the wilds and carry enough food to provide garrison-style meals for long. You hit the point of diminishing returns very quickly in the buffer zone. The more food you haul along, the more animals you need to carry your supplies, the slower you travel . . . and the more food you have to bring along. Supper, a bedtime "snack," and breakfast—we would stuff ourselves at all three meals, and try to top it off at Basil and before we rode out of Thyme. The bloated feeling we started with would pass all too soon, and we would ride with an edge of hunger until we returned to someplace with civilized kitchens.

When we stepped through to Cayenne, Joy and Timon were still hauling their booty through from Louisville. I let Joy hold the passage open and pitched in to help Timon cart everything through.

"What did you do, clean out the city?" I asked as I carried two cases of Pepsi through.

"I tried," Joy admitted cheerfully. "That was fun, a real binge."

"We filled up the wagon *twice*," Timon said as we passed, me going back for another load, him carrying one through.

"I got a lot of Pepsi and pizza mixes, and junk food and books, *good* coffee, cocoa, powdered milk, German wine, two cases of beer for you, and a lot of other goodies."

"What's the latest news?" I asked, hauling through the two cases of Michelob. It was in cans. I always buy the bottles, but cans meant that I could take some along on the road without worrying that it would get busted and wasted.

"They're tracking the radioactivity across Florida and they're burning thousands of acres of orange and grapefruit trees. They say that a lot more than a half million people were exposed to radiation at dangerous levels. The hospitals are all full, and they're rushing to get all of the bodies buried as quickly as possible. The UN Security Council is debating a resolution calling for member nations to take 'all necessary measures to eliminate the threat of organized terrorism worldwide,' whatever that means."

"It means a lot of bloody fighting," I said.

"Everyone seems to think that it will pass."

"Then you'd better be damn sure you get your family moved through as quickly as you can Saturday. Don't dally in Chicago."

"I won't. Oh, I cleaned the supermarket out of Hershey Bars and Milky Ways too."

"They'll come in handy. Chocolate's good for quick energy." I was quick to decide that we'd have to sneak some of the candy bars out for our trip.

"Powdered hot chocolate mix, a bunch of canned food, today's newspapers—*USA Today, Wall Street Journal, Chicago Tribune, Louisville Times, New York Times.* This week's news magazines, and I don't know what-all else. Some clothes, shampoo, personal things." She hesitated a minute. "Gil, I think I spent more than two thousand dollars."

"Is that all? The way you kept listing stuff, I figured it would be more than that. But I didn't know I could get that much out on my bank card in one day."

"You can't. You had about six hundred in your wallet and there was a little over a thousand in cash in that lock box you brought over from Chicago, and I had some cash of my own."

"Don't worry about it. Money's no problem. I told you that. You could have taken the credit cards too."

"I didn't think about it or I would have," Joy admitted with a smile.

Timon and I brought the last of the loot through, and Joy let the doorway close. We kissed and then she started digging through all the stuff to show me what she had bought.

"We can look at it all later," I told her. "It's supper-time."

"Oh, I got a bunch of those big square batteries for the lanterns too. You said batteries wear out fast."

"If you want your Pepsi cold, you'll have to coax Parthet to come over and freeze a block of ice for you," I said as we walked downstairs to eat.

"I didn't think about ice," she admitted.

"We've got a closet fixed up something like a shower stall, with a watertight door. Fill it with water and Parthet does his abracadabra bit and turns it into a solid chunk of ice. Chip off what you need either to put in a glass or to chill bottles in one of the coolers. Takes about ten days for the ice in the closet to melt and drain away."

Joy kept talking all through supper, but she still managed to wolf down her share of everything. "Shopping makes me hungry," she said, as if living in Varay wasn't excuse enough for eating as much at one meal as she used to eat in half a week. She hadn't noticed the way everyone's bellies puffed out and then deflated in the hour or two after a meal—like recurrent, transient beer guts. When she first saw herself that way, she was likely to panic. Joy put a lot of stock in her trim figure. So did I, for that matter, but I knew just how ephemeral the bloated stomachs were in the buffer zone.

I couldn't see how Joy had managed to buy everything she did and get it transferred to Varay in one afternoon. Timon said that they had filled the van twice, and they must have really packed every cubic inch both times. Of course, most stores would have help to get the purchases out to the van, but Timon and Joy would have had to unload the van at Mother's house, carry everything to the doorway leading to Cayenne from there, and then do it all again. Timon had already hauled through quite a lot before Lesh and I got back from Basil. There were ten full cases of Pepsi beside the two cases of beer and everything else Joy bought.

No wonder she was so hungry.

But the way Joy carried on at the table solved one problem. I had to talk with Lesh, Harkane, and Timon about our quest, and I didn't want to do that with Joy around, and questions would have been asked during supper if Joy hadn't monopolized the conversation. I also had to leave instructions for the people who were staying behind to make sure that things went as smoothly as possible for Joy. She had even thought to buy small gifts for all of the people who worked at the castle—nothing extravagant, but enough to let everyone know that she had thought about him or her. It's not the kind of thing I ever remembered to do. She must have pumped Timon for a lot of information, because she knew just who we had and how many children they had over in the village, and just about everything else about them.

I was impressed, and then some. Joy was going to make a very popular chatelaine at Castle Cayenne.

There was even a special treat for dessert, ten gallons of ice cream that Joy had brought back in a couple of new camping coolers. It was enough to give everyone in the castle a good taste with enough left over for the people with children in the village to take some home with them.

It was a jolly party, almost enough to make me forget what the morning held in store.

But then Mother joined us, just as the party was breaking up.

"Why didn't you tell me that there's a dragon flying in our world?" she asked.

"I haven't seen you since then." I turned to Joy. "Did you hear any more about it this afternoon?" She shook her head.

"Why is it so important?" I asked Mother. "I mean, beside the obvious evidence of how screwed up everything is getting."

"There are Varayans in that world."

"I know about Doc McCreary."

"He's not the only one. There are"—she made a quick, impatient gesture with both hands—"nearly two dozen Varayans, and their families, some from here, some from there. This dragon will have them in a panic."

"More than the *Coral Lady?*"

"Yes, especially just after that."

"You think some of them will want to come back here?"

"It's likely. I'll have to go home and call each of them, find out. I'm their only contact."

"Be careful."

"I'm aware of the danger," Mother said, coolly. Our relationship remained rather touchy. I make no apology for that. But we tried to keep it from completely destroying the family ties. It took work on both sides.

"Grandfather is still in danger," Mother said, changing subjects abruptly. "Frankly, I don't see how he has lasted this long."

"I told him that I'm not ready to take over his job," I said, softly enough that almost anyone but Mother might have missed it. *She* could hear a whisper through a chorus of air hammers.

"You can't carry him forever like that," she said. That started something ticking inside me. Mother actually believed that I had the power to affect Pregel, to hold off death. That she believed it was frightening. That she might be right was even more terrifying.

Mother was in a hurry to get to Louisville so she could do her Paul Revere bit on the telephone. Joy went upstairs to put some order to all the things she had bought. That gave me a chance to talk with all of the castle people and with my three traveling companions. I needed more than an hour to make sure that everyone knew what I wanted them to know in advance. The four of us who were going on the road would pop through to Basil at dawn and have our breakfast there. I gave Lesh, Harkane, and Timon a full briefing on what we had to do, where we had to go, what was at stake, and who our guide would be. Carrying along the talking head of a dead elf was the only thing that visibly bothered anyone. It bothered me too, but the elf was our only ticket.

When I got upstairs, Joy was still working at her sorting, putting the different items in separate stacks, but she had changed clothes. She was just wearing a bathrobe, loosely belted now.

"The bath water's just barely warm, but if you hurry you might get enough," she said.

I nodded and went on through to the bathroom. She was right about the water temperature, but it was often worse. Since Joy had braved it, I wasn't going to cheat by going to Chicago for a shower. I didn't want to give Joy the slightest excuse for thinking that Chicago and its world might be safe, not while I was gone. At least the water wasn't warm enough to let me sleep in the tub, and I might easily have fallen asleep in hot water. I was tired, and even more exhausted by the thought of the trek I had to start in the morning.

Why? I had asked myself that question quite often, starting as soon as I saw that all the craziness was building up to what looked like a suicidal mission for me. Why was I willing to head off on this impossible quest? I could have taken Joy back to the world we grew up in. We could have found a secluded place—too out-of-the-way for terrorists, far enough from any major target to have a shot at surviving anything, even all-out nuclear war. We could forget about elflords and chickens that laid dragon eggs, and kids who literally grew up overnight. I had the training to be a top-notch survivalist if it came to that. And it would probably be safer than continuing as I was.

The first time I went tilting at windmills it was different. I started out trying to rescue my parents from some then-unknown difficulty, then I went on to avenge my father's death, and other things got done along the way, *by* me and *to* me. I didn't even know what the hell was going on until it dropped right on my head. In a way, that was really an advantage. This time I had a fairly good idea of what was in store. *The omens said that we were rapidly moving toward Armageddon or Götterdämmerung or Judgment Day or whatever; the End of Everything*. If you believed the advertising.

I wasn't quite positive that I did, but the arguments were too strong to bet against them at house odds.

That still didn't make my decision to attempt something even less likely against longer odds very logical or intelligent, but it did let me sleep nights. Annick once told me that I did what I did from a sense of duty. The word embarrassed me then, and I tried to shy away from it whenever I could, even in my thoughts. I guess I still do. It sounds too abstract, too impersonal. "Duty, honor, country"? Maybe, but maybe not. Maybe I *am* just stupid or crazy enough for this Hero business.

Or perhaps it all came from a sense of family. All the family I had left was in Varay—Joy, my mother, and her kin. Dad was an only child and so were both of his parents, and they were all dead. I had never known either set of grandparents. Mother's parents were killed back in the early 1940s. Dad's died about ten years later.

Whatever. There was a crazy, dangerous job to be done, the kind of Hero-work I had been raised and trained to do—even if it was by subterfuge and deception. My decision to try was never seriously at doubt.

I don't claim that I was being smart.

"Are you going to take all night in there?" Joy called from the bedroom. I guess that maybe I did come close to dozing off in the tub, lukewarm water and all.

"I'll be out in a minute," I said. I toweled off vigorously, and that perked me up a little.

Joy was already in bed, the covers pulled up to just below her breasts. Only a single lamp was burning, and it was low. Joy and I made love, but I can't claim that it was my best performance ever, and afterward I did something I never do. I just rolled off and went straight to sleep. I simply couldn't stay awake.

When I woke, much later, the night was at its most silent. The bedroom was dark, with only the faint glow of the clock's luminous face and the moon- and starlight filtering in through the window. Joy was awake, her head on my shoulder, one hand down under the blankets caressing me, stroking, teasing. I turned toward her and we kissed.

"I hope you were dreaming about me," Joy whispered in my ear. Her hand was still busy below.

"What are you talking about? I wasn't dreaming."

"You must have been. You got a big hard-on."

"I don't remember any dream, but if I had one, it must have been about you."

"You'd better prove it."

I managed to sneak a glance at the clock—it wasn't quite four-thirty yet—and then I did what Joy wanted. Five and a half hours of sleep is plenty for me most nights. And I would like to think that I redeemed myself after the evening before, even though I knew that it might be the last chance we would ever have.

"How long will you be gone this time?" Joy asked after we finished.

"I don't have any idea. I don't know how far into the

mountains we have to go, or how slow it will be. Several weeks at least."

"You realize that if I knew how to ride a horse, I'd be going with you."

"No!" Since Joy *didn't* know how to ride, I could have avoided that, but I knew where silence or agreement would lead. The second part of the quest would be by boat. "I would never risk you like that, Joy," I told her. "And I could never take a chance of getting in a position where I might have to choose between saving you and completing the mission. The penalty for failure might be too drastic—for everyone."

"You let *her* go with you." She was talking about Annick.

"Not exactly. And it wasn't the same. The choice wouldn't have been anywhere near as difficult."

"You mean because she knew how to fight and kill?"

"No, because she wasn't you and I never felt anything for her like I feel for you. Annick was driven by hate, and all she saw in me was that I hurt her enemies more than she had."

When Joy started to ask another question, I stopped her with a kiss—a long, hard kiss. And then it was time to get up.

Dressing for the road is quite a procedure, and I can always count on sweating a lot out riding in the complete get-up. I had layers of clothing, part from one world, part from the other. I started with T-shirt and jockey shorts, the heaviest denim jeans I had, wool socks, and comfortable combat boots. For casual wear, that would have been more than enough for an August day that would probably get into the high eighties. But that was only the start for a proper Hero going a-questing to do Hero-work. The next layer was a padded leather tunic that reached down past my butt (split partway up the back so I could ride a horse in it) and laced up the front. The complete costume includes the Varayan equivalent of chaps to protect my legs, leather studded with six-inch strips of metal to keep a chance sword stroke from biting too deeply, but I never wore those. The chain mail to go over the leather had to wait until I had experienced help. Getting that on and fastened was a two-man job. Anyway, I didn't want to start carrying that weight until we were ready to leave.

Joy finished dressing long before I got my leather tunic laced up. Then I went to check on my companions. They were up—dressed, ready to go, already armed and armored. Lesh would have seen to it that they were wakened in plenty of time.

My armor and weapons were in the great hall waiting. Timon had packed my chaps and helmet, knowing that I wouldn't be wearing them. The helmet is another heavy bit of metal that I avoid as long as possible. I dug out my lucky Cubs cap to wear instead.

We ate. All of the people who lived in the castle were there for the meal, even though it wasn't quite dawn yet. They knew something about what we were off to do, and sharing the farewell meal with us was one way of showing their support. We ate fast, not worrying about digestive problems, then finished getting ready to leave . . . so we could fit in another breakfast at Castle Basil.

"I'm having a bad case of *déjà vu,*" Joy said while Lesh and Timon helped me finish dressing. "This is like that scene in *Cat Ballou* where they're all helping Lee Marvin get dressed for the big showdown."

I wished that she hadn't said that. I have enough trouble keeping from feeling ridiculous when I'm all fitted out ready for a rumble, and I remembered the scene she was talking about all too clearly.

We got my chain mail on. It didn't hang quite as low as the tunic. Then my weapons: two elf swords over my shoulders, dagger at my waist on one side, quiver on the other. I would carry my compound bow until we got to the horses. I had a pistol and a box of cartridges packed, but that was just old habit, since I didn't expect to use the gun.

"You look like something out of a comic strip," Joy said when I was ready to go. She didn't quite manage to swallow her laugh. She had been holding it back for ten or fifteen minutes by then.

"Prince Valiant?" I suggested with an exaggerated grin.

"No, Hägar the Horrible." This time, Joy didn't even try to hold back the laugh. "You didn't even shave."

"I probably won't until we get back." Joy and I just

looked at each other for a moment. "We're going to be late for breakfast," I said finally, mostly to break the tableau.

"We just . . ." Joy started and then she just shook her head.

We had quite a load of gear to take through to Basil. Joy held the passage open while Lesh, Harkane, Timon, and I shifted everything through with the help of a couple of our other people. Baron Kardeen had people waiting on the other side to carry everything to the great hall and then out to our horses.

When we made our entrance into the great hall, the room fell silent and people turned to stare—even the servants who were starting to haul in the breakfast victuals. I always got some stares—the Varayans all saw me as a big shot, the local equivalent of a rock star, I guess—and Joy is always worth a stare. I didn't let it bother me most of the time, but Joy wasn't used to that kind of intense attention.

"It always makes me think that my fly is open," I whispered, and she relaxed a little.

"Maybe it is," she whispered back.

"No, I already checked." We both laughed and went on in to eat.

The head table was more crowded than usual that morning. Parthet, Aaron, and Mother were there. Even Kardeen came out to eat with us, and that was unusual.

Joy kept staring at Aaron, but so did I, and nearly everyone else. He may have received more attention than I did. In two days, he had apparently aged ten years. He was as tall as me but not as heavy. His hair had grown considerably too, into a modest "natural." His voice had deepened and he spoke more slowly, considering his words, but he still smiled a lot and didn't seem bothered by his magic spurt of growth—though everyone else was concerned about it, including me. There couldn't be any question of taking him home to his family now. They would never believe that Aaron was really Aaron.

And *eat* . . . Aaron packed away as much food as any two of the garrison soldiers, and *their* appetites were legendary.

Breakfast went on for two hours, a little longer than usual, and afterward I said private farewells to Kardeen,

Parthet, and Mother, and asked each of them to keep an eye on Joy. I went upstairs to see the king. He was asleep, but he was breathing easily and there was more color in his face. Encouraging. When I went back to the great hall, I talked with Aaron for a few minutes, incredibly curious about how he was taking everything that had happened to him. I was still curious after our talk. It really didn't seem to faze him in the least.

Then I went off alone with Joy while Lesh and the others finished loading our horses in the courtyard.

"I don't suppose it would do any good to tell you to be careful," Joy said.

"I'll be as careful as possible," I said. We both knew how empty that promise might be.

"I'm too new a wife to be a widow." And then she came into my arms and started crying.

We couldn't share much of an embrace with all the metal I was wearing, but I kissed her eyes, tasting the salt of her tears. Then we kissed for real, but she was still crying.

"There's more to me than you might think, Joy," I said. "When you get a chance, ask Uncle Parthet to tell you about the magic that the Hero of Varay has. And remember how quickly I healed from that stabbing and the operation. It almost drove the doctor crazy."

We held hands as we walked out to the courtyard. Quite a lot of the garrison and staff came out to watch us leave. Seven horses were ready, four to ride, three to carry our supplies . . . and the head of the dead elf. His birdcage was perched atop the packs on one of our packhorses, tied in place. The eyes turned to meet mine, and there was anger in his look.

"I will not forget this humiliation," the elf said, and Joy screamed.

"What is that?" she demanded, clinging to me. Well, I *had* mentioned the elf to her, it had been impossible to avoid all talk of him, but seeing—and hearing—the reality was still a shock for her.

"That's what's left of the elf who stabbed me," I said, leading Joy off to the side, out of sight of him.

"That head talked."

"Parthet provided part of the magic. Apparently the elf improved it a little. He's our guide, the only one who can make it possible for us to find the relics we're looking for."

"How can you trust him?"

"I can't, but he has every reason to help us. He wants his head and body to go home to his father for a proper send-off, and the only way that can happen is if we succeed and get home safely. The rest of him is locked up in the castle, and if we don't make it back, terrible things will happen to it—at least things that the elf considers terrible."

Joy was shaking as if she had fever and chills. I guided her over to my mother, and Mother knew what was wrong. I kissed Joy, told her again that everything would be all right, and hurried to my horse—Electrum, son of Gold.

I had help mounting, and as soon as I was up, my companions mounted, also with help. We could have made it unassisted, but we were too loaded down with armor and breakfast to make it alone without looking terribly undignified. The others started walking their horses slowly toward the gate. The magic doorway to Castle Thyme was down in Basil Town. I turned Electrum around and walked him over to Mother and Joy.

"I will be back," I said, projecting all the confidence I could muster. I *would* be back, at least once or twice—I hoped.

Then I turned my horse again and followed the others off to the main gate. The way was open, doors pulled back, portcullis raised, the short drawbridge to the top of the path down.

There was a commotion on the ramparts above the gate and in the gateway itself before we reached it. People were pointing down the side of Basil Rock.

"Someone's coming, running hard," one of the guards shouted. I caught up to my companions and reined in to wait. Lesh, Harkane, and Timon were each leading one of the pack animals. Lesh had the one that carried our elf's head.

After a moment I rode out onto the drawbridge that crosses a small gap at the edge of the rock. On the top switchback below, a youngster was running hard up the lane. I looked on down to the town and saw a group of people, several of them pointing up. Whatever the runner was about, the townspeople knew.

I rode Electrum down to meet the runner. He couldn't have been more than twelve or thirteen years old. He stopped when he saw me and fought to catch his breath.

"What's wrong, lad?" I asked.

"You're the Hero?" he gasped. I nodded. "It's terrible, lord, terrible." As his breathing settled down, his voice got stronger, his speech more coherent.

"It's forest trolls, Lord. A mighty band of them. They attacked Nushur and put it to the torch."

11

Precarra

I reached down and pulled the kid up behind me. Then I turned Electrum around on the narrow lane and trotted back up to the courtyard. I let the boy from Nushur down and listened while he told his story again, in more detail. The trolls had hit Nushur in the night, screaming and burning, but showing more organization than usual. A few survivors thought that they had seen a warrior directing the attack, someone so large that he had to be an elf.

When he finished, the boy came to me and clutched at my leg.

"You have to come, lord, or they'll return and finish us for fair."

"I'll send a patrol," Baron Kardeen said. "They can reach Nushur well before sunset."

"We need the Hero of Varay," the boy said, his voice getting shrill.

Kardeen looked to me.

"I guess we can ride that way," I said. The boy's fingernails were biting into my leg. "I'll take a look and see what I can learn. Your patrol can follow up. We'll ride southeast from Nushur. Shouldn't add more than a day and a half to the journey."

"Looking for another sword to strap to your puny back?" the talking head asked scornfully.

"Maybe for a more cooperative guide," I told him. That ended *that* conversation.

"You stay here, boy. Ride out with the patrol that follows us." I looked from him to Kardeen. The baron nodded.

"Wait five minutes and I'll send a man with you," Kardeen said. "He can ride back to meet the patrol if you follow after the trolls. Save a little time."

"Fine." I turned to the boy again. "You'd best go inside and get some food and rest while you can."

"You're going to Nushur?"

"I'm going," I told him, and he finally let go of my leg.

It did take no more than five minutes for Kardeen to get the extra rider out, armed, armored, and mounted. I led the way to the gate again after another wave at Joy. She was still looking worried and scared, standing next to Mother. The story the boy from Nushur told couldn't have helped Joy's nerves. Most of the crowd followed us to the gate. A few people came out onto the drawbridge to watch as we rode down to the town of Basil and beyond. On the second switchback, I looked up and saw both Joy and Mother at the top of the path. From there, they would be able to see us until we crossed the Tarn River east of town and got to the first curve on the road to Nushur.

We took the path down the side of the rock slowly, spaced far enough apart that none of the horses would feel crowded and perhaps get skittish—five riders, eight horses, and one unencumbered head. The lane leading down from Basil Rock is steep enough to require caution at any time.

As we rode through town, people watched silently. Maybe they were impressed with how quickly their Hero could ride to the relief of Nushur. Or maybe most knew that something was already in the works.

It was a silent start to the ride. I didn't feel much like talking, and none of my companions tried to start a conversation. We crossed the Tarn and the thin strip of farm fields that separates Basil from Precarra Forest east of town. It was a familiar road. I had covered the entire distance between Basil and Thyme three times when I first arrived in Varay, and I made it a point to ride to Nushur to visit the magistrate and the village's inn two or three times a year, the way I tried to visit every population center. Nushur was one of the hardest places to reach, because the nearest magic doorway was in Basil. Few places were farther by road from a portal.

The morning was already warm, and I started to bake before we had traveled a mile. Once we got into the forest, things were a little better. There are no carefully maintained rights-of-way along the roads of Varay. Trees crowded the trail and big trees forced the dirt lane to detour. Early in a particularly hot and dry August, the creeks that the road crossed were all low, hardly wet enough to count. We rode at a moderate pace and let the horses take it easy, stopping occasionally to let them rest and drink. That's the way any long ride starts. Riders and horses both need a chance to build up to the demands of the road. Push too hard at the start and you might not finish. In any event, you can count on the journey's taking longer than it has to.

I had no special warning from the danger sense that is part of the stock in trade of the Hero of Varay. After three years and a couple of months, that sense seemed as normal as the routine five. It wasn't perfect. It could be fooled just as the others can be. That meant that we kept our eyes open on the road and we would post sentries when we camped.

The ride to Nushur was uneventful. We had the road to ourselves but for a couple of farm wagons early in the ride. We stopped to rest the horses halfway to Nushur and took time to have a light meal ourselves. After that, we picked up the pace and reached Nushur with more than an hour of good daylight left.

Nushur was still smoldering, more than thirty-six hours after the attack. Two-thirds of the buildings had been burned to the ground. Once a fire starts in one of those cottages, there is no putting it out. But there was also nothing left of the magistrate's manor or the pub but stone foundations and hearthstones. The survivors hid until they saw my pennant on Timon's lance. Then they came out of the ruins slowly, alone or in small groups, to stand in the center of their village and wait for me to say something.

But what could I say?

I surveyed the village, looked around. A couple of times I had to close my eyes for a moment. Finally, I dismounted and greeted the few residents I recognized.

"How many were killed?" I asked.

"Nigh on thirty, lord, including my master," one of the boys who worked for the innkeeper said. Tearstains streaked his dirty face, and new tears started.

"And the injured?"

The boy shrugged. A woman came forward.

"Not many, lord. Those as was bad hurt ha' died already." That was the way of things where medical attention was hard to come by.

"The magistrate?" I asked.

"Him and all his family died," the woman said. "And my man and babes." She turned and walked away, but without tears. She was beyond them.

Maybe this disaster couldn't compare with the tragedy of the *Coral Lady* and the Tampa Bay area, but these people had never heard of those. This was their home, *their* disaster. It was as real as any disaster could be, as devastating, as total, as important to them.

It was important to me too. These were my people.

I took a slow walk through the remains of Nushur, accompanied by Lesh and Jordro, the man Kardeen had sent along. There didn't seem to be much food left in Nushur. The raiders had carried off much of what they hadn't destroyed. As I talked to the survivors, I learned most of the story. The trolls came through the village on foot, throwing torches, swinging their long knives and battle-axes at random. They hardly stopped, just long enough to grab whatever was handy, and then they kept moving due south, apparently aiming directly for the Titan Mountains.

"You need anything more before you start back?" I asked Jordro when we got back to the horses.

He shook his head. "We'll have to bring food as quick as we can. And the faster I start, the faster they'll fill their bellies."

"And anything else the baron can think of," I said. "They've really been wiped out."

"Just hope the trolls keep going south toward the mountains. There aren't many folks living south of here."

"We'll try to prod them along, as long as we can stay on the track," I said. "Just make sure that the rest follow as soon as possible."

"You won't have much of a track to follow," Jordro said. "Trolls won't leave much evidence of their passing."

"What about this elf on horseback?"

"Believe him when you see him, lord," Jordro advised. He spoke softly and looked around to make sure no villagers were close. "Anything happens out here in the countryside, someone's sure to yell 'elf' every time."

I glanced at our elf in his birdcage. "And sometimes they're right," I said.

"I'll start back now," Jordro said. "The sooner off, the sooner help arrives."

A few villagers got agitated when Jordro galloped back toward Basil, so I explained that he was going to get relief supplies, especially food, lined up. I also told the villagers that more soldiers were coming, and that I was heading south on the trail of the trolls. It seemed to ease a few anxieties, but most of the survivors were in shock yet from the attack.

I had to be careful in my phrasing. I didn't want to make promises I might have to break. There was a limit to how much time I could devote to the pursuit, especially if the trolls changed direction and headed drastically away from the course I had to follow to accomplish my original mission.

"Trolls can move fast when they've a mind to, lord," Lesh said as we rode out of Nushur. "With a day and a half lead, it may be too much for us to catch 'em, horses and all."

"I'll be satisfied if they keep heading south," I said. "If we catch them, that's a bonus." A Hero has to make sounds like that, I suppose. If we caught them, we'd have a fight on our hands, and I never looked forward to battle with anything but distaste.

"Folks back there was sayin' there was a hundred of 'em," Lesh said. "Mayhap not. Scared folks in the night may count three for one, but they must still be a fair number to dare attack a town, even a village so small as Nushur."

"It's not normal, lord," Harkane said. "Trolls don't attack towns less they got someone pushing hard." He glanced at our elf, who stayed out of the conversation.

Bad as it was, Nushur's tragedy could have been worse. The food shortages would only be temporary. The trolls hadn't burned the fields, and the coming harvest would see plenty of food for the village. The livestock had been run off, but some of the animals might return, and even if they didn't, meat would be available as soon as the villagers got up the nerve to go into the forest to hunt.

Game was plentiful in Precarra. And Baron Kardeen would certainly see to replacing the lost livestock. Once the villagers got to work, they could get the houses rebuilt in just a few days. Only the more substantial buildings, the manor and the inn, would take longer. But those buildings were less important. They wouldn't be needed until Nushur had a new magistrate and innkeeper.

The dead couldn't be replaced so easily, and they certainly wouldn't be forgotten in Nushur, but life would go on. Probably. That might depend on whether or not I succeeded in my primary mission.

The forest trolls didn't leave much of a trail, but there were signs enough. Not far south of Nushur they had stopped to butcher a couple of the cows they had driven off. They hadn't bothered with a cooking fire, but bones had been dumped over the next several miles as they were chewed clean. I couldn't get any real idea of the size of the raiding party, but enough feet had passed over the same summer-scorched grass to leave marks. Where the ground was soft, near the frequent pitiful creeks, there were occasional bare footprints visible—splayed troll feet.

And we saw marks of a single shod horse overlying troll prints in a couple of places. It looked as if there *was* a rider with them, driving them along.

Then we found the body of a troll who had apparently been killed by an arrow through the neck, though we didn't find the arrow. Trolls don't use bows normally, and I thought that an elf would be more likely to use his sword if one of his troops had to be executed. The long claymores, like the two I carried, seemed to be *de rigueur* among elf warriors.

"Some elves do use bows," Lesh reminded me. "That party we raided in Fairy, you recall?"

I nodded, but I still wasn't completely satisfied.

Not long after we found the body, we made camp for the night, moving well off to the side of the trolls' track. We set up in a clearing next to a creek. My danger sense was quiet except for the tiny tickling of distant peril that I had felt since arriving in Nushur. Our supper was the most perishable of the food we had brought from Basil. We ate, rested for a couple of hours, then rode on slowly, taking advantage of a moon that was just past the full . . . *two* moons just past the full. A couple of hours before dawn, we stopped again to get a little sleep.

I almost missed the second dead troll. If I hadn't moved well away from our campsite to relieve myself, I might not have spotted the body rolled off against the edge of a bramble patch. With the aid of a flashlight, I saw that this troll had died the same way as the first. There were matching puncture wounds on the chest and back, the kind of holes an arrow would make. But, once more, there was no arrow. I showed the body to the others at dawn, before we started riding again. Huge brown eyes stared sightlessly out of the porcine face. Large canine teeth protruded in front of bluish lips.

"Takes a powerful bowman to put an arrow through chest and back like that," Lesh said, pushing the body over with his boot.

"Or a long spike of some kind?" I made it a question.

Lesh shrugged. "Never heard of no weapon like that."

We mounted up and started riding, following the trail and keeping watch for any more bodies. One troll corpse was interesting trivia. Two made it a real mystery.

By noon, the forest started to thin out. Occasional patches of rocky ground intruded on the greenery. Lesh said that we were getting close to the wild southeastern quarter of Varay, a region inhabited mostly by shepherds, grape farmers, and miners.

"Forest trolls can't go much further," Lesh said. "They're like to trespass on other tribes soon."

But the trail did go on, bending a trifle to the west, staying in the forest. The trail seemed to be getting fresher—meaning that we were gaining on the trolls—but none of us had enough tracking experience to know how *much* closer. My danger sense wasn't shouting alerts yet, though.

Conversation was limited to the most essential information while we rode, observations about the trail, the condition of our horses, suggestions for breaks, that sort of thing. Normally, we did a fair amount of talking on the road. We spent so much time together that I knew Lesh, Harkane, and Timon better than I had ever known my own parents. But we didn't do much talking on this trip. Our elf inhibited the talk more than the trolls that were somewhere up ahead. At least our elf wasn't overly talkative either.

We found three more dead trolls that day, each killed the same way, at widely separated spots.

"Someone else is tracking them," I decided, and Lesh nodded. "Someone a lot closer than we are."

"Someone from Nushur, like as not," Lesh said.

It was possible. The Nushurites were peasants in the classical sense, people of the land, but it wasn't too far-fetched to think that one of them had found the gumption, or the hatred, to track the trolls and kill whenever he could do it safely. A village hunter would be a good shot with a bow, and he might be thrifty enough to recover his arrows so he could use them again.

Each time we found another dead troll, my danger sense got a little more active. By late afternoon, I was convinced that we were getting fairly close to the raiders.

"We may be only a couple of hours behind them now," I told my companions. The last troll seemed that freshly dead. I didn't want to overtake the trolls at night, so I decided to make camp before dusk and stay put for the entire night. That might let us catch up with the trolls the next day, before they ran out of forest.

"They turn one way or t'other soon," Lesh said. "Mayhap they even turn back on their own trail after whoever's killing them."

"They might not know what's going on," I suggested, "if the bowman's content to pick off stragglers . . . maybe trolls who stop to take a leak."

"I reckon even trolls got to stop for that now and again," Lesh allowed.

We rode on a little farther. I wanted to be choosy about our campsite, find a place that would offer a little protection. An isolated copse on a slight rise with plenty of open space around it would have been perfect, offering concealment for us but letting us spot any trolls coming in while they were still far enough away for us to put a few arrows into them. Harkane and Timon had both developed into fair archers. Timon didn't have his full strength yet, but within the range of his lighter bow, he was an ace.

We had to make do with what we could find, though. I spotted a little glen off the track we had been following.

There was no clear killing zone around the nook, but it was fairly well concealed from any angle but one. There were two exits, so we couldn't be bottled up easily and there was spring water coming out of a slab of rock to gather in a small pool below it.

While the others unloaded the horses and made camp, I climbed the rock above the spring to get a look around. I found a place in some scrub brush and turned slowly through a full circle, letting my senses reach out as far as they could. It was summer and we were in the south of Varay. There was a rich country smell to the air, a light breeze that felt wonderful after a day of hot riding. As I turned, my feeling for danger ebbed and flowed. We were close enough to the trolls that I could follow them just on the strength of the danger signal—like a radio direction finder. They were southeast of us, which meant that they had curved off to the left again. They were close, but not *too* close.

The Titan Mountains were closer than they had been too. They were a line across the south, individual peaks clearly visible in the foreground, higher ranges behind nearer lower ranges, ranked off into invisibility. The greens of mountainside trees blended away into a more distant violet. Clouds capped the higher peaks and swam in between, cuddling the mountains, obscuring them.

There wasn't a dragon in sight. The way things had been happening lately, that was almost a surprise.

It was beautiful country. Varay has a pastoral attraction that can only be weakly imitated by any place back in the "real" world. A lot of the buffer zone is like that.

When I climbed back down to our camp, Lesh had one of his smokeless fires going and he was heating water for coffee and warming our food—real food; we hadn't started on the packaged camping rations yet. The horses were on a picket line with room to graze and a chance to get at drinking water. The pack frames were still on our extra horses, but their loads had been taken off and arranged on a flat rock away from the water. The elf's head was perched there as well, and he was scowling.

"What's your gripe now?" I asked.

"You're wasting time."

"Not so much," I said. "And since I don't know exactly where we're going or how long it will take to get there, I can't decide if it's too much. Some things have to be done immediately."

"You're risking everything."

"You did your own share of stalling back at Basil. You haven't given me much incentive to hurry, not if it ends with me going to your father's lair."

He shut his eyes then, his way of ending the conversation.

Xayber's son hadn't said anything that I hadn't told myself at least hourly since we left Basil, following this diversion rather than jumping straight over to Thyme. Some good was coming out of it, though. The elf was showing his worry about the possibilities again. Farther along the road, I might be able to pull some advantage out of that. If I saved all of the realms of existence, I wanted to be around to enjoy them with Joy.

We ate and settled in for the night. I took the first watch, a habit. While I was on watch, I walked around the perimeter of our camp, irregularly, not like walking a fixed post. The Varayan night was no stranger to me any longer. I knew most of the dangers it might pose. I could recognize the normal sounds, the brief, soft noises of predators and prey acting out their life-and-death rituals. And after Lesh relieved me, I got right to sleep, thinking about Joy, missing her already.

When Timon woke me, near the end of the night, I felt troubled. My danger sense had perked way up, but the danger wasn't immediate yet.

"Wake the others, quietly," I told Timon. "Trouble."

Dawn was still an hour away. Lesh and the others started loading our horses, slow work in the dark. I could feel the danger drawing nearer. The easy guess was that the trolls had doubled back, but I couldn't be certain. We moved our animals back near the rock outcropping when they were ready, and where they would be as safe as possible.

"Trolls," our elf said in a loud stage whisper. "All around, moving in like soldiers. And something else, some*one* else." Eyes of Fairy: the dark was no handicap for him.

"One of your kin?" I asked.

"I think not." He was silent for a moment. "They are close."

I could tell that too. My danger sense was screaming. One of the things it was screaming was that if there *was* an elf with the trolls, Xayber's son might try to attract him, hoping to win an easier trip back home. It might all come down to a matter of how badly he wanted to be reunited with his body.

I drew Dragon's Death and held it out toward the edge of camp. The sword's battle song came to my lips as always, starting softly and building. The first wave of trolls came in a solid line. As soon as all four of us were engaged fighting that bunch, more came at us from behind.

It wasn't the sort of mad melee that my previous encounters with trolls had been. These moved as if they had someone ordering the battle, as if they had drilled extensively, and that was totally alien to the troll style. They might not have an elf behind them, but there had been somebody, sometime.

The first attacks ended. Survivors pulled back, but my danger sense got more frantic instead of less.

"They were just checking our strength," I said, just loud enough for my companions to hear. "The next attack will be the real thing, more of them." And the first engagement had taxed us. I looked to the sky. Dawn was closer, but there wouldn't be enough light for accurate bow work for another twenty minutes or more, and the trolls weren't about to give us that much time.

The second assault started.

Numbers? It's hard to count in the middle of a fight, even if you've got light. I started to think that the estimate of one hundred we'd heard in Nushur couldn't be far wrong. In any case, there were too many trolls, even for a Hero, his elf swords, and three valiant companions. We could slow them down, make their victory expensive, but there didn't seem to be any way to beat them.

Then my danger sense hit me with an extra twist, causing me to duck to the side just in time to miss an arrow flying through the space my head had occupied just microseconds before.

12

The Titans

The itch I felt in the middle of my back had nothing to do with the extra danger sense I inherited with the title of Hero of Varay. This was something much more primitive, a feeling that somebody had me lined up in his sights. I had chain mail on, but that won't necessarily turn an arrow. I had more experience than I wanted in the limitations of chain mail. The itch translated itself into frantic movement as I hopped around as much as the setting and the trolls permitted. Arrows in the dark didn't sound like an archer from Nushur. There was no one in Nushur who had the eyesight of an elf.

I saw a second arrow go past me and pierce the forehead of a troll. There may have been more arrows. It wasn't light enough that I could expect to see them but by chance or extremely close proximity. I shouted a warning to my companions. My frantic gyrations had separated me from them. An elf sword demands a lot of room, and I had moved away from Lesh and the others at the beginning of the fight, long before I felt the need to take extra evasive actions. My sword song got louder and more intricate and I started to clear a larger circle around me.

The trolls finally noticed that there was an archer involved in the fight. It seemed that each arrow found one of them, but I was slow to pick up on that clue. At first, I might have dismissed it as the inevitable consequence of there being so many more of the trolls than there were of us. But the earlier trolls, along the road . . . in the heat of battle, they slipped my mind far too long.

A little more light. I could see the attacking trolls and the growing stacks of their dead. I didn't have to count on the instinctive awareness of where everyone was. My people were all on their feet, still fighting. Timon and

Harkane were back to back, covering each other, moving as a unit. Lesh was off to the side, jabbing with a short spear held in his left hand and whirling a battle-ax in his right.

I finally quit my mad gyrations when it sank in that the archer was aiming at trolls and not at me. I didn't want to make it any harder for him than I had to. I would feel foolish dying by mistake when there were so many ways to die intentionally—by someone else's intention.

Dragon's Death seemed almost weightless in combat, eager to move in answer to my will. I pulled more volume from the battle song as the fight went on, apparently drawing energy from the tune. The blade glowed brightly from the blood that washed it, but the sword's glow lessened as the light of dawn increased. Drawing the second sword, the blade taken from the son of Xayber, was purely unconscious. I shifted my grip on Dragon's Death to hold it in my right hand alone, and reached over my shoulder to draw the second weapon with my left hand. Two sword songs intertwined themselves—and I'll never know how my throat managed both at the same time. I was whistling a duet by myself, even though the elf head was also whistling the song of his sword off to the side.

I moved into the heaviest concentration of trolls, slicing left and right, propelling myself forward with the force of the swings. I've read accounts where the hero went through a wild melee and was then able to describe his every move in technical fencing jargon. Bull. At a time like that all you can do is make every move you can think of to keep your head on your shoulders. If you're competent with your weapons, the moves come faster than you can think. Reflex and instinct, carefully honed by training and practice, do the job. There's little chance of remembering every sequence afterward.

More light made better targets. When I could spare the odd nanosecond, I tried to spot the archer who was helping us. But I didn't have any luck until the attack ended. One troll screamed a series of guttural sounds and the whole troop, those who were still able to, broke off and ran, chased by several more quick arrows. I turned and saw the archer on the next rise.

Annick.

We stared at each other, maybe sixty yards apart, for

a frozen time. Before I recovered enough from the surprise to say anything, she had mounted her horse and ridden off out of sight behind the rise. I caught one more glimpse of her through the trees and she was gone.

"That was Annick," Lesh said—as if I might have failed to recognize her.

"Either her hunting tastes have changed or elves are out of season," I said, almost gasping the words. I was still short of breath from the fight.

So were the others. A quick inspection showed that Harkane was the only one with anything worse than scratches. He had a long gash along his right forearm, a cut that ran almost from wrist to elbow. Along the center of the slice, the wound looked dangerously deep, but the bleeding was seepage, not the gushing that would have indicated a severed artery. It was serious, but not as bad as it might have been.

"I'm going to have to sew that up," I told Harkane after I cleaned the wound. There was a fairly complete first-aid kit in our supplies. Timon found it for me. After I gave Harkane a long swig of the local painkiller—a foul-tasting brew called something that the translation magic rendered as *numb-er*—I put in several butterfly stitches to draw the sides of the wound together, then doused the cut with antiseptic again and bandaged it. There were tears at the corners of Harkane's eyes until the numb-er took effect, but he gritted his teeth and didn't make a sound. As long as the wound didn't get infected, he would be okay.

"What now, lord?" Lesh asked when I finished with Harkane and the rest of us had treated our scrapes and scratches with iodine. "Do we keep after the trolls and finish 'em?"

I looked at the bodies strewn around us.

"No, we've got to get on with our main job. Just make sure that all of these are really dead." I got caught by a troll playing possum once. I didn't want it to happen again.

Lesh grunted and set to work. It was a task that didn't seem to bother him, and it *would* have bothered me to do it—I had done it before and wouldn't hesitate to do it again if I had to, but as long as I didn't *have* to, I didn't even want to watch. Timon and I rechecked the loads on the horses to make sure that there had been no mistakes in the dark. An unbalanced load would be miserable for the horse, and if things started falling off, we might lose time or more.

Then I went over to our elf head.

"What will you do about the bowman? Who is he? I couldn't see." Xayber's son was more agitated than I had seen him since our fight, and his death.

"I'm not going to do anything," I said. "And the archer wasn't a he, but a she. That was the niece of Baron Resler."

"*That* hellbitch? His voice climbed two octaves. Annick would have been pleased to know the effect she had.

"You know of her?" I asked, trying to keep my voice flat.

"I know of the banshee. We all do."

"She must be slipping," I told him. "If she had spotted you, she would have slipped an arrow between your eyes just for the pleasure of it." Xayber's son closed his eyes. I had a curious thought. I wondered if his body, back at Castle Basil, was shuddering from the revulsion he so clearly felt for Annick.

"There's thirty-four of 'em dead, lord," Lesh reported. "Twelve were killed by arrows, all clean shots chest, throat, or head. She was a wicked eye with a bow, lord."

"How's Harkane doing?" I asked softly, not turning to look.

"He'll be right soon enough."

"Let's break out a beer apiece before we start riding. The beer should be halfway cool and we can all use a little boost."

"Aye, lord."

Lesh knew just where the beer was packed, which was no surprise. One beer wasn't nearly enough for me, or for the others, but we had only one case of Michelob along and I had no idea how long it had to last, how long it might be before we got back out of the mountains.

Then it was time to ride.

The surviving trolls had run northeast. Annick had headed due north. We went southeast.

"We've got a long way to go to reach the proper pass

into the Titans,'' our dead elf told us. ''You've come too far out of the way.''

I had no intention of resuming that argument, and when I didn't respond, he closed his eyes.

We rode at a good pace that day, trying to make up ground. When we started to come upon long open stretches near the edge of Precarra, we angled more to the east. Riding took the nervous lumps out of my gut after the early-morning fight. When we stopped for lunch, I checked Harkane's arm—so far, so good. There was no bleeding and no trace of infection, though I didn't know if infection would appear that soon. He didn't complain of pain, and he seemed too alert to be hiding much, so I just gave him aspirin rather than another dose of the Varayan numb-er. *That* stuff was potent, but I wouldn't give or take it unless it was absolutely necessary. Our supply was limited and we might have worse injuries to deal with by the time we got back to Basil.

Despite what I had told our elf, I *was* worried about the time we had lost by riding to Nushur and then chasing the trolls. I didn't know how much time we had until the general craziness and deterioration reached whatever critical mass it needed to trigger the End of Everything. I didn't know how long we would need to reach the shrine in the Titans, then the shrine out in the Mist, and finally to do whatever had to be done with the family jewels of the Great Earth Mother in order to reverse the magical entropy, or whatever it was that put the real world and the buffer zone at risk of annihilation. Dad used to say that it's crazy to worry about things you can't change, but it's hard to avoid it sometimes.

There weren't any real roads in this section of Varay. There simply was too little traffic to keep nature from reclaiming any path. Grapes were hauled out in the autumn, wool in the spring, metals in small quantities every couple of months. Mostly, the trails there were led to the nearest stream that would float a small flat-bottomed boat and the goods went downstream to villages nearer the center of Varay. Supplies came back upstream over the same routes.

''We'd better top off our water bags every time we see good water,'' Lesh said after we finished lunch. ''Out in the wilds ahead, we can't count on finding much this time of year.'' With Harkane injured, Lesh was leading two packhorses and Timon handled the third.

Before we left the forest for good, we came across a small pack of the seven-foot lizards, the almost-dragons, like the one that had been my welcome to Varay when I came through the first time. The midget dragons scuttled off ahead of us, their tiny wings fluttering madly even though they were too small to get the dragons off the ground. Lesh speared one—''Just for practice,'' he said.

The land started getting wrinkled before we left the forest, and beyond Precarra there were deep folds, and the kind of fissures that earthquakes can cause. Layers of adjacent rock might be separated by a hundred feet, horizontally or vertically. Finding a secure path took effort when the land was at its wildest. This was a part of Varay I had not seen before, rugged but tempting, like the Badlands of the Dakotas.

But there were also islands of green, sometimes quite extensive. There were small stands of trees, pastures, the very rare farm. Lesh warned us not to expect hospitality in this quarter of Varay, and he was right. Not even the king's Hero got more than a surly greeting or a grunt. And those were the more genial ones. Usually, we were pointedly ignored. ''They're uncommon independent sorts,'' Lesh said, understating beautifully.

Near sunset, we had to start detouring to find a place to cross one river that did meander through the wilds. It ran in a narrow canyon between steep walls. Even if we could have worked our horses down to the river, the waters was too swift and too deep to ford.

''Comes down off the mountains,'' Lesh said. ''It'll be cold water too.''

We followed the canyon upstream, toward the mountains, looking for a place to cross. We didn't find it that afternoon. We just went on until we found a decent place to camp, in an area of broken rock, boulders the size of houses scattered around.

''Can't sleep just out in the open,'' Lesh said. ''Even if those forest trolls aren't chasing after, there's rock trolls and always the chance of a dragon flying over looking for a feed.''

There was no fuel handy for a fire, so we made do with cold food. Lesh lowered a canvas bucket to the river on a long rope, several times, to water our horses after they cooled off. The water was frigid. I thought about hanging a six-pack of beer down to cool in the river, but decided that we had better save it for a while longer.

The night passed without alarm, and we got an early start in the morning. A couple of hours later we crossed the river and turned east again. There were other rivers, creeks, and dry canyons to cross, but eventually we managed to get over each. We spent a full week riding east like that before our elf finally said that it was time to angle south to the mountains. We were near the pass we needed to use to enter the Titans.

When I first arrived in Varay, all that anyone had to say about the Titans was that they were impassable, unscalable, the southern boundary of the buffer zone, an *absolute* barrier. No one knew how far south they extended or what might lie beyond. No one went there. At least, no one came back. Gradually, I learned that there were qualifications. The Titans weren't simply a blank wall. There were foothills, and then a progressively higher series of mountain ranges, one beyond the other. People did go into the nearer reaches. Some folks lived on the lower slopes of the northernmost mountains. There were a few villages, collections of people with their farms, their sheep and cattle. There were also the mines that produced the metals, precious and common, that Varay and the other kingdoms needed. To the people of the buffer zone, the steel, tin, and copper found in the mountains were as important as the gold and silver. Our precious metals weren't draped with the same mystique in the buffer zone. Gold and silver were used as money, but barter was more common. The standard of exchange was more likely to be weights of corn or wheat than weights of gold or silver. The metals were measured against the grain, not the reverse. Mostly, gold and silver were considered useful for paying Heroes, for occasional trade with the mortal realm, and for decorative purposes. It was local currency only by default, when something more compact than grain was required. That was one of the things about the seven kingdoms that I had the most trouble adapting to.

The Titan Mountains. You could see them from any

prominence in the southern half of Varay, which made it easy to keep your directions straight. There was always a line of white and purple and brown separating sky from ground in the south, though the intersection was often blurred or hidden by clouds or haze. The closer you got to the mountains, the more impressive they became, always reaching into the sky, towering. Until you got so close that the mountains overwhelmed everything else.

As we approached the bulwark, we crossed two ridges in the foothills, then went down a long, deep valley that left us in shadow from midafternoon on. The way led downhill to the base of the first range of the real mountains. I spent so much time looking up toward the peaks that my neck ached. The way ahead of us did seem to be nearly sheer, but I knew that it wasn't.

When we camped for the night, the sky overhead was still bright, but the shadows in our valley made it seem like twilight. The trces in the valley were all stunted, perhaps from the limited sunlight they received. Lesh collected enough wood to keep a decent fire going through the night. We thought it might be quite chilly.

"It'll be worse when we get up into the mountains, and we can't count on being able to run a fire every night, even if there's wood," I reminded him.

"But no sense freezing when we don't have to," Lesh said. Then, " 'Less you think it's too risky."

I thought about it. The idea of a fire made me nervous on general principles, but it didn't cause any recognizable twitching of my danger sense. "We'll try it, tonight at least," I said. We were going to light a fire to heat supper, so we might as well let it burn afterward.

I was glad for the fire when I got up for my second sentry turn a couple of hours before dawn. It might be August, and we might be in the southernmost reaches of Varay, but we had already picked up a couple of thousand feet of altitude, and that night was chilly, maybe even in the low forties. I put several extra branches on the fire and brewed fresh coffee to carry the warmth inside. My danger sense was absolutely quiet. For the moment at least, we were probably safe.

"You know, there's one benefit about coming this way," I told Lesh when we started riding again. "We're far enough south that it's not so bad going on field rations. The food will last that much longer."

Lesh grunted. "I'd still like a good Basil breakfast."

"Well, so would I, but it could be worse."

"And will be soon, like as not," Lesh said. It was an easy prophecy.

But our first days in the Titans were glorious. I quickly wished that I had found time to make the journey when there was no deadly threat hurrying me along. The lower reaches of the mountains were mostly gentle. We rode basically east, but along a curved and climbing path, edging gradually farther south. From one mountain to the next we rode through heather and scrub trees, sometimes through vast fields of wild berries that were ripe and tasted something like strawberries, but not as tart. The path we followed wasn't the best-defined route I had ever seen, but animals both wild and domestic had climbed it. People used it. We found the remains of campfires in several places, ages of fires built in the same premium locations.

The view looking back out of the mountains was even more spectacular than the view coming toward them. All of Varay and Dorthin lay spread out below us, endless miles of green and brown, distant plumes of smoke, more distant fluffs of clouds, blue sky, and sunlight. The sun felt particularly hot on bare skin, but the mountain breeze remained quite comfortable all day. The chain mail and leather padding weren't nearly the burden they had been down in the flatlands.

We couldn't travel very fast even though the path wasn't particularly dangerous, and each afternoon we camped at spots where others had camped before us, many times.

Each day took us higher, farther south, deeper into the mountains. By the third afternoon like that, we had high peaks on both sides and we were riding above a steep-walled valley that might have seemed at home in Switzerland. Where sunlight hit the patches of grass and wild flowers, the colors were brilliant—greens and yellows and golds, fewer blues and reds. Once we saw a shepherd and his sheep, sixty animals or so, on the opposite slope, north of us. On a straight line, they were probably only a quarter mile away, but we would have had to travel at least three miles, most of it on foot and nearly vertical, to get to them. The shepherd watched us carefully but didn't return our greeting.

"We must be almost south of Carsol by now," Lesh said when we made camp that night at our highest point yet. Carsol was the chief city of Dorthin.

"But the mountains aren't part of any kingdom," I said.

"As far as folks normally go, they are," Lesh corrected me. "When we get back into the high parts, then nobody owns them."

"Tomorrow," Xayber's son said. It was a way of getting our attention. "If memory serves, you'll see what real mountains are like then. There'll be a high pass. This path will continue on below it, leaving the narrowest of tracks up to a high pasture. The horses won't be able to go any farther than that. There's grass and water for them there. You'll have to block this end of the pass enough to keep them from wandering over the edge. Then you'll have to walk on to the shrine of the Great Earth Mother."

He certainly had our attention. It was the most information he had ever given out at one time.

"How far do we have to go then?" I asked.

"That depends on how long you can survive up there," the elf said. "Once you go beyond that high pass, the defenders of the shrine will know that you are coming. And none may enter without their permission."

13

The Shrine

"You might have mentioned that before," I said.

"And what good would it have done?" the elf asked, scorn oozing from every word. "Would it have stopped you from making the attempt or merely distracted you at a time when your puny mind could stand no additional distractions?"

"Puny mind?" I challenged. "Whose mind is on the platter and whose is still on his shoulders?" I went on before we could get bogged down in a useless argument. "Who are these defenders, and what can we expect from them?"

"They are the Keepers of the Shrine, beings created by the Great Earth Mother for just that purpose. And for what you can expect, you can expect to lose your lives, your minds, and the very fabric of your souls."

"Which will cheer you no end," I said.

He made a spitting sound, but it was dry. "Though I am dead already, I have more to lose than you ever could."

We were setting up camp in a narrow cave that promised some protection from the wind. The days had been comfortable in the mountains, but the nights were getting colder. With sunset still a half hour off, the temperature was close to freezing and the wind chill made the mountainside feel like Soldier Field on New Year's Day. I couldn't wait to get into thermal underwear. We had packed sets for each of us. But changing into them meant a few moments of really freezing exposure.

"Can you be more specific about what we'll face?" I asked.

"Only in part," the elf said. His cage was resting on a pile of supplies just inside our cave. The wind didn't seem to affect him. At least he said nothing about it and his teeth didn't chatter.

"The defenders will offer whatever measures they believe necessary in order to destroy you. Maybe they will think that their routine precautions are enough. The shrine itself is at the center of a deadly maze—a labyrinth that can't be unraveled by logic or intuition. Acceptable visitors are escorted through by the defenders. And the inside of the shrine is defended by one of the Great Earth Mother's prime eunuchs, and you have yet to see *their* like in any world."

Cheerful sort. "I've been in plenty of her shrines," I said. "None of them had any fancy defenses."

The elf snorted. "This is no hovel thrown together by peasants with shit-stained feet. This is one of the very pillars of creation, erected by the Great Earth Mother herself, bordering on her own realms outside time and space."

I had heard stories about the Great Earth Mother since I first arrived in Varay. Her cult was the only religious or quasi-religious one in the seven kingdoms. Although there was no organized priesthood or dogma, she had shrines in every castle, town, and village, with more scattered around the countryside—like the cave I first entered Varay through. But I had never given the Great Earth Mother any more serious though than I might have given the gods and goddesses of Greek or Norse mythology. Even when all the talk about finding her balls started, I never thought of the Great Earth Mother as a real being. I knew a lot about the buffer zone after three years there, and I had been in Fairy, but it wasn't until that evening in a shallow cave maybe four thousand feet above the plain of Varay that I had a real gut realization that I might be out to plunder the greatest treasures of an immortal being who might actually be a real goddess and the creator of all the universes.

It wasn't a good feeling.

"And if we succeed here, then we have to go through the same thing at the other shrine?" I asked. My voice didn't want to say the words. My voice didn't want to have anything to do with the rest of me.

"Not precisely the same, but the same," the elf said. His voice sounded very satisfied, which didn't make sense if he really believed that he had more to lose than we did.

I stood there for a moment, the outside cold forgotten, the inner chill growing, threatening to freeze me from the inside out. Lesh and Timon had finished unpacking our things and had tethered the horses just outside the cave. There was a wide shelf out there, but we couldn't let the horses wander. The drop beyond was more than five hundred feet. Harkane was sitting at the back of the cave. The others, still solicitous of his wound, wouldn't let him do any of the work. There did seem to be a slight trace of infection in his cut now. The skin along the wound was an angry red, and there was a little seepage of pus. I had been treating it with penicillin and I didn't think that he was in any real danger, but I'm not a doctor, so I was still concerned.

Maybe the mountain cold contributed to the sudden depression I felt. I was twenty-four years old, newly married, a computer specialist who had got lost through an accident of heredity and dumped in an alien world with an impossible job. And I was freezing my butt off in a cave high on a mountain getting ready to challenge the Great Earth Mother on her home turf.

"I'll get a fire going," Lesh said.

He startled me. I was so lost in my brooding that I had lost track of my immediate surroundings. "Good idea," I said when I recovered. "Is there enough fuel around?"

"Plenty of deadwood. These scraggly little trees don't take much killing."

"You need the flashlight?"

"Not all that dark yet, lord," Lesh said.

I turned and looked back out. No, it wasn't that dark yet.

"Something wrong?" Lesh asked softly.

"No, just lost in thought," I said.

It didn't sound very convincing, but Lesh didn't argue the point. He collected the wood, arranged loose rocks to protect his makeshift hearth and hold the heat, then built a small fire inside the mouth of the cave. The breeze going past sucked out enough smoke to keep the cave bearable. We heated our food and ate in silence. Afterward, Lesh and Timon took the flashlight and collected more of the stunted, bent wood so we could burn the fire all night. That helped, and so did the thermal underwear, but we were all still cold.

We didn't reach the track up to the high pass until late the following morning. We had to dismount and lead our horses up a steep, narrow path to reach the higher level. We found a beautiful alpine meadow at something over a mile high. A series of small creeks came down from the ridge on the west side of the pass and combined to flow south and dropped in a waterfall that must look spectacular from below or from the next mountain to the southwest. The grass in the high meadow wasn't too high, but the horses seemed happy to get at it.

"Seems an awful poor spot to leave the horses," Lesh said while we walked the animals across the meadow toward the east side, where the meadow bent upward into another mountainside.

"Looks pretty good to me," I said. "Water, grass."

"Just look around, lord," Lesh said. He made a wide gesture with one arm. "It's so *open.* Dragons could spot them from miles off. We get back, we're like to find naught but a few odd bits of bone and hair."

"There are plenty of caves." I pointed at a couple. That's where we were headed, toward three caves that were close together. "They've got places to hide."

"Horses are too dumb to find caves in a panic," Lesh said. "They see a dragon—or just a big shadow from a cloud—they're like to run off the end and smash themselves to bits."

"Our elf did say we'd have to block the trail," I said after we turned the reins over to Timon and Harkane. Lesh and I walked off away from the others.

"There's plenty of places else they can kill themselves," Lesh insisted. That was true.

"Well, we can't take the horses any farther and we can't afford to leave anyone here to tend them," I said. "I doubt that we could find a better place to leave them than this. We'll show them the caves, bring them inside, let them sniff around. Maybe that'll be enough for them to remember." I paused a moment. "Anyway, as long as one horse survives for each of us, we can all ride back out of here."

"How we gonna tote his high-and-mightiness now?" Lesh asked.

"It'll be awkward, however we do it, but we have to find a way. There's no use finding things wrong now, Lesh. We have to go on one way or another, and we need him with us."

We walked a large circle, looking over the meadow.

"Anyhow, we can't count on anything *he* says for true. He still wants to see you deader'n him."

"But he also wants to get home to his father, head and body, and the only way he can do that is to see us succeed."

"Hah. This could all be a trap for you. Mayhap he thinks the Great Earth Mother will whisk him home, or even set his head back on his shoulders."

"It's a chance we have to take."

"It could be the last chance we'll ever get."

"I didn't say I was thrilled about it, Lesh," I said, maybe with a trace of a sigh.

We spent the rest of the day in the pass and camped there for the night. We kept busy, unloading everything from the horses, putting together the items we needed to carry with us in backpacks, blocking the top of the path to keep the horses from leaving that way, caching the things we weren't taking in one of the caves, and so forth. We had to rest frequently too. The altitude was hard to get used to. Sure, we were only a mile or so above sea level, but that was ten times higher than we were accustomed to. There were no trees in the pass, so we made several treks back down to the lower level to gather wood for our barricade and for a couple of all-night fires—one for that night, one for when we returned. Positive thinking.

Harkane's arm was improving, and he seemed fitter in general. He had little pain and the redness was decreasing. Aspirin and penicillin seemed to be doing the trick. And, if my mother was right, maybe my fierce determination that he recover quickly helped.

That night was even colder than the night before, but our cave was better situated and the fire larger. At dawn we ate our fill for the first time since we left Basil. I thought that it would be easier to carry food in our stomachs than on our backs, and we would likely need that fuel before long. We left the beer sitting in the cave, a lure, a prize awaiting our return.

"I know how packhorses feel now," Lesh moaned when we were loaded up ready to go. We all had heavy packs and long coils of ropes, bunches of rough pitons, and climbing hammers/picks hanging from us in addition to our weapons. There had to be trade-offs or we wouldn't have been able to move, let alone climb. None of us wore armor, and I left my bow, arrows, and the second elf sword behind, making do with only Dragon's Death and my dagger. Harkane and Timon had their bows—traditional longbows that they could carry unstrung—but my fancy double-curved compound bow would be too damn awkward to handle while we climbed.

The elf remained in his birdcage. There was really no option to that. A short cord held the cage to the top of Harkane's pack. We had given Harkane a bit less weight to carry, and he volunteered to carry Xayber's son. Lesh and I were carrying the most weight. We were the biggest, the strongest. Harkane had less, mostly because of his injury. Timon carried the least. He was the lightest and youngest of us, far from full-grown.

"Okay, where do we start?" I asked Xayber's son.

"Southeast end of this pass," he said, so we started in that direction. I took the lead, with Harkane and the elf head just behind me, Timon next, then Lesh. The horses were busy grazing. They didn't pay any attention to our departure.

When mountain climbing first entered my awareness, when I was ten or eleven, my impression was that climbers were always strung out along a sheer rock face, looped together with ropes, scrambling to find minuscule finger and toe holds. Sometime not long after that, I mentioned it to Dad, and the next thing I knew we had two books on climbing techniques. We went through the books together, did a little easy climbing in Kentucky and Tennessee, then spent two weeks one summer—when I was fourteen, I think—out in Colorado at a climbing school. We took the advanced course the following summer. I learned what climbing was really about. Sure, the exciting and dangerous work on rock walls is part of it, but there is a lot more. Working your way across thick scree can be just as dangerous, and there is considerable technical knowledge you need before you have any business getting on a rock wall. And, often, you have to hike for miles on the flat or on deceptively gentle slopes before you even unlimber a climbing rope.

We moved south and east for nearly two full days before we did any of the bits that look so exciting on film. Most of the time we followed ledges that gave us room to walk almost normally. Occasionally, we had to clamber up or down a slope. During those stretches, we roped ourselves together for safety, and to get into the habit, but they really taxed nothing but our endurance and our leg muscles. Walking along a sideslope, or spending hours going up and down those *gentle* rises, can be agony. We all had charley horses from the strain.

Just past midafternoon of our second day on foot, we went into a blind canyon. At the far end, the walls came close enough together to form a chimney, a route up to the next level, a good 150 feet above. The chimney looked fairly easy, but for people with no experience it could be touchy.

"We're going up that?" Lesh asked.

I nodded. "It's easier than it looks, easier than some things we may have to do. I'll go up first with a rope, lower it back down."

"Just tell me what to do, lord. I'll go up first," Lesh said. "It's my place."

"Not this time, Lesh. I know how to do this. I've done it before."

When I was fifteen, I thought that shinnying up a rock chimney, feet on one side, back against the other, was the height of fun and adventure. Strange how it became draining work by the time I was twenty-four. I left my pack at the bottom, carried one rope coiled from shoulder to side, and paid out a second rope while I climbed. Dragon's Death would be in the way going up a chimney, so I had it slung at my side, where it wasn't *quite* as much of a nuisance. I stopped a couple of times to pound pitons into the rock for safety and laced the second rope through each piton. Lesh and Harkane were on the far end of the rope, ready to take up the slack if I lost my footing and fell.

The basic technique for climbing a chimney is simple. You walk up it, using the pressure of your back and shoulders on the other side to replace gravity. Move your feet, straighten up to push your back higher, and repeat as needed. If the walls of the chimney are at a comfortable distance, you can climb quite quickly—until the strain hits your shoulders and calves.

After fifty feet I had slowed considerably. By one hundred feet, I was wondering if I would ever finish. My breaks came more frequently and lasted longer. When my shoulders reached the top, I took a quick glance to make sure that I had somewhere safe to land, then pushed myself out of the chimney onto the flat and just lay there, perhaps for five minutes, before I tried to move. I stretched and rubbed at my legs to ease the aches before I looked back down and waved to let the others know that I was okay. I pounded two pitons into the rock on top to belay the ropes, the one I had strung coming up and the extra one to haul up our packs.

By the time everyone and everything was up—Lesh came up last and retrieved the pitons on the way because we might need them again later—it was time to look for a place to spend the night.

"Sure must not figure on folks coming to this shrine, or they'd make it simpler," Lesh said when he came out of the chimney and caught his breath.

The elf didn't bother to comment.

I was guessing, but I figured that we had to be about two miles up by then, maybe higher. We couldn't find a cave or much cover of any kind, so we had our coldest night yet. There were no trees, so there was no deadwood to make a fire with. We had several cans of Sterno, but that wasn't enough for warmth, just enough to heat water for our coffee and our freeze-dried meals. It was a long night, more than a match for our thermal underwear and the thermal blankets we used to save weight.

Luckily, that was the only night we spent totally in the open. The rest of the time we were able to find some cover, even if it was only a small niche in a rock face, open above and on one side.

Over the next three days we had a number of spots of hard climbing, some as touchy as anything I had ever attempted, like inching up a cliff along a six-inch-wide ledge that climbed at a fifty-degree angle, and a knob that I had to creep around with holds that were nearly imaginary just to set two pitons on the other side so my companions could use rope handholds to make it. Finally, at something approaching three miles up, we had to cross a sloping ice field, hacking out steps and using the primitive crampons Baron Kardeen had found for us. It was my first time on a high ice field, so my climbing experience didn't help much there.

"It's mostly downhill from here," Xayber's son said when we reached the ridge above the ice field.

It might not have been the top of the world, but it felt like it. I felt a giddy exhilaration that could hardly have been greater if I had been on top of Everest, a lightheadedness that was only partly a result of the thin air. We stood on the ridge looking around. There were mountain peaks in every direction. Many of the peaks south of us were clearly much higher than the one we stood on.

"How much farther?" I asked the elf. We were close to the midpoint on the food we had brought along and I hadn't seen any game larger than a squirrel in days.

"To the maze, one more day. After that, who can tell?"

One more day would take us right to the halfway point on our victuals. We might yet be tightening our belts before we got back to our horses and the cache of food we had left behind.

The crest above the ice field was relatively ice-free, so we walked along it, then down it, losing five hundred feet in altitude before we had to leave the ridge. My biggest concern then was carelessness. The slope wasn't extreme and there wasn't much ice on the southeastern side, but the way was steep enough that a bad slip might send any of us tumbling toward a drop so far I couldn't even estimate it.

But we found a dandy cave to sleep in that night, dry and deep enough to get us completely out of the wind. Harkane's arm was healing nicely by then. There was only minor redness about the center of the cut, no soreness, swelling, or seepage.

The altitude was telling on all of us, though. We were tired most of the day, and any stretch that called for real exertion required a long rest afterward. That night, in the cave, I told the others to forget about taking turns as sentries. I made up my bedroll nearest the entrance and decided to trust my danger sense—and perhaps the extra sensitivity of our elf. We all needed the sleep, except for him, and maybe even *including* him. I never asked him if he slept, but he did close his eyes for long stretches of time.

I didn't wake all night. In fact, I didn't wake until more than an hour after the mountain's early dawn. We all slept well and woke moderately refreshed for the last push on to the shrine and its guardians.

When we emerged from the cave, we had a surprise. Snow had fallen during the night and the sky was still overcast. "I know we're awfully high, and we've already crossed ice, but this *is* still August, the height of summer. What are we doing with fresh snow?" I wasn't speaking to anyone in particular, but Xayber's son chose to answer.

"It might be natural, of course. At this altitude, snow is possible any month of the year, but it might also be your first greeting from the defenders of the shrine."

"Or maybe Santa Claus is coming to town early this year," I replied, irritated by the elf's tone. Snow was a nuisancc, but unless we came to some really tricky stretches, it might not be that great a danger.

"Their *first* greeting," the elf said. When I didn't reply, he added, "We are getting close to the maze. Angle down this slope to the east. When we round that next shoulder there, we may be able to see the temple and its maze."

It was closer than I thought.

The next shoulder was more than a mile away, and we had to take the slope very carefully because of the snow, losing another few hundred feet of altitude in the process and all but a dusting of snow. Then we maneuvered around the shoulder—a rock outcropping half the size of Basil Rock—along a path that was nowhere wider than two feet, and some places only half that. The drop at our right increased as we went along, and the earlier slope got precipitous. Before we made it around the hump, the drop at our side looked like several thousand feet straight down.

There was a long, broad valley beyond the rock shoulder, though, a high valley climbing slowly to the east-southeast beyond the end of the chasm at our side. There was a similar drop from the valley side, down to those unfathomable depths, and then a vista almost as inviting as the meadow where we left our horses.

"No snow there," Lesh observed.

There was even lush, healthy grass visible in the nearer half of the valley. Beyond that, everything was rock—slabs of rock like dominoes lying on their edges, or maybe like underfed children's blocks, a dense field of regular stone formations.

"That is the maze," the elf said. "And look beyond if you can."

"Doesn't look like much of a maze to me," Lesh said.

I didn't pay much attention to him. I was up on tiptoe trying to see what lay at the heart of the maze. The elf said that we might be able to see the shrine. There was something large and brilliantly white off in the distance, but not enough of it rose above the gray stones for me to tell anything about its appearance.

"That white?" I asked, glancing at the elf. We moved on a few steps to the end of the narrow ledge around the shoulder, where we had a little more elbow room.

"That white," he agreed. "It is the entablature of the shrine. If you climb a few feet higher on this rock behind us, you should be able to see most of the facade."

I looked at the rock to see if I could get up it without much loss of time or energy.

"We'll see it soon enough," I said. Then I had second thoughts. "But maybe I can get a better idea of the lay of the maze."

The elf laughed. "Little good that will do you. You could map out every twist and turn and it wouldn't help you in the least when you finally got down into the maze."

With that kind of challenge, I had to try. I spent twenty minutes getting ten feet up the wall and finding an anchorage that let me turn my head to look. The maze was complex, much too intricate for me to hope to memorize even a small portion of it from my present perch. But I did have a a slightly better angle on the shrine.

"How far off is that temple?" I called down.

"Straight line, less than three miles," the elf replied. He didn't shout, but I had no trouble hearing him.

I whistled mentally. I had thought it might be a third

of that, half of it at most. At one mile, the shrine looked like a Greek temple. At closer to three miles, it had to be colossal.

"How did anybody manage to build something that big up here?" I asked when I rejoined the others.

"The Great Earth Mother gave birth to it," the elf said.

Any further comment I might have made would only have left my companions as depressed as I felt, so I kept my mouth shut.

14

The Defenders

"You know where we need to enter the maze?" I asked the elf as we started across the green end of the valley. We were lower than we had been while we skirted the rock shoulder, so now we were climbing an easy slope toward the nearest wall of the maze. The temple itself was out of sight.

"Choose as you will, Hero. It makes no difference. Every opening leads to the shrine and none gets there."

"Is there a point to this riddle?" I asked.

"The maze lives, breathes, thinks, moves. It is the first defender of the shrine. It can admit anyone it chooses to admit. And if it doesn't choose to admit you, the only way by is to kill it, and it can't be killed."

"The way you elves can't be killed?" I asked.

"The maze has been there since before the beginning. It is promised that it will remain after the end."

"And if we don't get in there, and back out, the end is upon us, right?" I asked, to remind him of our position. His good cheer was really beginning to annoy me.

"And worlds lost or won!" he boomed. That such volume could come from a mouth with no lungs below it still astounded me. "Think what a tale they'll tell of us in the Netherworld!"

"He's fey," Lesh said.

"He can't be fey, he's already dead," I said. "Despite his feeble boasts, what more can he lose?" I didn't try to keep him from hearing me. "Let's get there," I said, without giving the elf a chance to add another wisecrack. "If I listen to much more of this crap, I'll teach him what soccer is all about." That was for my own benefit. I didn't expect the elf to understand the reference, and apparently he didn't, but Timon got a laugh out of it.

There were tiny white flowers scattered throughout the

grassy part of the valley. In some places, the flowers were so thick that there was hardly room for the grass. I knelt down in one patch and pulled a flower on a four-inch stem. I couldn't smell any scent from the flower, but I slipped it into a buttonhole on my jacket. I was going to have *something* to show for this trek.

My danger sense had been relatively quiet until we rounded that rock shoulder and I got a good look at the shrine. It started doing a tarantella as we started moving toward the maze. Then the feeling built. I tried to deal with the concept of a field of rocks being a living creature and failed absolutely. Our elf was not being allegorical. The way he spoke, I was certain that he believed what he said, that the maze was a living defender of the shrine. The *first* defender.

"Where's its brain? Where's its heart?" Lesh asked, almost shouting at the head just in front of him.

"Wherever it chooses to be," the elf replied.

"If you want to hold any hope of getting home to your father, you'd better come up with something better than useless riddles and inane patter," I said. "If that's all you can provide, we might as well dig a hole and bury you here, save ourselves the bother of toting you around and listening to the sound pollution you spout."

He hesitated a moment before he answered. That was promising, even if his words weren't.

"I can't give you hope that doesn't exist," he said. "If you find your way through the maze, it will only be because another defender feels confident of destroying you later. I can only sense faint hints of their minds, but they have their politics, like all sentient gatherings."

I reciprocated by taking my own time considering what he said before I spoke again.

"Can you guide us through the maze?"

"For what good it may do," he said. "I can sense the proper course to take at any specific moment. An elf can't be lost. But the maze *can* shift, and any correct choices can be made incorrect at its whim."

I thought of one possible loophole, but I didn't say anything, just in case the maze had good hearing. If it could read minds, we were out of luck anyway.

A mile isn't far to walk on a sunny day, even if you're loaded down with a heavy pack and a heavier heart. But not all miles are equal. We got to the top of the slope, and it looked as if we had a mile to go to the beginning of the maze. But that last mile was extraordinary. After ten minutes of level and then slightly downhill walking, we were still just as far away and the rock we had started from appeared to be a mile behind us.

I stopped walking. My danger sense had been getting progressively more agitated about what I would expect as I covered the distance separating me from a threat. But my eyes were telling me that the enemy, the wall, was no closer. The easy guess was that my eyes were wrong.

"What is it?" Lesh asked.

I told him. He looked at the wall of the maze, then back to where we had started. Timon and Harkane went through the same motions. Harkane's movements gave the elf his chance to judge the distances too.

"You realize, of course, that we are almost on top of the maze," the elf said.

"I figured that out," I said. "That's why I stopped. But my eyes don't agree, so I have to try something else."

There weren't a lot of options popping into my head. All I could think of was *If my eyes are lying, I've got to try it without them.* I drew Dragon's Death and closed my eyes while I started pacing forward carefully, sliding one foot in front of the other.

"Stay close to me," I warned the others. I took only five steps before my blade encountered stone. I opened my eyes and the outer wall of the maze was right there.

"How did you do that?" Lesh asked.

"What did it look like to you?" I asked.

"It looked like the maze came tearing straight at us and ran itself right into your sword."

"I'm impressed," Xayber's son said. "I would have thought that you would need much longer to think of that."

"Maybe if you hadn't been so quick to assume that our minds are puny, you wouldn't be in the position you are," I said quietly—trying to avoid making it sound like an insult. The insult was there, of course, I simply wasn't trying to emphasize it at the moment.

There were two openings into the maze about equally distant from where were. I mentally flipped a coin and headed for the entrance to our right. I kept my left hand on the outer wall of the maze to make sure that it didn't zoom off on us again. The wall *was* stone, cold, hard, and smooth. I didn't feel any throbbing pulse, any rise and fall of breathing lungs. I still couldn't conceive that it might actually be alive.

"Stay close together," I said before we entered the maze. "Keep a hand on the back of the man in front of you. Grab a strap or something. If this maze *can* shift, I don't want to let it separate us."

We were near the center of the north wall. Our straight-line distance to the shrine couldn't be more than a mile and a half, not that straight-line distances would mean much in a maze. My danger sense clanged like a fire alarm at the entrance, then settled down to something bearable, leaving itself room to signal a panic if the occasion arose. I hesitated for a long time at the start of the maze, trying to feel something of this *creature* we were about to enter, to violate. I even tried communicating with it, tried to project a thought ahead of us.

Why don't we make this simple? Make it easy. I'm already suitably impressed.

I didn't hear any replies.

One foot in front of the other. Shuffle off to Buffalo. Or someplace. Put your left foot in. Put your left foot out. Walk the line. There was no static, no resistance, no fireworks as we entered. I walked straight ahead along the first passage, staying close to the wall on my left, touching it, dragging my hand lightly along the rock about half of the time. Whenever we came to a choice of paths, I let the elf decide which way we should go. He might have been leading us in circles, or into any number of traps, but I *thought* that he was doing his best to keep his end of the bargain. True, he had damn little to gain by helping us if our mission was as hopeless as he claimed, but he had absolutely nothing to gain by betrayal. As long as he was intelligent and rational enough to figure that out, I didn't think that we had to worry about betrayal. But how rational can you stay when all you have left is your head in a birdcage?

The walls of the maze and the ground beneath our feet were a uniform slate gray. The walls were fourteen feet high and the passage seven feet wide. Negotiating a static maze like that, against a stopwatch perhaps, would have been a stimulating challenge as a game or intellectual exercise. The chance that the maze was alive, able to shift its configuration at will, and possibly able to throw more deadly obstacles in our path, made it much, much more. The tension I felt was maddening, waiting for something—*anything*—to happen. But the maze remained passive, quiescent. I wasn't sure what to expect—sudden trapdoors to deep pits, armed and hideous-looking creatures, extremes of one sort or another—*active* defenses certainly, not just boredom and the drain of nervous anticipation. For two hours there were no sounds but our boots scraping stone and the elf's terse directions—left, right, or straight ahead; second left, third right, when several passages appeared close together. Then we turned one corner, and a second, immediately, and the elf said to stop.

"The pattern has changed," he announced. "We have to backtrack."

I almost asked how far back we would have to go, but didn't.

"Which way is it to the shrine from here?" I asked instead. "Direct course."

The elf thought about it for a second, then said, "To your right." I pointed and he said, "Just a little more this way." I adjusted my aim and he said, "Precisely."

"Plan B," I announced, though I had never said anything about alternative plans. This was the possibility that had popped into my head before we reached the maze.

"Don't say anything, not one word," I warned my companions, though I had no real cause to believe that silence would provide any measure of surprise.

I took a rope from the side of Lesh's pack and a grapple from Harkane's. I attached the grapple, paid out forty feet of rope, then had the others each take hold of the line farther back, all without saying a word. It was going to be tricky doing this in a seven-foot-wide passage, but I coiled the rope at my feet and started to swing the grapple around my head, building up momentum. Finally, I launched the grapple over the wall in the direction of the shrine. The hooks clanged softly on the other side, and held when I drew back on the rope.

"Quickly!" I said, and pulled myself up the rope first. When I reached the top, I crossed to the middle of the seven-foot-thick structure and stood on the rope to make sure that the hooks didn't pull out while the others climbed—Timon first, Harkane with the elf, then Lesh. I had one hand on my elf sword, but no opponents appeared to challenge us.

I coiled the rope and slipped it over my shoulder, ready for the next time. We were closer to the shrine than I would have guessed, about two-thirds of the way across the maze, and we were able to gain another fifty yards moving on top of the labyrinth before we had to climb down again.

"When the deck's stacked against you, cheat," I told the elf. I was feeling pretty smart just then.

That was before the wall fell over on us.

My danger sense gave me just enough warning to scream "Down!" and to drop to the ground myself. It was lucky that we had stayed in the habit of remaining next to a wall at all times. The wall that fell hit the wall next to us but didn't shatter. We were able to run to the next intersection, past the fallen section of wall, before it folded in and collapsed completely.

I looked back. The wall had not broken. There wasn't even a crack at either end of the fifty-foot-long collapsed section. The wall had simply warped at each end, then folded lengthwise to cover the passage we had been in.

We moved on, turning left, right, then left again.

"This way to the shrine?" I asked the elf, pointing. I was trying to keep track of directions, but I wasn't positive.

"That way," Xayber's son agreed.

I got the rope with the grappling hook set to throw again. I didn't know if the same trick would work twice, but I was going to try. There was an intersection behind us, so I had more space to stretch and swing the hook. It didn't catch the first time, but it did the second. I gave the rope a tug . . . and pulled the wall over. Halfway. It rested against the side of the opposite wall. We backed off and waited to see if this section would collapse the way the first had, but it didn't. And the grapple held, so we climbed to the top and moved along the canted section to where the wall remained upright and level.

When we had level rock under our feet again, we were very nearly at the inner limit of the maze. There was one more passageway, and one more wall, between us and the temple yard. And I could see an exit in the final wall, not twenty yards to our left.

"Let's try for it," I said. We scrambled down from the wall and ran for the opening, still linked together. I expected the opening to close in our faces, but it didn't. We got through and ran on far enough that a maze wall couldn't fall on us from behind.

Then we stopped to catch our breath before the next threat, whatever it might be, turned up.

The temple yard, hundreds of acres, had carefully manicured grass, a number of rock-bounded formal gardens full of blooming flowers in a dozen colors, and many wandering pathways of gravel that was a brilliant snowy white. A hundred and fifty yards away, more or less, the shrine of the Great Earth Mother rose more than a hundred feet high, gleaming white marble without visible seams, almost blindingly reflective in the sunlight. The columns along the facade were merely half-columns attached to the main wall rather than freestanding pillars, but the effect was still reminiscent of an ancient Greek temple. Gold double doors in the middle of the wall we were facing provided the only hint of color against the white.

"The shrine of the Great Earth Mother," the elf announced in deep, important-sounding tones.

I fought back an almost irresistible compulsion to go down on one knee to bow my head toward the shrine. Lesh also stayed on his feet, but both Harkane and Timon went down.

"Get up," I told them quietly, and they did, but they didn't take their eyes off of the shrine.

"The jewel will be inside?" I asked Xayber's son.

"The right one," he said. "Inside, in the shrine's most secret recess. I can feel its pull now."

The double doors swung open without any evidence of anyone touching them. Twelve soldiers marched out in double ranks. They wore leather skirts and gold chestplates and helmets, outfits that looked Roman in design.

Short swords hung at their sides, and each soldier carried a spear taller than he was.

"More defenders?" I asked quietly.

"I don't think so," the elf said. "These are merely their tools, created for the moment. Disposable."

"Then let's dispose of them," I said. "Don't drop your packs until we get close, though. Our supplies might disappear."

"And be careful of me," the elf said. "I may be able to help you if I can see what's going on."

Harkane looked to me, and I nodded. "Set him down so he can watch the fight when it starts," I said.

The odds weren't really twelve to four. Timon and Harkane together were about as effective as one fully trained, moderately experienced soldier. They worked well as a team, though, Harkane taking the brunt of any attack, Timon covering his back, making up for Harkane's youth with his own. But even if you viewed the odds as twelve to three, or twelve to three and a half, you wouldn't be right. The Hero of Varay isn't just some big dumb sucker who has to do everything just with muscle. I'm not that damn big to start with, and I hope I'm not that dumb. But the Hero of Varay is, according to the advertising, invested with a certain magic that comes down from the first of the line, Vara. And the elf sword I inherited on the Isthmus of Xayber after I killed my first dragon also possessed its own potent magic. If the soldiers marching out to meet us had been everyday mortal soldiers, the odds would clearly have been heavily against them. But they weren't common mortal grunts, and I didn't know how to figure in whatever magic the defenders of the shrine gave them. Of course, I have trouble handicapping a horse race too, and after growing up in Kentucky, not much more than a couple of stone throws from Churchill Downs, I find that embarrassing.

Harkane and Timon started using their bows when the soldiers were eighty yards away. Scratch two pseudo-legionnaires, one with an arrow through his throat, the other with a kneecap messed up. The other ten started running silently toward us.

"Let them do the running," I said softly. I drew Dragon's Death, and the sword song started to work its way past my lips. We slid our packs off and got ready to meet the attack. Harkane set the elf down, facing the right way to watch the fight.

Harkane and Timon had swords, good weapons forged of low-carbon steel back in my world. I had Dragon's Death. Lesh used a short sword in his left hand, mostly as a defensive weapon, and swung a battle-axe with his right. Although Lesh had to be closer to fifty than forty, he had stayed in top fighting condition. He didn't tire easily, and he was *good* with his weapons, experienced and cool.

Behind us, Xayber's son started a chant that wasn't quite his sword song. I couldn't tell what conjuring he was doing, but I hoped it would work.

There was nothing extraordinary about the mechanics of the fight. The spears the guards carried were wood. They couldn't stand up to sword or battle-axe. And their swords were shorter than ours, and not just shorter than my claymore. Their body armor wasn't enough to make up for the deficiencies of their weapons. They all went down, most terminally.

We retrieved our packs and went on to the shrine's entrance.

"What's next? This eunuch you were talking about?" I asked our elf.

"Perhaps," he replied, "or there may be other surprises. The building may have its own traps for unwelcome visitors."

The golden doors had remained open, so we didn't have to worry about picking locks or breaking the doors down. We walked right in and stopped just inside.

The inside of the shrine was brightly lit even though there were neither lamps nor skylights—no apparent source for the illumination. Columns ran along all four sides of the hall, different kinds of columns—round, square, fluted, smooth—setting off the outer portion of the building as a series of aisles, like the side sections of a cathedral. The central part of the shrine was one immense chamber, at least sixty feet high, one hundred and twenty wide, and maybe three hundred long . . . the size of a football field. The ceiling was a complex vault, but there were no central pillars to support that expanse. It was impressive.

"You could get a Super Bowl crowd in here," I mumbled, more to myself than to my companions. I cleared my throat, then asked, "Where's the jewel?" louder.

"Below us," the elf said. "It's in a basement or vault, something of that nature."

"You have any idea where the stairs are?" I asked, hoping that there *were* stairs. We weren't equipped to mine our way through a marble floor.

Xayber's son closed his eyes and took what seemed to be quite a time considering that. When he opened his eyes, he said, "It feels like there are several passages to the lower levels, but I can't tell which leads to the repository. In here, the magic of the defenders is much stronger than my own."

"Another maze?"

"In effect." If he still had shoulders under his head, I'm sure he would have shrugged them.

"Booby traps or just blind alleys?" I don't know how the translation magic rendered those terms in the elf's language, but he didn't hesitate.

"I can't tell. There is danger everywhere within these walls."

I already knew *that* much.

It was time for another mental coin flip. We went left, clockwise, staying out in the aisle area that girded the huge central chamber. There were echoes, and echoes of echoes, as we walked. Whenever a blade scraped against wall or column, the clang seemed magnified in the distance. It wouldn't take a supernatural talent to know that we were there. There were a lot of doorways off to the side. Most led to small side rooms. Some led to stairways, up or down, most of them up. The side rooms weren't nearly as high as the aisles or the central chamber. The building was a rectangular block on the outside, so there was a lot of room above us on the sides, maybe as many as eight or ten floors' worth.

We checked eight doors before we found the first stairway leading down. The stairway was as brightly lit as the rest of the shrine, still without any visible source. We went down forty-three steps before we reached the bottom, and three more doors. Xayber's son didn't have any certain feelings about which, if any, of the doors might lead us to the jewel, so I started with the right-hand door. It led to more stairs, down another thirty steps.

"It's above us now," the elf said when we reached the bottom. "Unless there's another stairway, or a ramp, leading up, this is the wrong way."

There was a long corridor at the bottom, with a number of doors on either side. We opened each door. Some led to sleeping rooms—no beds, but with cushions and blankets on the floors. There were other rooms that seemed intended for people to spend waking time in. The corridor had a blind end, maybe halfway across the shrine, so we retraced our steps, went back up the lower flight of stairs, and tried the middle door. There was just a single room leading off of it, as bare as could be. Xayber's son said that the jewel couldn't be in there. It still felt too far away.

When we tried the third door, my danger sense went off the scale, completely berserk, and I couldn't see the threat. Neither could the elf.

"The jewel isn't in there," he said. "I am certain of that."

That was a relief. And no, I didn't have the slightest urge to go in and find out what the terrible danger in that room was. I may be a certified Hero, but I am not a certified idiot.

We went back up to the main level and continued our circuit. A little farther on, we found another stairway leading down and took it. This one turned out to be as fruitless as the first. All we did was lose time.

On the way back up those stairs, Xayber's son shouted, "Stop!"

We stopped and waited for his explanation, looking around, weapons out, ready to meet any threat.

"The jewel has moved," the elf said. "It is above us now, on the main level of the shrine."

"Someone has moved it, you mean," I said.

"It can only be a defender, the Great Earth Mother's eunuch," the elf said.

"Found hisself one ball, has he?" Lesh said, trying to make a joke. Nobody laughed.

We got back to the main level and moved toward the large central chamber. As I moved around one column, I saw the defender standing in the middle of the room, with all that elbow room around and above him.

The Great Earth Mother's eunuch needed all the room

he could get. He was one big sucker, twelve feet tall and six times my weight—at least. He had a sword in each hand that made my claymore look like a toothpick. A gold chain hung around his neck with a brilliant ruby hanging from that.

"The ruby is the right ball of the Great Earth Mother," the elf said.

"That figures," I mumbled.

"All you have to do is take it off his dead body."

"I thought he was immortal," I said, sliding off my pack and drawing my sword again, while my companions made their own preparations.

"As far as I know," Xayber's son said, "he is."

15

The Magnet

I could hardly avoid the thought: *One of these days I'm going to run into an immortal who really is, and I'll be up shit creek when I do.* Elves were supposed to be immortal, but I had watched one die after a run-in with a dragon and I had lopped the head off of another elf—who might or might not actually be dead, depending on your definition; he was certainly talkative enough yet. Dragons were also supposed to be immortal. At least, they were allegedly unkillable by mortals. But I had finished off the one who killed the elf warrior, then another one that had been imported by the Dorthini wizard to do me in. Neither immortality was absolute, and if that seems to stretch the definition, I can't help it. Fairy and the buffer zone run by their own mutable rules of logic and semantics.

The big eunuch waiting for me was supposed to be immortal. Maybe he was no more immortal than dragons or elves, but after all, the eunuch was alleged to be a special creation of the Great Earth Mother, engineered specifically to safeguard one of her two most prized possessions.

He was naked but for the swords in his hands and the ruby hanging on his chest. He was totally hairless and had skin that was almost pumpkin orange. Twelve feet tall, he had to weigh more than a half ton, and very little of it looked like fat. His legs were the size of my torso. He had been very thoroughly emasculated. Not only had his testicles and scrotum been removed, he had been left with only a tiny stub of a penis. He was made eunuch, not born that way. The scars were obvious and a vivid red. His breasts were enlarged, his eyes nearly an albino pink. He looked angry. I bet he was that way all the time.

I took a couple of steps out into the center of the shrine,

but I wasn't ready to get far from the pillars. I didn't want to have too far to run when I needed cover. Lesh was off to my left, far enough away that we wouldn't get our weapons tangled, close enough that we could both engage the eunuch at once. Harkane and Timon were behind neighboring pillars, twenty feet apart, arrows notched to bows, waiting for a signal from me before they did anything hostile.

I tugged on my Cubs cap to make sure it was seated firmly.

"You don't belong here," the eunuch boomed. Castration certainly hadn't turned him into a soprano—or maybe that *was* the soprano range of someone his size.

"How do you know I don't belong here?" I asked, willing to delay the fight as long as possible. But the eunuch was in no mood for games.

"What name should I carve on your tombstone?" he demanded.

"If you don't know who I am, then you won't need my name. And I'm not about to waste a week burying you, so I don't even care to hear your name—if you have any idea what it is."

"It is Baddassus who will kill you!" he shouted, and I started laughing my head off and couldn't control the fit.

The eunuch roared and started whirling his sword even faster—like a *Saturday Night Live* parody of one of those Japanese chefs who work in front of their customers with twirling carving knives.

"They call *you* Bad Ass?" I asked when my laughter finally ebbed. "Someone has a terrific sense of humor."

"I'll show you humor. How dare you mock my name!"

Very softly, I whispered, "Timon, eyes and throat. Harkane, try for his heart or a major artery, maybe the ones on the insides of his thighs."

Back with our packs, Xayber's son started chanting up a spell.

The fight started.

Lesh and I moved farther away from the pillars as Baddassus lumbered slowly toward us. To keep a sword extended toward each of us, he had to expose his whole front to Harkane and Timon, and they started pumping arrows into him as quickly as they could. The shafts didn't seem to do much damage—a few minor, short-lived spurts of blood appeared and dried up, and each seemed to infuriate the giant eunuch that much more. He brushed at the arrows, breaking them off, then he roared again and advanced toward the pillars at the side of the shrine's main expanse.

I moved to get in his way, and he swung one of his swords at my head. I ducked, but his aim was high anyway, and the blade bit into the marble column as if it were a rotten tree. While he was freeing that sword, and while Lesh kept his other sword busy, I ducked in to get a shot at his tree-trunk legs. My mouth was pumping out the sword song full blast as I hacked at the back of the eunuch's left knee—which seemed only slightly narrower than the columns holding up the ceiling.

For all the good I did, I might as well have been trying to cut down a tornado with a butter knife. My blade bit into the eunuch's leg, but not deeply. I certainly didn't come close to amputating the leg, and that had been my intention. Dragon's Death had the sharpest, strongest blade I had ever seen, and I had put every ounce of my strength into the swing. It *should* have been enough. That blow would have cut through a foot-thick tree trunk.

The eunuch jerked his sword free of the marble and brought it down toward my head. I twisted out of the way and feinted toward his groin.

Baddassus brought both of his swords around to block my blade. His reflex gave Lesh an opening to move in and chop at the back of the eunuch's knee with his battle axe, the same knee I had attacked.

"Harkane, give him a stick to piss up," I yelled, circling to force the eunuch to turn.

Harkane's arrow found the eunuch's groin. The eunuch screamed and doubled over to jerk out the arrow. That gave Lesh and me each one hack at the back of Baddassus's knee, one slice from each side. There was blood and a wicked gash visible, but it didn't slow the eunuch at all. The muscles had to be tougher than spring steel. He started spinning, screeching a war chant, and twirled his swords at blinding speed. There was no way any of us could meet him steel to steel. His blades would either snap our weapons or knock them out of our grasp.

Suddenly, without warning, the eunuch dropped one sword and grabbed at his groin. He bent over to look at himself, astonishment appearing on his face.

"Hurry," Xayber's son said. "I can't hold this magic for long."

Lesh raised his axe and hacked at the side of Baddassus's suddenly reachable neck. It was a blow that would have severed any other head, but even though the axe blade bit deeply into the neck, Baddassus hardly seemed to notice. I drove the point of Dragon's Death into the eunuch's armpit, and he dropped the other sword. But he didn't move to defend himself. He didn't turn on either Lesh or me. Instead, he grabbed at his groin with both hands—not in pain, but with surprise. The look on his face was impossible to read. Harkane came out from behind his pillar and drove an arrow through the eunuch's left temple at close range. Baddassus fell forward then and seemed to shake the entire shrine when he hit the floor.

The next swing of Lesh's axe finally cut the eunuch's spinal cord. While he finished hacking head from neck, I retrieved the chain and the ruby. I hung the chain around my own neck to get it out of the way . . . after I cleaned off the blood.

"What did you do?" I asked the elf while Lesh finished removing the eunuch's head and booted it away from the body.

Xayber's son had closed his eyes to avoid watching the final stages of the decapitation, an understandable aversion. I turned the pack under his cage and he opened his eyes again.

"I gave him the one thing he always wanted but could never have," he said, "an erection. How else would you deal with an immortal eunuch."

"Lesh, leave off," I called. "Let's get out of here." Lesh had turned his battle-axe against the body of the giant.

We hurried to get into our packs and jogged to the gold doors. I heard a mighty moan and turned to look. The eunuch's body was getting to its feet—up on one knee, then all the way up. Both hands were jerking the air in front of his groin. The head on the floor rolled over so it could watch. The head sighed in what sounded like great relief as the body spasmed and trembled in the eunuch's first orgasm. Then the eunuch got down on his knees and started crawling toward his head. We didn't wait to see if he would make it.

Outside, we had to fight the same dozen soldiers again. They had risen—wounds still gaping but not bleeding—and formed ranks to meet us. Just the sight of them was more than I wanted to face just then. The open, bloodless wounds reminded me of the appearance of the Congregation of Heroes in the crypt below Basil. That was just how I saw them in the unnerving dream/vision/nightmare that I experienced before the Battle of Thyme.

But I had to face these soldiers. Once more we fought. Once more we had to kill all twelve of the shrine's legionnaires, because not one of them thought to surrender or run. If they could keep rising from the dead, they had no incentive to quit. My companions and I lost too much time in the fight. As we finished off the last of the soldiers for the second time, the gold doors opened and the eunuch charged out, roaring his rage. His head was firmly, if not tidily, back on his shoulders again; there were bits hanging out that shouldn't have. He had swords in both hands. His tiny stub was dripping.

We ran for the maze. This time we didn't waste time trying to beat the maze by the "rules." We followed passages when they were convenient, but stayed up top as much as possible. We lost ground to the pursuing Baddassus every time we had to go down into the maze to cross a passageway.

But the eunuch wasn't very fast on his feet. At his size, every step had to send shock waves through his entire body, especially at any kind of speed. And he kept stopping to look down at himself, to touch his stub. His preoccupation gave us time to get clear of the maze and to start running for the narrow ledge around that rock shoulder at the end of the shrine's high valley. There was no way that the eunuch could get his bulk around that. But we hurried on quite a bit farther before we stopped to rest.

It wasn't until we were out of the reach of Baddassus and had time to quench our thirst and share a quick meal that I took off the prize hanging around my neck to examine it. The gold chain weighed about four pounds, and the pretzel-sized links were soft enough to make me think they might be very nearly pure gold. The ruby was translucent, brilliant against the light, and about the size of a pecan, held by a gold band and linked to the chain—a smooth ruby nut.

"You're sure this is what we came for?" I asked Xayber's son.

"I'm certain. You hold the right testicle of the Great Earth Mother in your hand."

A relic after all, not the real thing, I thought. It was a relief . . . and also something of a disappointment.

"One down, one to go," I said.

"Don't count your balls too soon," the elf said.

That's an easy kind of thing to say when you're in a spot like ours. And three hours later, we had a dragon after us.

We did luck out on timing. We had just found a cave and decided to camp for the night. The dragon came over the next peak and dove straight for us. For me: that's how it felt. We got into the cave and sat with our blades toward the entrance while the dragon took its time figuring out that there was no way it could reach us. I made thankful noises about real dragons not being able to breathe fire the way fairy-tale ones do. That cave wasn't deep enough to get us away from much more than a pocket lighter's flame.

At least the dragon didn't camp on our doorstep, so we did get some sleep. The next morning, we made a couple of hours on the trail before the dragon returned. I assumed that it was the same one, though I couldn't be positive. Dragons aren't exactly common, even in the buffer zone, and none had bothered us all the way out to the shrine.

This time we were working our way through a narrow crevasse and we stayed put until the dragon gave up and flew on. But that dragon, or a different one, was back before sunset. This time we were out in the open with no place to hide. I didn't have much room to swing my sword, either. The shelf we were edging along was only about thirty inches wide, with a wall behind us and a sheer drop in front.

It was not a good place to be. I had Dragon's Death

out, but all I could hope to do was fend the dragon off for a short time. It dove at us, then had to pull to one side or the other. At least it couldn't hover, and there was no room for it to perch on the ledge with us or really use the advantage of its claws and teeth.

"Can you make this beast think we're a bigger dragon that it is or something?" I asked Xayber's son.

"I can try," he said, not bothering with a wisecrack for a change.

The dragon tried flying parallel to the shelf, trying to beat at us with the end of a wing. But it kept pulling the wing away from Dragon's Death, so that tactic didn't work for it either. It made a couple more passes, trying to figure out some way to get its claws into play, then it suddenly veered off, pulling for the sky with all the strength it could get into its wings. I guess our elf scored an ace.

"How long is that bastard going to dog us?" I asked when we finally got camped in a tight little cave. No one had an answer, and the cat-and-mouse game continued, day after day.

Dodging the dragon slowed our progress. Sometimes it would keep us penned up for hours before it flew off. Our food ran out, and in the buffer zone, even as far south as we were, that is almost as immediate a crisis as a dragon. But we still couldn't hurry. We didn't dare try the most exposed of the tricky stretches until we were certain that the dragon wasn't close. We had gone two and a half days without eating, and another three days on extremely short rations, before we finally got back to the valley where we had left our horses and the rest of our supplies.

The dragon found us again just as we reached the high pasture and were looking forward to a badly needed meal.

"I guess we have to deal with it," I said, resigned to the attempt. I don't care how many dragons I had faced before, or how many I might face in the future, I don't think a time could ever come when I would look forward to it. When you play in that league, you only get one loss. Even Roman gladiators had a shot for a thumbs-up reprieve when they lost if they put on a good show.

My companions knew the drill. We dropped our packs and spread out. The dragon circled low once, then climbed and came in for the attack. This dragon wasn't nearly as huge as the behemoth that the Etevar's wizard had summoned. This one might not even have been quite as large as the one I had finished off for the elf warrior on the beach up on the Isthmus of Xayber.

But it was big enough.

Timon and Harkane used all of their remaining arrows on the beast. Lesh and I had at it with our blades. Maybe hunger sapped some of our strength, but it didn't lessen our determination. I was almost hungry enough to rip off a drumstick for lunch.

The dragon aimed for me on each pass, which was no surprise. I would move to one side or the other and swing Dragon's Death. When the dragon turned its head to come at me, Lesh would dash close to plant the blade of his axe in whatever patch of dragon hide he could reach, then pull the blade free and get out of the way. It was slow going. I was reluctant to take the gamble that I had taken with the dragon at Castle Thyme—the maneuver that had cost the elf warrior in Xayber his life. The idea was to get the dragon used to its foe jumping to one side or the other at the last instant, then to stand still and swing the blade straight into the dragon's snout, let its momentum rip its head open enough to make it vulnerable to the only stroke that could kill it, a deep lunge through an eye, aimed at the tiny brain in the middle of the back of the head.

The elf warrior in Fairy had died bringing down his dragon. I had come close to the same fate when I tried it at Castle Thyme. The same kind of injuries now, up in the mountains, days from help, would certainly be fatal. Parthet wasn't close to keep me going with his magic until the healing magic of the Hero could take over.

My companions and I were also in no condition for a marathon battle. As easy as Dragon's Death was to wield, I couldn't do it forever after two and a half days without food.

"We've got to try something different," I shouted as the dragon was coming in for another pass. "Go for the wings."

Lesh only hesitated for an instant before he nodded.

This time, I didn't try to swing at the dragon's head.

Instead, I ran the other way and ripped Dragon's Death through the membranes of its wing, holding the blade up and letting the dragon rip its own hide. On the other side, Lesh was doing the same thing, though I couldn't see him doing it. There was too much dragon between us. The dragon pulled up then, trying to get altitude again. The skin of its wings continued to tear. It started to pull up, then fell, got a little air under its wings, and banked around.

But it couldn't stay in the air.

The dragon came back down so fast, so completely out of control, that the collision was headfirst and it ended up on its back. Before it could recover, or even start to flop over, I ran up to the head and drove Dragon's Death into the nearest eye—at a convenient height for a change.

When it was over, we collected our horses and went to the cave where we had stashed our equipment and supplies. Only one of our horses was missing. That was better than I expected, and we had eaten enough of our food that the other animals wouldn't be overly burdened when we left the high pasture—the next morning, after two good meals and one full night of sleep.

Once we had horses under us and an easier trail, we all felt better, less tense. Half of our quest was finished, and we knew that it *was* possible to get into one of the Great Earth Mother's special shrines, nab a jewel, and get out. It *could* be done.

We were back on the flat, not more than three hours south of Thyme, before the next dragon started to pick on us. It just circled high overhead like a buzzard, keeping pace with us but not diving to the attack. It made us nervous, and nearly panicked the horses, but there was nothing we could do as long as the dragon stayed in the air. I hadn't packed any surface-to-air missiles.

We kept riding, and we kept looking over our shoulders.

"That is no ordinary dragon," Xayber's son said after the creature had followed us for more than a hour.

"Tell me something I couldn't guess," I said. Dragons that attacked you on sight were ordinary. Dragons that flew on by without a second glance were ordinary. A dragon that waged a war of nerves was *not* ordinary.

"Very well," the elf said. "it *may* not be a dragon at all—but notice the stress on the auxiliary verb."

"Okay, stress noted. But if it's not a dragon, what is it—Dumbo?"

"I'm not familiar with the reference, but don't bother to explain. I'm sure I'm not interested. I simply meant that it might be one of the defenders of the shrine waiting to reclaim that which you wear around your neck. It is even conceivable that it is the Great Earth Mother herself, in disguise, waiting to decide how best to deal with, uh, *our* effrontery."

"Do you consider either possibility likely?" I asked, watching the circling dragon as I spoke.

"The first, perhaps. The second, probably not. They are merely off-chances to consider."

"Long shots," I said. "Consider them considered. And I'm getting a sore neck from it all." It wasn't my intention, but that comment shut the elf up. He was sensitive to talk about necks, sore or not.

"Folks at Thyme won't be happy at us bringing a dragon by," Lesh said. "They think they got troubles enough, I'd guess."

"You know anyone who *doesn't* think he has troubles enough?" I asked.

"I reckon not, lord," Lesh admitted.

"We can't do anything about this dragon, or whatever it is, as long as it stays up where it is. And, quite honestly, I hope it does keep its distance. I've already bagged my lifetime quota."

I was wearing the gold chain and ruby under my chain mail, and it was uncomfortable, a constant irritant like a pebble in a shoe. But even if the jewel was only a precious stone and not really what it was cracked up to be, I would have put up with the discomfort. A ruby that size had to be worth a fortune. I didn't want to put it in a pack or pocket, afraid that I might somehow manage to lose it.

"We'll be in and out of Thyme quickly," I said a few minutes later. "That should end the matter. Once the dragon loses track of us at the passage, it should lose interest in Thyme." It sounded like a good thing to say. If the thing was something other than a dragon, it might even work that way.

I was looking forward to getting home and unwinding for a few days before we started out to steal the other jewel of the Great Earth Mother. Since we got out of the mountains and back on the plain of Varay, I had thought of little else but spending a little time with Joy. I knew it wouldn't be much time, but I wanted to savor however many hours or days we might have before I had to leave again.

But the dragon overhead kept me from fully enjoying my thoughts of Joy. It was great that the dragon wasn't attacking, but it also posed a continuing threat. For all the elf's theorizing, it might be a real dragon. Why it might be following us the way it was, I couldn't explain, and I couldn't be certain that it would head back to its normal haunts when we disappeared through the passageway from Thyme. It might savage the village, even the castle. But on the other hand, if we stayed on the road and took the long way back to Basil, it might savage Basil Town. I couldn't tell what it might do and I couldn't do anything about it in any case. We could only do what we had originally planned to do, go to Castle Thyme, take the passage through to Basil Town, and climb the rock to the castle . . . regardless of what the dragon *might* do. I couldn't fight it if it didn't come down, and if it came down after I left, I still couldn't fight it.

The villagers of Thyme were not as happy to see me as they usually were. But then, I didn't usually bring a dragon in my wake. We hurried past the village and straight into the castle, where I had put in a gateway to the town of Basil. Folks nodded and greeted us politely enough, but they kept looking up at the distant dragon. We didn't linger. I opened the doorway to Basil, we all got through with our horses, then we mounted again and rode up the rock to the castle.

There was no dragon flying over Basil.

As soon as we reached the courtyard of Castle Basil, we turned our horses over to the grooms from the mews and went into the keep with our elf. We headed straight for the great hall, needing food after our time on field rations. At least, all of us needed food except Xayber's son. The elf had no stomach to satisfy anymore. I didn't bother to look for Parthet or Kardeen. They would hear of our return quickly enough and come looking for us. And as soon as we took the edge off our hunger, Lesh, Timon, Harkane, and I would be off to Cayenne, to regroup, refit, and pig out until our guts were ready to burst—unless Kardeen or Parthet had news so dire that we couldn't afford but one night and the meals on either end of it.

We were too early for supper, but there's always food available, and we soon had a couple of pages hauling it out for us—cold meat and fried potatoes, bread, cheese, and plenty of beer. The beer was right there in the great hall, so we started on that first, which suited me just fine.

I was still building my first sandwich—more or less a submarine, a whole loaf of bread split down the middle that I stacked with just about everything the pages fetched from the kitchen, ham, beef, cheese, onions, a tomato-based sauce that no one could *ever* mistake for ketchup, lettuce, and pickles—when Baron Kardeen arrived and sat at the table across from me. I paused in my culinary construction long enough to pull the ruby out from under my mail and let it hang down in front.

Kardeen stared at the jewel.

"That's what we went for," I said, and he nodded.

"Have there been any more strange happenings here?" I asked before I bit into my sandwich.

"Everyone has tales of strange happenings," Kardeen said. He shrugged and continued to stare at the jewel. "Most are things that always happen and no one pays attention. Until now."

That was something I could have anticipated if I had thought of it. I nodded to give me time to swallow. "But is any of it really odd, ominous?"

"We're still getting a few dragon eggs every day, not nearly as many as that first time, maybe one in four dozen. There were snow flurries around Arrowroot. And we had one peculiar sighting of something in the air that was big and noisy. Not a dragon."

"It was an airplane," Parthet's voice said from behind me. I turned and looked. He had sounded as if he were right at my ear, but instead he had just entered the great hall, some forty or fifty feet away. That was a trick I had heard before. I got down a couple of quick bites of food before he neared the table and reached around me to get the jewel and hold it up so he could see it better.

He didn't try to take the chain off my neck.

"You see this airplane?" I asked.

"No, but I questioned the people who did, and believe me, it was an airplane, possibly a military jet, flying low enough that I got a description of numbers on the bottom of its wings."

"Any reports of a crash?"

"Not yet. The engines were apparently still running when our people saw it. They *heard* it first."

"And I can't even get a butane lighter to work here."

"We have a ship waiting for you at Arrowroot," Kardeen said when I went back to eating. "It's not the largest or fanciest craft that plies the Sea of Fairy, but it is seaworthy. I looked it over myself. It carries a single sail for when the wind is with you and eight oars for when it isn't."

"Eight oars?" I asked around my food.

"And the sailors to man them. They're all soldiers, but they've all had at least some previous experience with boats and they've been drilling together for two weeks now. So they're ready to go whenever you are."

"I guess we can leave the day after tomorrow," I said, giving us an extra day to shove calories down our throats. "That leave enough time to stock the boat with food and such?"

"Time enough," Kardeen said. "Either Parthet or your mother can open the passageway for us here. I assume you're going on to Cayenne?"

"Right now," I said, getting up as I crammed the last of my sandwich into my mouth.

"We'll have everything ready for you," Kardeen said.

I washed down the last of the sandwich with beer. "How is Grandfather doing?" I asked. If the news had been really bad, I would have heard it already.

"His Majesty is much the same as he was before you left," Kardeen said, and his face got a little longer. "He has never remained so ill for this long before."

I looked at Parthet.

"I'm doing everything I can, and your mother has brought Hank McCreary over twice to help," Parthet said, very softly. I nodded.

I knew that I should go up to see Pregel, but I wasn't up to that yet. I needed to get more food into me, and I needed to get back to Joy, hold her in my arms.

"I'll stop back tomorrow, maybe even later tonight," I said. "I'll see grandfather and tell you about this trip, and catch up on everything else. Right now, I have to get back to Joy." We had been gone more than a month. August had ended, September begun.

"Of course," Kardeen said. He escorted us to the doorway back to my place, and I told him about the dragon we'd left circling over Thyme.

"I'll ask Parthet to check on it," he promised. At the moment, Parthet was taking care of our elf. I wasn't about to take Xayber's son home with me.

There are two separate doorways between Basil and Cayenne. One connects my bedrooms in the two places. The other opens on the ground floor of Cayenne, in the stable. Since I had Lesh and the others with me, we took the lower route, just in case Joy might be up in the bedroom. It also gave us a chance to pass through the kitchen to make sure that the cooks knew we were back—and uncommonly hungry.

I had started loosening my armor and other gear before we left Basil. I finished getting rid of all my extra weight as I climbed through Cayenne, looking for Joy. None of the items would get lost. They would probably be collected and returned to their proper places within minutes. The staff at Cayenne was small, but it was efficient, sometimes *too* efficient.

Joy was all the way up on the battlements, just starting back down when I met her at the top of the stairs. We hugged and kissed and talked about taking time for ourselves before supper to complete the reunion properly, but ruled that out because it was already close to mealtime and I was still starving. Then I realized what was missing. Or *who*.

"What happened with your parents?' I asked. "Didn't you bring them over?" It spoiled the mood.

"I brought them," Joy said. "Mom and Dad. My brother and his family couldn't make it to Chicago that weekend."

"What happened?"

Joy looked away from me. "It was terrible. They got to Chicago just before noon that Saturday. At first, they were upset that you weren't there. That was before I could tell them anything about Varay or bring them here. And *that* was a real mess." She paused and buried her head against my shoulder for a moment, hanging on. When she continued, her voice was muffled, the words coming in almost-separated groups.

"I tried to tell them about this place first, warn them, and they both thought I was crazy. Then Mother decided that she wanted to see our marriage certificate, like she still didn't believe that we were really married, and she wouldn't get off the subject. And Dad started grumbling because he figured he wasn't going to get to the ballpark." Joy pulled her face away from my shoulder and looked me in the eye.

"Then I opened the doorway here." She stopped and twisted around in my arms, looking away from me again. "Scared doesn't even come close to describing what they were like. It was all I could do to get them to even step through to look at the place. But I had to make sure they knew I was telling the truth, that I wasn't on drugs or crazy. We came up here so they could look around and know that we weren't still on the Chicago lakefront. I told them about you and Varay. They held on to each other and they listened and they looked."

Joy stopped talking again, and we went on down to our bedroom. Sunset was near and there weren't any lights on inside, so the shadows were thick, concealing. I waited for Joy to continue. She went to the window and stared out.

"Daddy didn't say much of anything the whole time here, and nothing at all after we went up top. He looked kind of green around the edges. Mother was scared and didn't hide it. She talked a lot, but not much of it made any sense. I showed her the marriage certificate you got from Baron Kardeen, and she carried on about how she couldn't tell her friends that we got married someplace that doesn't exist and all that."

Another silence, this one shorter than the others.

"I told them that we could get a place for them to live here, and a place for Danny and his family, because the other world might get even more dangerous than it already was, more nuclear bombs, more terrorists, maybe even all-out nuclear war. Daddy doesn't think that nuclear war is even possible anymore, not with all the changes in Russia and everywhere. I'm not sure they believed one word I said about all that. They've never thought much of my opinions. They wouldn't even consider moving here. Daddy had to be back at work Monday morning. Mother couldn't cut herself off from all her friends in St. Louis. And what kind of place was this for Danny to bring up his kids? What kind of place was this for *anyone?* I talked until I was blue in the face and crying from frustration, but it didn't do any good. Finally, I had to take them back to Chicago or just keep them prisoner here, and I couldn't do that, no matter how stupid they were being. Then Daddy tried to drag me off home with them, get 'help' for me. If I hadn't managed to slip through the doorway to your mother's house, I think he would have made it. I called the apartment from Louisville. Daddy was mad. Mother was crying."

I held Joy long enough for her to get her crying done.

"We'll try again," I said after a few minutes. I dried her tears with my hand. "They've had time to think about it. That'll make it easier. Come on, let's go eat. A meal will make you feel better." In Varay, no one missed a meal voluntarily.

There was a huge fire in the hearth at the head of the great hall, and the heat was welcome. It made me remember the cold of the mountains. And halfway through supper, there was a pounding on the door downstairs. Lesh went to check on it. When he came back, he pointed at the ceiling and said, "There's a dragon circling overhead."

16

The Shadow

I looked at Lesh, then down at the ruby hanging from my neck. I don't think that a light bulb went on over my head, but the realization came to me that fast. The *jewel* was actively calling dragons, somehow.

"What's this dragon doing?" I asked, without any great agitation.

"Just circling above, like the other," Lesh said.

"Sit down and eat," I told him.

"Aren't you going to do anything about it?" Joy asked.

"Not unless it comes down. I can't." I told her about the earlier dragons. "I guess that the one that followed us to Thyme has had time enough to fly here."

"You mean that ruby is attracting dragons to you?"

"Like a magnet," I said. "That has to be what's doing it. I've seen more dragons since we got this than in all the time I've been around here."

Joy had pushed her plate away when Lesh made his announcement, but when she saw that I wasn't going to interrupt my meal for the dragon, she pulled her plate back and started eating again. But she didn't have her heart in it. She nibbled and kept looking around. Some of the others at the table were just as nervous. At the moment, food was more important to me and my traveling companions than any dragon. Unless the beast came down and started causing trouble, I intended to fill my belly.

"The only way to get rid of the dragon is probably to take this jewel somewhere else," I told Joy. "If I'm right and it's the jewel calling the dragons. If this one is still overhead after we get done eating, we can step through to Chicago—no, better make that Louisville—for a while."

"Why Louisville?" Joy asked.

"In case there's someone looking for Aaron in Chicago," I said. "By the way, I didn't see him when we came through Basil today. He's still around, isn't he?"

"Yes, and apparently he's finally quit growing. He's taller and heavier than you. If I didn't know better, I'd say he was at least your age."

"Uncle Parthet still working with him?"

"Every day, almost constantly. Aaron is convinced that he doesn't have any choice but to become a wizard as fast as he can. I think Parthet did the convincing." Joy looked around the table, then leaned a little closer to me. "And some of the people at Basil are worried. They're afraid that because Aaron is black he'll practice black magic."

Varayans can be as superstitious as anyone, and they had more excuse. As far as I knew, Aaron was the only black to ever come to the buffer zone.

"That'll change as they get to know him," I said. "First time he does something special, all that will be forgotten. Varay doesn't have the history to make people bigoted over color."

We got through the rest of supper without any additional alarms. Before taking off for Louisville, I decided to go up to the ramparts to have a look at the dragon for myself. It was well past sunset, but I might still be able to catch a glimpse of the beast. I stopped upstairs to strap on my elf swords and to get the rifle that had misfired the last time I tried to use it on a dragon. I reloaded the magazine and carried the rifle up top with me.

The dragon was still floating around in lazy circles, more a silhouette than anything else, occulting batches of stars as it passed. I took the rifle, aimed, and fired. The gun actually worked for a change and the dragon flapped a few times to get even higher and started making wider circles, so maybe I hit it. I tried another shot but got nothing from the rifle. The third shot worked, but it didn't seem to have as much recoil as it should have. The dragon scarcely reacted to that shot, maybe just to the noise.

"Guess it don't want to be run off," Lesh said.

"I guess not," I replied. Harkane, Timon, and Joy had all come up to the battlements as well. Joy wanted to see a dragon for herself.

"Lesh, you think you can mind the store here for a day or so? Joy and I are going to Louisville. That ought to throw the dragon off."

"I'll handle things here, Lord," Lesh said.

"We'll take Harkane and Timon, I think. You want to come?" I asked them. Both nodded. Visits to the other world were still a treat for them.

"Lesh, there anything you want us to bring back for you?"

"I could use some of that beer in the big cans," he said. "You know the kind I mean?"

"The Australian stuff, Foster Lager, right?"

"Aye, that's it."

"Okay, Foster Lager it is," I said.

On one of our earlier visits to my world, Lesh and I had visited a fancy bar in Chicago that claimed to stock every brand of beer made in the United States or imported. The foreign beer list was alphabetized by country. Lesh and I started working our way straight down the menu. We were fresh out of Varay that evening, so we needed longer than usual to get stinking drunk—but we also needed another two nights of hard drinking to get all the way through the list. By the middle of our second session, the waitress hardly needed to ask for our order. She had a copy of the beer list. And on the third night, as we closed in on the end, we didn't even have to pay. We had an audience, with different folks picking up the tab for each round. It was a fun time, even worth the hangovers and all the people who said, "I hope you're not planning to drive." I assured them all that we had come by cab and would leave by cab, and I smiled and nodded, all of that. A couple of jolly drunks. We bought a round for the house now and then, and everybody was happy. Nobody much noticed when Lesh and I slipped into Varayan to comment on one thing or another. Who pays attention to jolly drunks? Oh, the folks who knew that we had worked our way through more than a hundred brands of imported beer in three nights all wanted to know which we liked best, but you can't make discriminating judgments when you've sampled most of the brands after you were already plotched. What Lesh liked so much about the Foster's was that it came in quart cans.

"A six-pack of that would really get you through supper" was the way he put it at the time.

Harkane and Timon ran off to change clothes. Well, Harkane didn't *run*. He would have considered that too undignified now that he was no longer a "kid." But he hurried, just the same.

"It'll just be for tonight and tomorrow," I told Joy. "The next morning, we're back on the road again, going for the mate to this ruby."

"Isn't one of those enough for whatever you have to do?" Joy asked.

"I guess not. Nobody knows yet what we have to do. All the elf has said is that we have to bring both of them together."

"You going to change first?"

"Yes, and I'm even going to take a quick bath to get some of the trail off me so I don't clog the drain at Mother's house. Why don't you open a passage to Basil long enough for Harkane to pop through to tell Baron Kardeen where we're going, and why. That way, someone can get in touch with us if necessary."

We set up Harkane and Timon in the guest room. That had double beds, its own bathroom, and a thirteen-inch television. TV fascinated both of them. If we hadn't just returned from a long quest, they would likely have stayed up all night watching the tube. Almost everything on TV was still new to them, even *Gilligan's Island* and *I Love Lucy*.

Joy and I had my old room. It was still "my" room even though I hadn't lived there since my first trip to Varay—actually, since I went away to college. I was only home for brief visits then, during school breaks and between semesters. I even took courses every summer.

After Joy and I shared a long shower and started to catch up on the long weeks of missed sex, I had an idea.

"You know, we could ease your mother's mind about one thing."

"What's that?" Joy asked drowsily.

"We could drive down to Nashville in the morning and get married again. No blood test or waiting in Tennessee."

"Can we get there and back in one day?"

"No problem. We'll take Mother's van. We can get

copies of the license and certificate and mail them to your folks."

"You sure you don't mind?"

"Not at all, love. Besides, it gives us something to do. And it will be nice to look at some mountains I don't have to climb."

"That'll be nice," Joy said. We made love again and then she went to sleep.

But I couldn't sleep. We had been back in the "real" world for three hours and I hadn't checked the news yet.

It was close to three in the morning, but Mother still kept the cable service paid up, so I got CNN and sat there to see what was going on in the world. There didn't seem to be any major current crises, nothing to preempt everything else for. There was still a lot on about the *Coral Lady* disaster and some reprisal raids that had been made. Apparently, those had been in August. The references assumed that any viewers had been in touch with the story all along, so some of it was too oblique for me to be sure exactly what had been done. There had been a series of raids, not just the one attack that had been on the news before I headed into the Titans.

There was no mention of the dragon that had been spotted over Chattanooga the last time I was in this world, no mention of a missing jet that might have strayed into the buffer zone. Maybe those dislocations had corrected themselves. I hoped so. Things were complicated enough.

It was five o'clock before I went back up to bed. Joy didn't wake. I set the alarm and crawled into bed. I still had time for a couple of hours of sleep. We planned to get up at seven to get ready for our trip south.

The drive from Louisville to Nashville wasn't bad, especially not since the speed limit on the interstate had been raised. We got on I-65 out by the airport, headed south past Fort Knox and Mammoth Cave, and crossed the state line into Tennessee just after eleven. We stopped for lunch at McDonald's just before we reached Nashville, ordered enough for twelve hungry people, and sat in the van to eat. When we went back inside to order seconds we drew stares from the kids working the counter.

I needed a half hour to find the courthouse, and we stood in line for another thirty minutes to get the license.

There was a preacher hanging around to marry couples who couldn't wait or who didn't have other plans, and the ceremony itself took less than five minutes. We had photocopies made of everything, then got a stamped envelope at the post office and sent the copies to Joy's parents. Next we hit a big mall on the edge of town, found a jeweler who had rings in Joy's size, and bought a set. We put more dents in my credit cards before we left the mall: clothes, books, playing cards, kerosene lanterns, and junk food. I planned to wait until we got back into Kentucky to buy the beer and some hard liquor.

After another big meal, this one a little more balanced, we started back north, just after four o'clock. I didn't push the van hard. We had plenty of time and I felt pleasantly full and contented. There was country music from a Nashville station and the day was beautiful, with some of the leaves just starting to turn to their autumn colors.

Then a Willie Nelson song was interrupted for a news bulletin.

"We have a report from Crossville on the Cumberland Plateau that Tessie has been spotted again, flying toward Nashville. An unidentified source at the FAA regional Air Traffic Control center confirms that the unidentified radar signatures match the August sightings there and in Chattanooga, and there have also been visual sightings this afternoon. We'll keep you right up to the minute with this as always."

The special report ended and the disk jockey came back on with, "Well, folks, we got us another dragon doo-doo alert goin' here. Ain't nobody got a pooper scooper big enough for Tessie. An' we're still lookin' for the first pile close enough for our crews to get to it. The reports we've had say Tessie can drop fifteen hundred pounds at a time." He stopped and laughed. "I shore ain't seen Tessie yet, an' I'm not sure I want to. She must not like country music."

"Tessie?" Joy asked.

"It figures," I said. "They call the Loch Ness monster Nessie, so Tennessee's dragon becomes Tessie." It was too transparent to be anything else.

"But they're treating it like a joke," Joy complained.

"What do you think they're going to do? They have to either laugh at it or think they're in the middle of a Japanese monster movie. It could be worse. After the *Coral Lady,* they could be shooting at clouds.'' I looked in all three rearview mirrors, then craned my head out the window. ''I guess we should be on the alert, though.''

''You think this dragon will come after you like the others?'' Harkane asked.

''I'd almost bet on it,'' I replied. Time for a sigh.

''I'll get your weapons ready, lord,'' Harkane said. They were probably all at the bottom of the pile in the back of the van, beneath everything we'd bought in Nashville.

''Tessie comes anywhere near Fort Knox, the Army is likely to blow him away,'' I said. ''I think that's still restricted airspace, what with the gold depository and all.''

''Can we drive through the base?'' Joy asked. ''Wouldn't it be simpler if they took care of the dragon and you didn't have to?''

I couldn't deny it. ''If we get that far. But we'll have to hide the weapons again and hope they don't stop us for a random check. The Army gets touchy about armed visitors.''

I hadn't been to Fort Knox in years. We used to drive out to look at the bullion depository every year or two, go through the George S. Patton Museum, and look at soldiers. Mostly, somebody in the family got the idea to go out there every time *Goldfinger* was on television. I knew that we had to get off the interstate quite a bit south to go through the base and depository area, but I had never gone in from that side, so Joy had to check the map to find out that we needed to turn off on US 31W at Elizabethtown.

Tessie didn't cooperate, though. We were just south of the exit for Abraham Lincoln's birthplace when Timon spotted the dragon coming up from the southeast, a little off to the right and behind us. We weren't going to outrun Tessie. I was already doing sixty and it was overtaking us easily.

''I have your sword and gun, lord,'' Harkane yelled right in my ear.

''Rest area coming up,'' Joy said. She was watching the signs.

''It's either the rest area or we fight out here on the

road,'' I said. I floored the gas pedal and the van shuddered a little at the sudden acceleration. ''Make sure that there's a shell in the chamber and that the safety is off,'' I told Harkane. I had taught him the basics of handling firearms, enough to get the weapon ready for me. I hadn't known that the rifle was in the car until Harkane mentioned it. That must have been his idea.

''There's the exit,'' Joy said.

I kept my foot on the gas until the last possible instant, then braked hard and pulled onto the ramp. There weren't many vehicles in the rest area—a couple of tractor-trailer rigs, one camper, and two cars. We went past all of them to the far end of the lot. I turned the wheel hard and stood on the brake, and we skidded to a stop.

I swung my door open and Harkane handed me the rifle, another .458 magnum like the one I had at Cayenne. The van was between me and the other vehicles. At the moment, there were no other people out in the open. I hoped that any witnesses would be too busy watching, or running from, the dragon to notice when I started shooting. I figured that the odds were pretty good.

''There's a box of shells in the glove compartment,'' Harkane said. Joy got the box out and open. I didn't know if I would have time to empty the magazine, let alone reload, but . . .

But there was no more time to plan. The dragon was on a steep glide, its wings tucked back, aiming straight for me. There wasn't going to be any hovering and circling for this joker. Of course, this dragon had been out of the buffer zone since before the rest of the nonsense started.

I wrapped the leather sling around my left arm and steadied the barrel on the roof of the van. The only thing missing was a telescopic sight, and that was hardly essential. I lined up on the dragon's left eye and worked to keep the pupil lined up in the notch of the sights while I waited.

I waited until the dragon was within a hundred yards before I started shooting—*after* I heard the first scream in the parking lot. I squeezed off all five shots, as fast as I could aim and shoot accurately.

I hit the dragon, every time. It jerked to the side, flipped over, then righted itself and came down hard, but not hard enough. It was still alive. It got up on all four legs and started toward me again. I moved out from behind the van, and Timon passed me Dragon's Death while Harkane reloaded the rifle. Harkane had never fired a weapon that powerful, and I hoped he wouldn't pick this time to start. He'd be as like to hit me as the dragon, even though the reptile was twice the size of the riverboat *Belle of Louisville*.

I moved out toward the dragon, but slowly, content to let it do most of the traveling. There were sirens blowing in the distance, coming our way, so someone had called the cops. A lot of good a state trooper was going to do, even if he had a shotgun or one of those briefcase submachine guns. Anyway, the sirens sounded too far off to reach the rest area in time to do anything but pick up the pieces.

The dragon stumbled and went down on its front knees—or whatever the proper terminology is for a dragon. It got up, and fell again. Its head slammed against the pavement, hard enough to crack it—the pavement, not the head. Lower teeth pierced its upper lip. Black blood oozed out.

''Give me the rifle,'' I called. Harkane was there in a second. I returned the sword and took the rifle. I went to within six feet of Tessie's snout and put five more rounds through the eye. Before long, I was going to be the Dirty Harry of the dragon-slaying business.

''Okay, let's get out of here before the cops arrive,'' I said, hurrying back to the van.

We got inside and I started the engine. ''Bury the rifle and sword back there,'' I said as I put the transmission in drive and goosed the gas pedal.

''You're just going to leave that thing lying there?'' Joy asked.

''Damn right. This isn't the time to get messed up in red tape.''

''But what are they going to think?''

''Maybe they'll think that dragons are for real,'' I said. I didn't really care. ''Check the map. Find us a back road into Louisville.''

17

The Mist

By the time we got back to my mother's house, the story was already breaking. The telephones and CB radios must have been busy. Most of the Louisville television and radio stations had crews on the way, and two TV stations with news helicopters were already on the scene. There were live shots of the dead dragon on TV when I switched the set in the living room on. There was no chance that anyone would be able to suppress this story—assuming that any military or governmental types might have tried out of conditioned reflex. The carcass appeared on the evening news of all three networks as well. I had the distinct feeling that Tessie would be much more than a nine-day wonder. Before the late news came on, dragon sightings had been reported in every state but Hawaii . . . and there had been two "sea serpent" sightings there.

"You think any of those are for real?" Joy asked.

"No. they would be swarming all over us by now if there were more." Maybe that was just my pessimism.

I switched over to CNN. The Air Force had finally admitted that a fighter plane had been missing for two weeks, lost while attempting to intercept a Tessie radar return over the Great Smoky Mountain National Park. A small coastal freighter was missing without a trace in the Adriatic. There had been no storms or reports of trouble from the ship before its disappearance. No wreckage had been found. An attempt to hijack a SAC B-1 bomber had been foiled by Air Police and the FBI. The Soviet Union was making "almost an accusation" that American forces had either sunk or sabotaged a new frigate in the Indian Ocean near Diego Garcia. Despite the improved relations of the last few years, the rhetoric was fairly heated. Radio and television signals had been mysteriously jammed, off and on, for nearly two hours throughout Iberia. The Tokyo Stock Exchange had suspended trading for three days after the Nissei Index doubled in five days. Duluth, Minnesota, had recorded its first significant September *summer* snowfall—nine inches and counting. A few hundred miles away, Milwaukee and Chicago were breaking record high temperatures, not just for September, for *any* month.

I would have liked to listen to more news, maybe even spend the night in civilization, but I had to get back to Varay. I got Joy, the others, and all of our loot through to Cayenne, stopped to talk to Lesh for a few minutes, then went right over to Basil while Joy organized a late supper at Cayenne.

Supper was just ending at Basil, but there was still food on the table, so I grabbed a snack, then went looking for Kardeen. He was in his office, still working.

"Sorry I'm late," I told him. "I keep attracting dragons." I pulled the ruby out from under my shirt. I hadn't taken the jewel off since I got it. Varay isn't big on safe deposit boxes. "They seem to be drawn by this. Even in the other world." I told him about Tessie.

Kardeen nodded, and gestured me into a chair without saying anything. He looked overworked and tired. He was always overworked, but he usually kept it off his face.

"I'm going to need Parthet along on the boat or we'll never get to the other shrine," I said when I finished talking about Tessie. "He has a spell to hide people from dragons. He used it when we rode to Thyme that first time. If the spell will work around this ruby."

Kardeen sent a runner for Parthet and Xayber's son, then filled in the time by telling me about our boat and the strange things that had been happening around Varay the last few weeks. A lot of little things had been reported. It sounded vaguely like the weird reports back home. In one case, they merged quite clearly. Fishermen had reported seeing a gray steel ship drifting without power in the Mist.

"Russian, most likely," I told Kardeen. "They're missing a frigate back home." I started to list the other ways the worlds were bleeding into each other but stopped, chilled by a sudden realization.

"That ship may have nuclear weapons aboard." The chill came from wondering what the Elflord of Xayber might do if he got his hands on weapons like that and found a way to make them work in Fairy or in the buffer zone.

"It's all coming apart at the seams, isn't it?" I asked.

Parthet arrived just then, carrying the elf head—still in its birdcage—and Aaron was following close behind. Aaron was as large and mature-looking as Joy had said. Kardeen repeated my question for Parthet.

The wizard nodded. "We're running out of time, even sooner than I feared. I have yet to convince myself that we have enough time left for you to complete your work and get back here."

"Have you figured out what we have to do with the jewels when we have both of them?" I asked.

Parthet shook his head. I turned the question on the elf, and he said that he wasn't positive of the precise steps either. There was nothing in the collective memory he could tap and nothing in the written records Parthet had available.

"The answer is there to be found, though," the elf said before I could accuse him of being less than honest with us. "I would not have agreed to any of this without that certainty."

"We're going to need you on the boat with us, Uncle," I told Parthet. "We need you to shield us from the dragons this rock draws."

"Not me," Parthet said. "Aaron will have to go. I couldn't sustain that magic long enough to help. I think Aaron can. You have no idea how quickly he's grown into the craft. And it will be his initiation test, the journey into the Mist and back."

I stared up at Aaron. He hadn't said anything but hello so far, standing back out of the way. His hair was clipped short now, and he had traces of beard stubble on his chin and cheeks. He seemed assured of himself and his place in the scheme of things. But I remembered the frightened eight-year-old he had been less than two months before. In some peculiar way, I could even see the boy as a ghostly overlay on the man.

"What do you think, Aaron?" I asked.

"I know the magic," he said. "I can't say how long

I can hold it until I try.'' His voice was deep but soft, his words precise, unhurried. I had the impression that he considered each word individually, but without losing time at it.

''He knows virtually every spell I can recall,'' Parthet said, speaking just as softly, but without the sense of deliberation. ''And he knows many more I had forgotten. He has pored through all of my old books and his memory is—so far as I can determine—exact.''

''This is what I was born to do,'' Aaron said.

There is something about that kind of utter certainty that always scares me.

''Has Parthet told you the price?'' I asked.

Aaron shrugged. He knew what I was talking about. ''I will be my own children. The little boy in me is not completely lost. He never will be.''

It was going to take an effort to avoid thinking of Aaron as that little kid who kept popping into Varay from Joliet, even though his maturation seemed to be mental and emotional as well as physical. But I stood and stuck out my hand. Aaron was four inches taller than me and his hand dwarfed mine. We shook.

''I'll say 'Welcome aboard' now, even though I haven't seen our boat yet,'' I told him.

''I might have been better off marrying a traveling salesman,'' Joy said the next morning when I was dressing. ''They're home more often.''

I kissed her. ''It's not always like this, dear. When things are going well, I can be idle for months on end.''

''Do things *ever* go well here?'' I guess the question was inevitable.

''I'll show you when we get this flap nailed down,'' I said. I didn't add all of the qualifications. Joy would worry enough without them.

There was a dragon circling over Cayenne at dawn, but the beast the other night had done no harm and my people were getting used to feeling privileged to ''serve'' the Hero of Varay. I guess they considered the honor guard overhead part of the price.

We stepped through to Basil—Lesh, Harkane, Timon, Jaffa and Rodi, Joy, and me. It was breakfast time, naturally, but Joy and I left our companions to start eating while we made a quick trip upstairs. Mother was with the king. Pregel was either asleep or comatose. Mother said that there wasn't much difference between the two for him anymore. Sometimes he was almost alert. Sometimes days would pass without his opening his eyes. He had aged visibly. He seemed to be only a half step short of mummification.

"He can't last much longer," Mother said. "I've seen the records. It's how his father died, though at nearly twice the age."

"No, not yet. I can't stay here to take his place. I have to go after this other jewel. It's the only hope for any of us." I spoke much louder than I needed to for Mother to hear. I wanted Pregel to hear as well, if he could, and Mother had to know that was what I was doing.

"I know," she said. She met my eyes without adding anything else. I couldn't read the emotion in her eyes. The loss of understanding that came when I discovered the world that had been hidden from me had made us strangers. Nothing had changed.

I turned and left.

We ate a hearty breakfast downstairs, knowing we were going back out into the wild. Baron Kardeen assured me that our boat would carry more than enough food for the four of us and for our crew, food for nearly two months—though much of it would seem monotonous, salted meat and hardtack. I hoped that our sailors were good fishermen.

A crowd of us went from Basil to Castle Arrowroot on the shore of the Mist. Parthet and Joy were there to open the way back to Basil for the others. Even Kardeen came to see us off, and he rarely left Basil.

Kardeen had given me a description of our boat the night before, but I had never seen it. The Varayan designers made it easy on themselves by designing half a vessel and using two of them together. The boat was fifty feet long, eighteen wide in the middle, and it had a single mast precisely in the center. The ends of the boat were identical, pointed something like the ends of a Viking dragon ship but without the carvings and fancy paint. A steering oar could be attached at either end. The sides were lapstraked, like clapboard siding on a house. There were five shallow extensions below the waterline in place of a single keel or keelboard. There were benches along both sides for the rowers, an open-ended cabin through the middle of the boat, and six separate storage bins that were not quite holds. The mast carried a single sail, and the spar could be rotated all the way around the mast. You never had to worry about turning the boat around if you wanted to head in the opposite direction. Just move the steering oar to the other end, turn the rowers around on their benches, and swivel the spar and you were ready to go.

But the sight of the boat stirred my danger sense. Not that I could avoid getting aboard and setting sail, but my danger sense was making sure that I knew I was doing something foolish.

We walked over to the boat—the name *Beathe* was painted on the side of the cabin—from the castle, taking along much of the off-duty portion of Arrowroot's garrison and a few dozen townspeople as spectators. The only sea traffic that normally put out from Arrowroot was the fishing fleet, and they never sailed out of sight of land. Apparently, everyone knew we were going farther out.

Walking on the pier. my first impression was that there was very little boat showing above the waterline, and there were still five of us to climb aboard, weighted down with weapons and armor.

"You sure we're not overloading this thing?" I whispered to Baron Kardeen.

"Not at all." He smiled. "It may not look like much, but this is the most seaworthy class of boat sailing the Mist or the other seas. And you'll be lightening the load daily as you eat and drink."

"In other words, the longer it is before we run into heavy seas the safer we'll be."

"This ship will take a lot, loaded down or not," Kardeen said.

Beathe's master was a grizzled fisherman named Hopay—*young* and grizzled. He was thin but his arms were muscled like a comic book hero's. He rattled off the names of his eight rowers, but there was no way I could remember them all from one exposure. I've always had trouble with names.

I said my farewells to Parthet, Kardeen, and Joy, taking quite a lot of time with Joy. Parthet had some last-minute instructions for Aaron. Aaron and I were the last to board *Beathe*. There was no "all ashore that's going ashore" because only the people who were sailing went aboard.

"Whenever you're ready, Master Hopay," I said, and he started shouting orders. The boat was pushed away from the dock, oars went down, and we moved out into the Mist.

Our departure was a protracted event. The breeze was against us, so we had to rely on our rowers. We could see people waiting back on shore. Joy and Parthet moved off to the side of the crowd. I waved a couple of times, and stared at Joy until I could no longer see her clearly. I waved again, just in case she could still make me out, then turned my attention to my command.

"Which way do we go?" I asked Xayber's son. His cage was tied on top of the cabin so we couldn't lose him overboard.

"West-northwest," he said.

"We'll have the wind in our faces most of the time," Hopay warned.

"That is the way we must go," the elf said.

"It isn't a matter of choice, Master Hopay," I said. "West-northwest it is. The elf is our navigator."

"Ain't but the least part of an elf," Hopay said, squinting at him. If he was worried about Xayber's son, he took care not to show it.

"Face me toward the bow and dangle the jewel in front of me," the elf said. I did as he asked and held the ruby out until he said, "Enough. Yes, this is the right way, but we have forever to sail."

"Aaron, you're keeping a lookout for dragon?"

"Since we left the castle," he said. "You know, I've never been on a boat of any kind before." He paused, then looked straight into my eyes. "My parents debated taking me with them on the *Coral Lady*, but it was to be a business cruise and they thought I was too young, that I wouldn't have any fun with them busy all the time. 'Next time,' they told me."

I nodded. "I've got some idea how rough it can be. I lost my father suddenly." I glanced away, then looked at him again.

Aaron was more a wonder than the talking head of a dead elf or dragons that could slurp down a string of cars like a strand of spaghetti. Even granting the visual impossibility that he could age fifteen years in a matter of days, it would be logical to expect emotional or educational lag, but Aaron showed neither. It was as if the magic that aged him also crammed a full education into his head and gave him the equivalent experience in living. I couldn't help thinking of the cliché about orphans being forced to grow up overnight. Aaron had done that in absolutely literal fashion. And he had absorbed "years" of apprenticeship as a wizard at the same time. Magic? Well, maybe that is the closest word, but it isn't close enough.

"There's something about me you should know," Aaron said a few minutes later. We had moved all the way to the bow of *Beathe*, where the sides rose to meet the nose. "You remember how I suddenly popped up in Varay?" I nodded. "Well, I can control it now, to some extent."

I needed a moment to consider that. "*What* extent?" I asked, amazed at how calm I sounded.

"I can use all of the doorways with the silver tracing—without rings or any of your 'family' magic. I can go to any portal from any other once I can picture the scene there. *From any to any,*" he emphasized, "not just through the paired doorways. Only Parthet and Baron Kardeen know that."

"I appreciate your trust," I said, marveling at the power. That was something Parthet had never even hinted was possible. I was sure *he* couldn't do it.

"You are Hero of Varay, and you will be king if we make it back from this voyage," Aaron said. "If I am to be your wizard, you have a right to know what you can expect from me."

I nodded slowly. I had to keep reevaluating my understanding of Aaron, a constant upgrading. I told him just what we had encountered in getting the first jewel of the Great Earth Mother, in detail. I finished off, "I don't know exactly what we'll meet this time. The defenses might not be identical, but they will be at least as thorough."

"Without a doubt," Aaron said.

"And no matter what problems we meet getting to the shrine, our most critical problem is time. We could win through up here, get the second jewel, and still have the worlds fall apart on us because there isn't time to get back to Varay and do anything with them."

Aaron appeared to go blank then, for maybe thirty seconds. His eyes remained open, he didn't fall over or anything, but there just didn't seem to be anybody home.

"Check with Wellivazey," he said when he finally came back from wherever his mind had gone. "Make sure that the boat is on *precisely* the right heading for this island we're looking for."

"Wellivazey?"

"Him." Aaron pointed at the elf's head.

"How did you know his name?" I asked. That was a secret Parthet had found too deep for him to come close to learning it. An elf's most closely guarded secret is his true name, for fear that an enemy might use it to conjure spells against him.

I don't know *how,*" Aaron said. "I simply knew it when you brought him back the other day. I looked at him and knew his name."

"How about his father's name?"

"I've never met his father."

"Does he know that you know his name?" I nodded slightly toward the head.

"I didn't speak it in his presence."

"That's good, I think. It might be best if he doesn't know that he has lost that secret. I'll check on our course."

I didn't know how to use it yet, but the name was a weapon if we needed it. In Fairy, to know the true name of your enemy was to hold the ultimate weapon over him. I went back to Wellivazey and asked about the course. He went through the same procedure as before, staring through the ruby and chanting, and then he confirmed that we were aimed directly at the island shrine—though it was still an unknown but considerable distance away.

I passed the news to Aaron. He nodded, stared up into the sky behind the boat, and started chanting softly. I couldn't understand any of it, of course. The translation magic of the buffer zone doesn't extend to magic spells.

Aaron kept chanting, gradually building in volume, but it was fifteen minutes before I noticed any result.

The wind had been in our faces since we left the dock at Arrowroot, but that died off and a new breeze started coming from behind. At first the two winds met and swirled around each other. Then the breeze from behind offset and finally overpowered the headwind. Master Hopay got the oars in and the sail raised. *Beathe* picked up a little speed, then more. The bow seemed to rise a little as we sped across the Sea of Fairy.

"Is this too much?" Aaron asked when he quit chanting and noticed me again.

I asked Master Hopay, and Hopay said that we were fine now but that if the wind got much stronger *Beathe* would be hard to handle and we might be in trouble then.

"It will get no stronger," Aaron promised.

An hour later I could see no sign of the coast on the southern horizon, even when I climbed up on top of the cabin and stood on tiptoe, holding the mast for support. There wasn't a trace of land to be seen.

Life aboard *Beathe* was far from comfortable. Fourteen people were crowded into an area that would have seemed inadequate for seven. The "beds" were merely shelves under the deck, narrow spaces that opened off of the cabin under the rower's benches, like bookshelves, slots no larger than the burial niches in the crypt below Castle Basil. The difference was that these slots were open on the side, not sealed at the head. But the similarity was enough to disturb my sleep and spoil my dreams. There were only eight beds in the cabin at that. Two more people could sleep on the long benches, and anyone else had to make do with a stretch of passageway down the center. Meals were eaten in shifts, and when we were under sail, at least three of the nine seamen (including the master, who took a regular watch) were always on duty, one at the steering oar and two to tend the sail and act as lookouts. The toilet was over the side, and using it could get comic and dangerous at the same time.

The wind remained constant in direction and force and didn't require Aaron's continuous attention. We only spotted one dragon, very late the first afternoon, and it remained far to the south, almost at the limit of vision.

Aaron put up a hazy, shimmering shield like the one Parthet had demonstrated in Precarra almost three and a half years before.

Master Hopay was reluctant to continue under sail after dark, and he remained nervous when I told him that we had to. He had no experience at sailing at night. It just wasn't done. Mariners in the buffer zone put in to shore every evening. Sailing out of sight of land was bad enough. Sailing after dark out of sight of land was inconceivable, according to Hopay. He wanted to furl the sail and drag a sea anchor through the hours of darkness. I conferred with Aaron and Wellivazey, more for form than because the decision needed a conference, then overruled Master Hopay.

"There are no obstacles in front of us and we can't afford to waste time," I said. If I had been anyone but the Hero of Varay, Hopay would have refused, or at least carried the argument on longer. But he gave in. He grumbled a lot, though, the first night and every night we continued to sail.

Every night. When we started, we had no idea how long the voyage might be. Even after Aaron came up with his wind I had no expectation of a quick passage. Neither Aaron nor the elf could tell how far away the shrine was. After a week at sea, the elf said that the pull of the left jewel of the Great Earth Mother was stronger than before, but still too distant to gauge.

At least we hadn't run into any serious challenges yet.

"They didn't come for us until we were close before," Xayber's son reminded me. "The forest trolls don't count. You brought *that* peril on yourself."

That made me think about Annick. I wondered what kind of torture she was inflicting on herself now, why she had been out in the wilds of Varay hunting trolls, where she was now, where she might pop up next. That last view I had of her, standing off an arrow's flight away from me, she had looked more sad than angry.

We went through the dowsing routine with the ruby three or four times a day. I dangled the jewel by its chain in front of the elf's head and he confirmed that we were still aimed in the right direction. Aaron started looking into the ruby after the elf each time, but said that he couldn't tell anything from it. Each time, Aaron qualified that with "yet."

The second week ended.

"No mortal's e'er been out so far from land," Master Hopay said. "Leastwise, none's e'er come home from so far out."

That was old news.

Lesh, Harkane, and I had taken to standing watches of our own, in case the danger appeared right aboard our boat. Our sailors were nervous and unhappy. But Baron Kardeen had apparently chosen them wisely. Every man grumbled and talked of his fear and his wish to turn about and go home, but no one went beyond talk.

On the eighteenth day, the sea developed a chop, a surface roughness we had not seen before, and Aaron's wind had competition that took his full attention for several hours. That night, for the first time, Aaron called off his wind and we took in the sail and dragged a sea anchor to keep us from drifting too far.

"I need the break," Aaron told me as the sail came down. "In the morning, I'll build the wind again—if we still need it. I think we're getting close though."

Maybe he needed the break, but he certainly didn't use the time to sleep. Aaron spent most of that night in the bow of *Beathe,* staring out at the sea in front of us.

And on the morning of the nineteenth day, the Mist finally lived up to its name. Dawn brought the densest fog I had ever seen, worse even than the one that had enveloped Castle Arrowroot to give the elflord's soldiers cover to retreat three years back.

"We're very close now," the elf said. He didn't even need the jewel to judge that. Over to the side, out of the elf's sight, Aaron nodded his agreement.

Aaron tried to raise his wind again but failed, so it was back to the oars. Our rowers hadn't worked much through the voyage, so they were able to put a lot into the task for this push. Lesh and Harkane took turns on the benches too, which let everyone take an occasional break and kept us moving at a decent clip.

"I can't budge this fog," Aaron confessed after perhaps two hours of effort. "I can't even *grasp* it." I wasn't sure what that meant. The two of us were standing at the ship's bow again, trying to see through the fog in front. "It's not a natural fog."

"I know." The fog had set off my danger alarm. For the first time in two weeks I was wearing both of my elf swords and my lucky Cubs cap, ready for anything and certain that "anything" was close. My bow and quiver were handy, and the others had their weapons where they could reach them in a hurry.

"Someone is reaching out to us," Aaron said a little later. "I can feel her mind probing."

"Her?" I asked. Aaron nodded.

"Then it must be the Great Earth Mother herself," I said. It didn't make me feel any better. Something tugged at my mind then, and I turned to look at the elf perched at the forward end of the cabin. His face had turned ash gray in the fog. His eyes bulged out so far that it looked as though they might actually pop out of his skull. And now, he seemed to be choking—without a throat to be constricted.

"Are you okay?" I asked, moving to him. The question was so ludicrous that I must have blushed bright red. Wellivazey's eyes rolled up in his head. A strangled sound escaped from purple lips.

"Aaron, can you help him?" I asked. We had to have the elf to identify the other jewel: *someone of the blood of Fairy, pure and true.*

Aaron started chanting. After a couple of minutes, his lips pulled back from his teeth in a fierce grimace. His eyes narrowed as he squinted, staring at the elf, his forehead wrinkled in concentration. Some color came back into the elf's face, gradually, but his eyes remained closed. He remained silent. Aaron started to sweat, and the temperature couldn't have been more than fifty on the deck of *Beathe*.

At the stern of the boat, Hopay shouted, "We have to turn back, lord!"

"No!" I yelled back. "Don't waver an inch from our course."

"We *have* to turn back!" Hopay repeated, panicked.

Timon grabbed his bow, notched an arrow, and aimed it straight at Hopay's heart.

"The Hero of Varay said we must go on," Timon said.

Most of the rowers stopped rowing, waiting to see what would happen.

"Put your bow down, Timon," I said. I walked to the stern. Hopay's eyes were wide with terror.

"Master Hopay, we must go forward. There is no alternative. We have to reach the shrine, and *it* is still in front of us." I tried to sound reasonable—encouraging, not threatening—but Hopay had to feel the tacit threat. I stared until he nodded.

"Aye, lord, we'll go on as you say."

"And when we reach the island," I said, dropping my voice almost to a whisper, "you remember that there is no way you can survive to get home without us, without the wizard, the elf, and me. You know that as surely as you know your own name."

He resisted even longer before he nodded this time. "Aye, lord, I know it. And maybe not e'en then."

I knew what he meant. I continued to stare at him. I didn't like the idea that my danger sense, or perhaps just my innate suspicious nature, forced on me. I didn't like to think of the possibility that Master Hopay and his crew might abandon us when we went ashore to get the other jewel. I couldn't let that happen.

"Gil!" Quickly!" Aaron shouted.

I turned. He gestured and I hurried back to the bow.

"He's recovering, for now. I'm afraid it's only temporary, but it's the best I can do. The strain . . . He's held on to the spark inside far too long already. My magic won't hold him long. A matter of hours, no more, and if that other power grabs him again . . ." He shook his head.

I looked at the elf. He opened his eyes.

"I heard," Wellivazey said, "and I could tell even without his words." His voice was thick and weak, barely understandable. "You'll remember your vow, Hero." It was no question.

"I'll remember if you hold on long enough to fulfill your part of the bargain," I said.

"Get me to the shrine." His eyes closed again, just as the bow of the ship emerged from the fog.

The demarcation was as clear as it had been with the fog that shrouded Arrowroot while Wellivazey's father pulled his troops away from the siege there. As we emerged, I could see the shrine of the Great Earth Mother dead ahead—a huge white building that looked to be the identical twin of the shrine in the Titan Mountains. But this temple was surrounded by white sand and gray rocks. The island was low, scarcely more than a sandbar, and not a hell of a lot larger than the shrine. It looked like no more than fifty yards from shore to shrine at the widest spots.

There were no troops waiting to bar us from shore, no outer maze for us to penetrate, but the shrine was not without its defenders. As *Beathe* cleared the fog, a scaly green sea serpent showed itself. The beast surfaced quickly. It was wrapped completely around the island, and its head reared up over its tail.

Our boat could have sailed straight into its mouth with the sail up and full of wind.

18

Plus Two

I prayed for the first time since I was a little kid, and I wasn't sure who or what I was praying to. The fangs on the sea serpent had to be fifteen feet long—four fangs, two upper and two lower, and there were long rows of sharp-looking teeth as long as Dragon's Death to go with them. The beast had a snake's tongue that it flicked out to test the air in our direction, and the tongue was as long as our boat.

"That son of a bitch must be more than a mile long!" I said, awed even more than I was frightened. None of our weapons could hope to hurt that monster. Naval artillery might not faze it.

"This looks like my initiation test," Aaron whispered, but his words didn't register right away. My attention was locked too fully on the mouth of the sea serpent.

Our rowers had stopped rowing again, but none of them had left their seats. They stared at the serpent, hypnotized by it, as was Master Hopay. Lesh, Harkane, and Timon came to the bow of *Beathe* to stand with Aaron and me. Harkane and Timon had their bows. Lesh had his battle axe. Despite the hopelessness of the challenge, we were all armed to face it as best we could.

"What do we do, lord?" Lesh asked.

I shook my head. I didn't have any clue what we could try that wouldn't be instantly suicidal. This sea serpent made the biggest dragon I had faced look like a $1.29 chameleon in a pet shop. Then Aaron's words penetrated my skull. I grabbed his arm.

"What do you mean, this is your initiation test?" I demanded.

"Something every apprentice must go through to become a full wizard," Aaron said, so calmly that he sounded half asleep. "He must face an impossible challenge and surpass it with only his craft."

"Impossible is one thing, but that monster is outside the normal rules," I said, trying to turn Aaron so he wasn't staring at the sea serpent. I didn't succeed. Aaron was simply too strong for me to turn him without his cooperation. The monster seemed to fill Aaron's eyes. I could see it reflected there.

"No, this is my challenge." Aaron used his other hand to peel my grip from his arm, and he was too strong to resist. He pulled my hand away as easily as if he were the brawn-over-brains hero and I were an eight-year-old kid. "There's no other way," he said, not taking his gaze from the sea serpent for a second.

No other way? I couldn't even see that *this* was a way. But I had trouble finding words to use.

The sea serpent continued to watch us, its body undulating, though it wasn't really doing anything more than treading water. Its eyes, set in knobs on top of its head, were as big as those round plastic sleds. Its nostrils flared larger than hula hoops.

"Parthet said that I would meet my test on this voyage," Aaron said, finally releasing his hold on my wrist. I wanted to argue with him, but I couldn't—and that was before I had any inkling *how* he planned to deal with the sea serpent.

"How will you do it, zap him with lightning?" I asked, hoping it would be that simple . . . but not believing it.

Aaron frowned and thunder rumbled in the distance, which made me think of Parthet.

"No, I think not," Aaron said. "Give me a moment to myself." He gestured, and the rest of us backed off as far as we could without abandoning the bow section of *Beathe* altogether. I glanced at the elf. His eyes were barely open. His nostrils flared and relaxed as if he were having difficulty breathing. And he had no breath at all.

Aaron stared at the serpent and started to chant softly. He broke off after only a moment and turned to me, but he spoke loud enough for Master Hopay and the rowers to hear as well.

"When the way opens, drive through as hard as you can, right up onto the beach. It's the only chance any of us has."

I nodded, and Aaron turned to face the monster again. Aaron resumed his earlier chant, or started a different one. I'm not sure which. The rhythm was different, but it had the same sort of *feel.* The spell he wove was hypnotic. I felt the words in my bones, jarring, adhesive, but my tension seemed to recede. It became more difficult to worry, more difficult to listen to my danger sense or to watch the sea serpent. It was hard to do anything but pay attention to the chant.

It lulled me so completely that I had no chance at all to hold Aaron back.

He put his hands on the gunwale and vaulted over, dropping into the sea. Aaron sank to his shoulders, then started moving forward. It wasn't until he had come back up to waist level that I came out of my trance and realized that he wasn't swimming, he was *walking,* and his feet were nowhere near the bottom of the sea.

Aaron continued to move forward through the water and he continued to rise, just as if he were walking ashore through rapidly shallowing water. Magic was magic to my Varayan companions, but I had—in this case—the misfortune of knowing about a precedent for walking on water, and Aaron's mimicry knotted my gut more than the monster he was moving toward. He headed straight for the head of the sea serpent, chanting all the time, his voice getting louder with every step.

The beast slowly closed its mouth and lowered its head until its eyes were on a level with Aaron's head and chest. The huge eyes were the same amber color as a dragon's eyes.

Aaron's steps slowed as he neared the monster's head. He held out both hands, palms open and facing the beast. Then Aaron stepped onto its snout, which was almost level with the sea's surface. He moved back along the snout, reaching toward the beast's eyes. It was a stretch, even for Aaron. The eyes of the sea serpent were set as far apart as Aaron could reach.

The monster started to sink below the surface.

"Push it!" I shouted, turning to call back to Master Hopay and the rowers. "Hurry, dammit! Get us through while we can!"

Master Hopay shouted orders. The rowers started pulling on their blades. I turned to watch the confrontation in the water again.

Aaron's hands seemed to almost sink into the pupils of the serpent's eyes. The creature's eyelids closed from both sides, narrowing to the barest slits, and Aaron's hands were right there. When the gaps were narrow enough for Aaron's hands to span them, he pulled the eyelids shut and leaned against the bony ridge between the eyes. The serpent continued to sink. Water rose to Aaron's waist, to his shoulders, then over his head. He didn't budge.

Pictures flashed through my head. I could see myself hurdling over the side of the boat into the sea, both elf swords flashing, to rescue Aaron and kill the sea serpent. The images were as sharp, as vivid, as reality, but they had to remain a fantasy. Some deeds are beyond the abilities of any Hero, and I had to think of my primary mission—especially now that Aaron had given the rest of us some chance to get on with it.

Beathe slowly picked up momentum as the rowers strained at their oars, panic giving them almost superhuman strength and determination. I hung to the side of *Beathe*, up in the bow, and continued to stare at the spot where Aaron had disappeared. There was a frothing of the water at first, then a string of bubbles that popped as they reached the surface, and then . . . nothing. The sea calmed until we crossed that spot and *Beathe's* wake rippled past to disturb the flat water. I could see the outline of the sea serpent as we rushed over it. By that time, more than five minutes had passed since Aaron's head had sunk beneath the Sea of Fairy.

I climbed on top of the boat's cabin after we crossed that spot and went back as far as the mast while *Beathe* continued to drive for the island. With one arm looped around the mast, I divided my attention between the spot in the water behind where Aaron had vanished and the shrine up ahead.

Our keel ribs grated on sand. *Beathe* lunged to an abrupt halt.

"Over the side," I shouted. Only my grip on the mast had kept me from being thrown from my feet by the impact. "We have to haul the boat up on the beach, out of the grasp of that beast."

There were thick nautical hawsers coiled in a box under the deck at the bow of *Beathe*. The crew, and my own people, dropped over the side as soon as Hopay and his men attached two of the hawsers to thick rings in the gunwale. We all dragged on the ropes as we waded through the shallows and up onto the packed white sand of the island. With thirteen of us pulling, and a little help from the sea swell pushing from behind, we got the prow of *Beathe* past the waterline, and the boat listed to starboard. Timon clambered back aboard the boat to get the elf. Lesh brandished two thick stakes he had discovered somewhere in the boat's stores. We drove the stakes into the sand and secured the ropes to them.

It had taken the efforts of *all* of us to get the boat that far. I didn't think that the crew would be able to free it alone, especially not if I kept Master Hopay and two of his rowers with me.

"The rest of you keep watch here," I said. The sailors—soldiers—all had weapons, their short swords at hand, their spears lashed to the sides of the cabin. With land beneath their feet and weapons out and ready, they were less prone to panic, but they were still frightened enough by the memory of the sea serpent that none of them argued with my orders.

Timon had Wellivazey in his cage. The elf's condition was deteriorating rapidly. His eyes no longer focused together. His mouth hung open and his tongue was darkened and swollen. He *looked* dead, finally.

We had just started marching toward the shrine when I heard heavy coughing behind us and an echo of distant thunder. I glanced over my shoulder, then stopped walking and turned all the way.

Aaron was wading ashore.

The six men I had left with the boat backed away from Aaron rapidly, fear flowing out from them in a wave I could feel. Aaron, still coughing and spitting water, stared at them for a moment, then joined the rest of us.

"The monster sleeps within," he said. Absently, he shook off water. His eyes were bloodshot and cloudy—murky. I couldn't tell what the cause was, but Aaron set off my danger alarm as wildly as the Elflord of Xayber ever had.

"I thought you were dead," I whispered, trying to

avoid showing him that the special sense of the Hero of Varay considered him a "clear and present" danger.

"No, not dead. I am a wizard now," he said, just as quietly.

"Hurry up," the elf croaked. "So little time!"

The gold double doors, identical to those on the shrine in the Titan Mountains, were on the south side of this temple. *Beathe* had beached on the east side of the island. Eight of us hurried across the sand, through the field of scattered rocks, toward the entrance. I was waiting for soldiers to emerge from the doors as they had at the other shrine. But no one came out to bar our way. Lesh and I tried to open the doors, but we couldn't budge them. They wouldn't move in or out. Then Aaron laid his hands on the gold and the doors popped open—violently. One door snapped off its hinges and fell into the shrine.

We stepped inside, past the fallen door. The empty cavity hit us with the echoes of the clanging door at our feet.

"Which way?" I asked, and my voice echoed just as strongly.

"The pull is weak," the elf whispered. "So weak."

"Which way?" I asked again, more urgently.

The elf's eyes wandered independently. Neither one seemed to see me. Aaron took the cage from Timon and set it on the floor. He unhooked the snaps, lifted the top off, and set it aside. Aaron started chanting as he picked up the elf's head. He stood and raised Wellivazey's head above his own at full reach. Then he brought it down slowly—and Wellivazey slipped over Aaron's head like a full Halloween mask. Nothing squirted out. Somehow, the elf's skull, brains, and everything else fit right over Aaron. Stronger eyes looked out of Wellivazey's face. They wavered a moment, then focused together. The elf's mouth moved, and Aaron's voice came through, subtly changed.

"It is above us, far above us," he/they said.

Timon gagged, then vomited. One of the men from *Beathe* went pasty white and fainted, hitting his head disturbingly hard. I didn't feel so good myself.

White face above black neck, no jagged fit—the line

between the two skins seemed perfectly smooth. A black hand pointed toward the side of the shrine's vault.

"There," Aaron's voice said through the elf's lips.

Master Hopay looked around, his head jerking back and forth as if he were having spasms in his terror. Then he bolted through the doors, running back toward his boat.

"Let him go," Aaron said, an instant before I could start after Hopay. "Follow me."

Aaron started walking quickly across the center of the shrine at an angle, aiming for a point along the west wall. The rest of us followed close behind him. Aaron went straight to a door that looked like all of the other doors along that aisle and pulled it open—wrenching the knob off and twisting one of the hinges in the process. Aaron showed none of the hesitation and uncertainty that Wellivazey had shown in the first shrine. We went up one long flight of stairs, through two small, bare rooms, then along a hallway that paralleled the aisle below, and up another flight of stairs, much longer than the first. At the top, we turned back the way we had come, moving back along the side of the shrine, and finally we started up one more short flight of stairs.

Those stairs came up through the floor of a room that was about sixteen by twenty-four and twelve feet high. The walls and ceiling were totally crusted over with precious gemstones—diamonds, rubies, emeralds, and others I couldn't identify by sight—and more were piled on the floor, in the corners, as if they had simply been swept aside and left. The stones were real, all of them. I knew that without scientific tests, a jeweler's loupe, or anything else. I simply *knew.* It was a fortune in faceted and smooth jewels.

Aaron/Wellivazey scanned the walls. Aaron's hand came up and pointed.

"That oval emerald, *there.*"

I went to the wall and touched a gem.

"This one?" I asked.

"That one," Aaron's voice assured me.

At first, I couldn't get a grip on the emerald. Only half of it was away from the wall, and it was fixed firmly and bounded by other gemstones. I tried to find some purchase with my fingers, without luck, and I was just about ready to use Dragon's Death to pry it loose when the emerald decided to pop off the wall on its own. It dropped right into my hand. The stone was warm, and it matched the ruby around my neck in size and shape.

I held the jewels next to each other, and the ruby slid out of its gold setting. When ruby and emerald touched, both started to glow.

"Not now," Aaron said. "We have to get out of here quickly. The world is collapsing toward us."

We ran down the stairs, through the midlevel corridor and rooms, down the last flight of stairs, and then we raced for the golden doors, slipping and sliding on the polished marble floor of the shrine.

Halfway across the huge central chamber we all skidded to a stop. A woman's figure appeared—first a ghostly wraith, then a more substantial figure. She seemed to have been assembled from badly mismatched parts, though. Her head, neck, arms, and shoulders appeared normal—attractive face, slender neck and arms—but watermelon-sized breasts hung from her chest, covering a wasp waist that I might have been able to span with my hands, over hips and buttocks that would have had to squeeze to fit through a hula hoop. Bulky thighs supported that construction, but the legs below the knees seemed normal, about right for the head and arms. Maybe the feet were a little too big. A caricature, a gross parody.

"Who disturbs my shrine and steals my treasures?" The voice was regal, haughty, and seemed to be in stereo.

"Not yours," I said, taking one cautious step closer to her. Obviously this was, or was supposed to represent, the Great Earth Mother. The devotional figures of her I had seen were all similarly distorted.

She studied me. "Vara, have you returned at last?" There was doubt, or maybe just wistfulness, in her voice, shattered when she shook her head and said, "No, you're not the one. You're just a thief. I will destroy you!"

"You'll have to stand in line, my lady," I said.

"She's just a mirage," Aaron said. "There is no substance. Hurry, to the boat."

We went past the mirage and reached the doors without catastrophe striking. But when we got out onto the marble walk that surrounded the building we had to stop again. The men I had left with *Beathe* had come up to the shrine, and they were cowering against the outer wall. Halfway across the beach, Master Hopay lay dead, his skull crushed by a boulder that was eight feet in diameter. His arms and legs were bent at unnatural angles, also obviously broken, though those injuries could scarcely matter to him now.

That wasn't the worst. Stones—everything from golf ball to basketball in size—were picking themselves up off the beach and smashing into our boat. There were already gaping holes in the sides of *Beathe*, and more appeared every moment. The stones hit with the velocity of artillery shells. Some went straight through, in one side and out the other. We weren't going to sail back to Varay in *Beathe*, not without a lot of time for repairs.

And time was one thing we didn't have.

"Look!" Lesh shouted. He was pointing at the sky.

There were hundreds, maybe thousands, of dragons of every size and description stretching off to the horizon in every direction I could see. And they were all converging on the shrine.

"Shit!" I said. I looked around at my companions, ending with Aaron/Wellivazey. "What the hell do we do now?"

"You have the balls of the Great Earth Mother." It was strictly the elf's voice that I heard this time.

"What do I do with them?" I held them up, both cupped in the palm of my left hand.

"Swallow them."

"That's impossible!" I mean, they were each the size of a pecan, shell and all, and there was no way I could get even one of them down without choking to death.

"Swallow them!" the elf's voice repeated, more insistently. "This is what you must do to complete your mission."

I looked at the two jewels. "Lesh, you remember the Heimlich maneuver I taught you?"

"Aye, lord, I remember."

"Be ready to use it on me if you have to."

"Aye, lord." He shifted his grip on his battle-axe.

On the beach, all of the rocks that hadn't hurled themselves at the boat were changing shape. It was something like Claymation. The rocks grew and turned into armed soldiers, and there seemed to be as many soldiers as there were dragons in the sky. The soldiers appeared as a cross section of human history. I saw stone-axe-carrying cavemen, Roman legionnaires, knights in mail and plate, red-suited musketeers, even a couple of olive-green uniforms topped by the flat helmets our soldiers used in the First World War and at the beginning of the Second.

And they were all coming toward us.

I popped both jewels in my mouth and swallowed.

It hurt. *Oh, God, it hurt!* I could feel them sinking, and I imagine it would have felt about the same if someone had crammed a baseball bat down my throat and pushed it all the way down to my stomach. The agony was beyond anything I could ever have imagined. The world around me seemed to dim, go faint. I was on the verge of passing out but didn't. I would have welcomed that end to my pain.

The burning went down my throat and straight on down through my gut. There was no twisting and turning of the stones following my digestive system. They *burned* straight down, like glowing embers sinking through butter.

Maniacal laughter echoed in my head. I knew that it was Wellivazey laughing, but there was nothing I could do about it. I couldn't move, couldn't contemplate movement, and speech . . . I didn't think that I would ever be able to speak again.

Fire and pain, a clear track, a straight drop, an endless agony—until the jewels came to rest. The burning and pain faded slowly. When I could finally bear to move, I had to reach down the front of my pants to check the damage. There was a very tender track down my abdomen, and an ache in my scrotum, a weight. I felt around cautiously, past the vibrating threads of pain, and counted—all the way to four. I pulled my hand out of my pants and looked at Wellivazey's face on Aaron's shoulders.

"You've sealed your doom now, Hero!" Wellivazey's voice said, but those were his final words. Aaron reached up and pulled the elf's head off of his own, then held it off to the side for someone to take.

Harkane took the head and tucked it under his arm.

I looked at Aaron. He had changed. The elf had left a

little of himself behind, a jagged streak of his pale white skin, running from a point at Aaron's left temple down the side of his face to the jawbone, where it came to another point. Along the cheek, the streak was maybe an inch wide. I took the head from Harkane and held it up to look. The corresponding section of the elf's face was black. Then—because I couldn't help myself—I turned the head over. There was no hole large enough for another head in there. I saw the end of the elf's spinal cord, the flesh and blood vessels, the bone of his skull, the dead gray of the bottom of his brain even.

I closed my eyes while I righted the head and looked at it again. It was not just the patch of skin that was different. At the top of the streaks, the two had also exchanged a small patch of hair—kinky black on the elf, smooth platinum blond on the wizard.

"It wasn't a perfect spell," Aaron said—his own voice back. "I held it far too long."

I reached out and touched his face, hesitantly. I couldn't hold back, though. There was no real break between white and black. The skin was smooth, unbroken, across the patch.

"We're still in danger," Aaron said, sadness in his eyes.

I looked at the sky in time to see the start of the rain of dragons. Suddenly, they were all falling, and many of them were changing into other creatures—chickens mostly, but I also saw cats and dogs, horses and fish fall onto the beach, into the sea, and onto our damaged boat. A huge bull elephant crashed through the bow of *Beathe,* permanently grounding it.

"No way home," I said, taking one step toward the boat.

"A moment," Aaron said. He held out a hand to stop me. Then he turned to face the horde of soldiers that had been created from the rocks. Their ranks had been greatly thinned by the falling animals, but there were still a couple of hundred of them. Aaron started chanting. After a moment, he went silent and opened his mouth as wide as it would go.

I still don't believe that I saw what I saw next. Impossible things happen almost routinely in the seven kingdoms and in Fairy, but this went so far beyond the usual impossibilities that I still can't convince myself that it actually happened.

Aaron exhaled in an incredibly long puff, but that wasn't what was so remarkable. That *sea serpent* emerged from a mouth two or three inches wide. As near to Aaron's lips as my eyes could place the beast, though, it was full-size—several times as tall as Aaron—and he just propelled it out onto the beach, where it started wriggling around eating the massed soldiery charging toward us. In a grossly magnified way, it was like one of those party noisemakers that you blow into and a paper tube expands and unrolls with a razzing sound.

This time, I think that all of us with Aaron vomited.

The serpent coiled back and forth across the beach, eating soldiers and the fallen metamorphosed dragons.

Before the tail emerged from Aaron's mouth, the island started to tremble and shake. *Earthquake.* I had never experienced one before, but I didn't need experience to know what it was, a powerful earthquake.

As soon as the last of the serpent was out of Aaron's mouth, I started dragging Aaron back, away from it.

"We've got to get out in the open, away from the building," I shouted at the others. There was a lot of noise, from the dining serpent, from the screaming soldiers, and from the rumbling ground.

Aaron gagged and coughed, and spit up blood.

"No!" he managed finally. "Inside the shrine. Quickly, inside."

"The building might fall on us," I protested.

"We have to take the chance," Aaron said. "We can't stay out here or that beast will eat us too, without any 'might' about it."

That settled it. Maybe the shrine would fall on us, but that didn't sound nearly as horrifying as the prospect of that sea serpent eating us the way it was slurping down all those soldiers and dead other things. We went back through the double doors. Lesh and I nearly had to carry Aaron. His guts were still convulsing. More blood came out of his mouth. Not all magic is painless, I guess.

"Find a single door that will open," Aaron said when he could, and then he went back to spitting and retching.

We had to try a half-dozen doors before we found one that opened without trouble.

Aaron straightened up, started chanting, and put his hands on the doorjamb—one on either side—in a gesture I couldn't mistake. There was no silver tracing around the doorway, but I knew what Aaron was doing. I wasn't nearly surprised when a familiar setting opened beyond the doorway.

"Get through, everyone," Aaron said, and the words seemed to be quite an effort.

I waited until all of the others were through—including Harkane, who had the head of our elf.

"Get through," Aaron told me. I obeyed, but I grabbed his arm and pulled him through into Arrowroot behind me, as the shrine of the Great Earth Mother started to collapse on itself.